Wellspring of Life

Book Five of the Towers of Light Series

Allen Brokken

Wellspring of Life
Book Five: The Towers of Light series
Copyright © 2022 Allen Brokken

Written by Allen Brokken
Edited by Sarah Grimm
Cover Design by Magpie Designs, Ltd
Edition 1
ISBN: 978-1-7378515-9-2

Dedication

To the families of the Wellspring Community homeschool co-op for providing a safe haven in a dark world for my children to grow and thrive.

Contents

The action-packed and suspenseful Towers of Light series should be enjoyed from the first book until the last. However, if you just can't wait to start your adventure, here's a summary of the previous books.

Book 1: _Light of Mine_

Our heroes, twelve-year-old Lauren and her brave little brothers, Aiden (nine) and Ethan (five), find themselves home alone on the frontier, when their parents disappear under mysterious circumstances. Farm life is hard, and the help promised to them never comes.

After discovering pieces of the Armor of God, they go to church for help, only to find a new Bishop and his Acolytes have taken over their little church, and the only help they recieve is from a snobby acolyte who must be reading from a different "good book" than they are.

A mystery unfolds as the shadowy Knight Protector stalks the farm, seeming to want to destroy the Tower of Light. As the story closes, a battle ensues where the true enemy is revealed. With the help of Knight Protector, our heroes win the day, but at a terrible cost.

Book 2: _Still Small Voice_

Our heroes believe in their hearts that the Still Small Voice is prompting them to light another tower in Blooming Glen. However, their Uncle arrives with a different plan. He doubts the Light and is determined to take them safely to Grandma's house at all costs, even if it means confrontation with Knight Protector.

As the children are swept away in what they believe is the wrong direction, the Dandelion Acolyte stalks them looking for an opportunity for payback from the previous battle. In the night, our heroes choose to help a diminutive Bjorn Born named Tok to save his bear from the Bishop's menagerie of evil. The children successfully release the circus animals, but miss the chance to save their parents. Their error is revealed in a battle with the giant Skull Crusher, as their Uncle seems to sacrifice himself so the children can find safety with Knight Protector in the refuge of Quinn's ferry.

Book 3: *Fear No Evil*

Knight Protector has gathered warriors to escort the children to Blooming Glen. However, Skull Crusher arrives, putting that plan to the test by destroying their ferry. Our heroes are separated and washed down the river in the battle's aftermath.

After coming ashore, the children make new friends; Lauren the giantess Tye, Aiden the Iron Priestess known as First Sister, Ethan the Bjorn Born Besta, and Lok. Our heroes' new friends and their faith give them the courage to overcome the dangers of the valley of darkness.

Meanwhile, the Dandelion Acolyte has locked the children's parents in Iron Mountain's dungeon and is reborn as the new Lord of the Iron Mountain, Refi'Cul.

With the help of First Sister, Aiden rescues their Mother from the dungeon in the Iron Mountain. Finally, our heroes reunite with Mother, Uncle, Knight Protector, and their new friends for a climactic battle against Skull Crusher.

Book 4: <u>*Armor of God*</u>

Our Heroes and their friends must now retrieve the lost Armor of God, before Refi'Cul's agent Prime Sister and her squad of Steele Brothers does. However, their Mother is more concerned about lighting the tower in Blooming Glen and saving Father than retrieving the armor. So the group splits up, attempting to tackle both objectives at once.

Our heroes and their mother go with Tye to gain the aid of the giants, only to have Tye disowned by her father, Master Warden, based on Skull Crusher's lies.

The family flees the giants' camp, and the forces of Darkness foil their plans to retrieve the rest of the Armor of God. In the battle, Prime Sister captures our heroes and corrupts their holy weapons with the Darkness of a Y'lohnu Censer. Mother and Lauren manage to escape, but Ethan is left in Refi'Cul's control, while Tye is turned to the Darkness in secret.

As the family tries to save Ethan, Tye turns on them, leading to a climactic battle where they free Father from Refi'Cul's control; however, the fight leaves him horribly burned over his whole body. Only the Wellspring of Life can save him.

It is in the aftermath of this battle that Wellspring of Life Begins.

Light Bearers: Anyone who has chosen to follow the Light as described in the Good Book. They can take up the Armor of God in defense of others and destroy the sources of the Darkness. While many Light Bearers are human, and humans are typical in many regions of Zoura, other races can become Light Bearers.

Minions of Darkness: Anyone who has gone entirely to join the side of the Darkness. This can be a conscious choice or through the corrupting effect of items infused with the Darkness.

Mighty Mercenaries: Will work for anyone if the pay is good, but their code tends to keep their actions in support of the Light, despite their neutrality as an organization. Some Mighty Mercenaries are Light Bearers.

Bjorn Born: Grow to the size of a young child and are humanoid, but they have grey skin and no hair. Males have a ridge of spines on their head that grows larger as they age, and females have two tufts of black whiskers that come out of either side of their head, similar to a Turkey's beard. The Bjorn Born live symbiotically with bears and are generally ignorant of the Light and the Darkness. However, when the Darkness corrupts them, they go to war against their bears.

Iron Priestesses: Women from the Iron Mountain transformed into iron by the pool of life. Men attempting the same process generally turn to dust, and not all women of the Iron Mountain become Iron Priestesses. They follow the code of the Iron Mountain, which is similar to the teachings of the Good Book, but they are not necessarily Light Bearers.

Steele Brothers: Men who have been transformed by the waters of the pool of life after Refi'Cul corrupted it. They are entirely Minions of the Darkness

Heath Wardens: These are giants standing nine to twelve feet tall. They generally protect the wilds east of the muddy river. They have a unique way with animals and plants that helps them preserve and guide things in the wilds. They have not heard the message of the the Good Book and the battle between the Light and the Darkness, and could join either side if they felt it was in the best interest of the wilds.

Lauren, *aka Sissy, La'Ren of the Tower*: Age 12, the eldest child in the family. Her spear knocks the Darkness out of people, then returns to her hand. Meow Meow, a tiny black-and-white kitten, is her pet. He is empowered to wake people at just the right time.

Aiden, *aka A'den*: Age 9, the middle child in the family. He lost his fiery sword that destroys machinery of the Darkness. He replaced it with a blessed tack hammer—it's power is yet unknown. Daddy Duck, a rare golden mallard with a white spot on its head, is his pet. The duck concentrates and directs the Light of the tower to shine the way in the Darkness or destroy sources of Darkness

Ethan, *aka E, E'tan*: Age 5, is the youngest child in the family. Ethan's shield creates a force field of Light that harms the Minions of Darkness. Sparkle Frog, a Zourian rainbow flying frog, is Ethan's pet who can heal bumps and bruises.

Father, *aka Champion*: is a farmer and Master Artificer, able to create amazing devices to fight against the Darkness. The Bishop captured Father and partially corrupted him to become a Champion of Darkness. Ethan rescued Father from this, but now the man is horribly burned.

Mother: In her early years, Mother was Light Bearer in her own right. However, when the children were born, she became a homemaker.

Parson: He has been the spiritual guide for the family as long as the children have been alive.

Bishop: He is the official overseer of the church organization region. However, he is a Minion of Darkness and the mastermind of its spread across the Heathlands.

Refi'Cul, *aka Acolyte of the Dandelion Order, Yellow Acolyte*: The Bishop's protégé, he has been manipulated into corrupting the pool of life in the Iron Mountains in order to use the pool to become the Lord over the Iron Mountain and be transformed into a body of Steele.

Nicolas, *aka Acolyte of the Violet Order, aka Violet Acolyte, Brother Flower*: A junior acolyte in the Bishop's group. He turns on the Bishop when his schemes become known, and Nicolas gives his life to protect the children.

Knight Protector: Father's elderly mentor and a member of the Mighty Mercenaries who spied out the Bishop's corruption and became a guardian of the children.

Uncle: Father's brother, a powerfully built frontiersman who became a Light Bearer after protecting the children from Skull Crusher.

Skull Crusher: A champion among the Heath Wardens, who has turned fully to the Darkness. He intends to crush the family for the shame he feels because they defeated him.

Tye: A teenager among the Heath Wardens and friend to Lauren, who became a Light Bearer while fighting alongside Lauren, Tye can wield the children's holy weapons. Refi'Cul used the Darkness to turn Tye against the Light temporarily, but she has become a Light Bearer again.

Master Warden: Tye's father chose to side with Refi'Cul in his war against the Light at the urging of Skull Crusher.

Iron Sister, *aka Prime Sister, Nurse Maid*: is an Iron Priestess who briefly joined Refi'Cul when the rest of the Iron Priestesses chose imprisonment. Her time caring for Ethan when he was wounded has made her a Light Bearer.

Y'olhnu Censers, *aka Censers*:

The Censers are a creation of the Darkness that pollutes the air with corrupting influence. Directly breathing in their vapors can turn a person or animal to serve the Darkness. The Bishop and his allies built a network of Censers across Zoura. Where the influence of two Censers overlaps, the Darkness becomes particularly powerful and is known as a double-Darkness zone.

Turing to Iron or Steele

The process that makes Iron Priestesses and Steele Brothers does not entirely turn a person to the metal. Their bones and muscles become stronger to support the weight of their new metal skin, but they are not made of metal entirely. To keep their skin flexible, they have to go through the hardening and tempering process. They also require regular exposure to high heat, or they risk freezing in place like a statue.

The Use of Titles vs. Proper Names

Throughout the series, you may notice that a proper name refers to children and teens. However, adults' proper names are never given. Instead, their title or a pet title is always used in the story. As a read-aloud, I wanted the adult reading the story to have just a little less barrier to putting themselves into the story as Father, Mother, Knight Protector, or any other character they resonated with, as a person watching over the children listening to them read.

Ethan woke with a feeling of dread he couldn't escape, some unknown force was weighing him down. However, the icy-cold fear faded as his consciousness returned to a warm, furry weight purring on the side of his head.

He reached up and carefully plucked Meow Meow off himself. Last night's roaring fire in the abandoned cabin's crumbling hearth was now just embers, but the morning twilight let him see the kitten clearly as it cried, "Meow." This brought a smile to Ethan's face that overcame his exhaustion from the day before just a little bit.

By the time his family, Knight Protector, Iron Sister, and Tye had gotten settled in the cabin last night, he was so tired he fell asleep still wearing his cotton button-down shirt, khaki pants, and blessed brown leather shoes. His clothes felt damp and sweaty in the cool, pre-dawn air. The cold sent a brief shiver through his body which shocked him fully awake.

With a sigh, he sat up—kitten in hand—and marveled at how the white of its paws and face shone brightly, while its black body faded into the darkness of the cabin.

"Why'd you wake me up, little guy? Shouldn't you bother Sissy?" he whispered, noticing he was the only one awake despite the hint of purple in the sky.

That puzzled him, because usually Uncle and Mother would be up before dawn. Then, as he looked toward the light, he realized it wasn't the sun he was seeing. Instead, off in the west, shone a glimmer of light, almost like a star had fallen to the ground.

He sat in wonder; it reminded him of the lantern in the Tower of Light. "Is that what you wanted me to see, little guy?" he asked the kitten in a hushed tone.

The kitten merely squeaked, "Meow."

Ethan set Meow Meow on the ground and cautiously got up for a better view. Then, he carefully padded across the weather-worn wooden floor, to avoid large splinters from the water-damaged floorboards. After destroying the Censer hidden in it, Uncle said it was still the best shelter in the area, but Ethan didn't think it would protect them from the rain with all the holes in the roof.

The word *danger* flitted through his mind, causing him a moment of doubt. Shouldn't he wake up Mother? But instead, he grabbed his silvery shield and hung it on his back. He cinched the brown leather straps tight, making himself stand up straighter. Something about that gave him the confidence to go out into the night. Then he tiptoed gently toward the light, and his soft leather shoes muffled any sound of him crossing the room.

When he got to the entrance, he noticed the doeskin-clad giantess, Tye, was sitting on the ground next to the door—asleep! She was supposed to be guarding them! Heat rose in his cheeks as he thought about how she'd argued that she was fine and could take a turn on watch.

The way Lauren said Tye had turned to the Darkness earlier concerned Ethan. Sleeping on her watch just proved she wasn't fine. However, even sitting, Tye was a foot taller than Ethan, and with one of the holy swords his Father made on her lap, the giantess would have no trouble forcing him back to bed if he woke her. With her head slumped forward and her hair covering her face, she had no idea he was even up. So he paused for a moment, and took a deep breath. *What should I do?* The light in the distance seemed to call to him.

He stepped outside onto the dew-soaked prairie grass and slowly walked to the edge of the cabin's hill. The icky feeling of his clothes got even worse, as the dew on the tall grasses began to seep through his shirt and pants.

A shiver went through him when he stopped at the hill's edge and peered toward the light. It took him a moment to focus on it, but it seemed to be coming from near the top of a building in Spring Fields. The city was a few miles away, but the ground rose dramatically from the side of the lake, giving him a clear view of the city in the distance.

He followed the road from the south of the city and scanned the two-and three-story wood and stone buildings that made up the city. Then, finally, he found the dock where they'd set off to this side of the lake. Ethan shuddered as he recognized the long street beside the dock. The memory of pushing the wheelbarrow over the cobblestones with Father in it, engulfed in flames, brought a tear to his eye. Would they be able to find the Wellspring of Life in time to save Father? His worries were interrupted when his eyes finally locked on to the source of the light coming from a building at a crossroads in the long street.

That light must belong to that little girl in the window with the lantern!

He wanted to meet that little girl. She'd saved him, and in a roundabout way, she saved his Daddy too. She was a hero. But how could he thank her? She was on the other side of the lake. The flat boat was just too big for him to push across.

Another shiver reminded him of his damp clothes, then he realized his feet didn't feel soggy. The blessed leather shoes Father made for him didn't seem to be soaking up the dew. That got him thinking. If the shoes didn't get wet, were they maybe like a rock? Could he go REALLY FAST and skip across the lake?

He looked around. Tye was still asleep, and no one else was stirring. If he ran REALLY FAST, he might be able to cross the lake and back in just a few minutes. Maybe the little girl had a special pet that woke her up too. Should he chance it?

The light twinkled across the lake. Ethan just knew he needed to see what was going on there. He looked over his shoulder one more time. No one was watching. So he crouched down and pulled the sloppy bows on his shoelaces loose. He cinched the coarse leather shoelaces extra snugly and felt his tongue on his upper lip as he concentrated on tying the bows just right. They came out lop-sided but were tight when he tugged them. So he took a deep breath, and sprinted down the hill as fast as his feet would take him.

He built up incredible speed. A whoosh filled his ears as he ran down the hill. Finally, he hit the water so fast he didn't even feel it below him.

Despite being on a secret mission, he couldn't contain his excitement. "I did it!" he yelled, "I'm running on water!"

A wake rose behind him as he blasted his way across the lake. The speed and excitement of running on water consumed Ethan's attention, so he overlooked the eleven-foot-tall giants patrolling the beach until he was almost upon them.

He had a moment of doubt and almost faltered, but his resolve to speak to the little girl was stronger. He concentrated on lining up to the street he'd run down the night before and blew past the brown leather–clad giants on watch before they knew how to react.

After a couple of blocks, Ethan took a peek over his shoulder. The giants were starting to give chase and blowing ram's horns in alarm.

He realized he didn't have much time. If he didn't get to the girl quickly, the giants would catch up, and she might be in danger. So he pushed himself harder and moved just a bit faster.

As he approached the three-story wood-and-cobblestone building on the corner, Ethan realized he'd spent so much time focusing on going fast, he hadn't thought about how to stop. By the time he started to slow down, his momentum had taken him a whole block past the little girls' house.

He turned and peered down the street. He could barely make out the forms of the giants running toward him. He had to hurry.

Ethan jogged back to the apartment, careful not to run at super speed. He mounted the uneven stone steps and knocked on the door, feeling suddenly queasy. Was it the crazy run or fear that they might not answer? If they didn't, the run was for nothing.

The wave passed when the door opened a crack, and a familiar face outlined by messy black hair peered out. "You're the little boy with the shield!"

He turned slightly and patted the top edge of his shield to show her. "That's me." He smiled with pride, "My name is Ethan."

"Hello, Ethan, I'm Sarah," she whispered. "Why are you here at this late hour?"

Ethan looked down the street, and the giants were becoming more clear in the distance. "Can I come in, please? Giants are coming!" He motioned in their direction.

The girl's brown eyes went big as she opened the door, waved him in, and quickly shut and locked it. They were standing in an entry hallway that had seen better days. Small pieces of plaster were missing from the walls, the wallpaper was torn in places, and the floorboards weren't in good repair.

She stood there, just staring at him while he took in the room. The brass lantern in her left hand illuminated her nightdress and messy black hair. She must have noticed him staring because she tried to pat it down with her free hand. A slight hint of pink colored her cheeks, and Ethan thought she was very pretty regardless of her hair. He felt his own cheeks heat up at that realization.

Then she started tapping her foot. "Well? What are you waiting for?"

Ethan stood there for a moment, stunned. He wanted to talk to the girl but wasn't sure where to begin.

"Um I saw your light." He pointed to the lantern, "You have a little light like we do. Well, like we did . . . er do . . . It's complicated." Ethan scrunched up his eyebrows. How would he explain the situation and sneak out of there without the giants knowing? Sweat broke out on his forehead.

"Complicated, huh? Why don't you just tell me about your shield? It was so bright last night I could hardly see what happened down there." She motioned toward a wooden bench along the wall; its edges were rounded from uneven use. He had to nudge the leather boots at its foot further under the bench to get close enough to sit down.

Ethan took the shield off his back, sat on the bench, and laid it on his lap. "Well, my Daddy made this shield for me to help protect people from the Darkness."

She reached out and traced the lantern symbol. "That looks just like my lantern." She held up the lantern over the shield to emphasize the point.

"Yeah, you shined your light last night, which helped me save my Daddy," Ethan replied. "Where did you get that light?"

"Well, my family and others met a blacksmith, and he talked to us about the Savior and how we could shine his Light. Then, he taught me a song to help me remember always to shine the Savior's Light," she explained.

"Light of Mine!" Ethan blurted out.

"Shhh, don't wake my parents. But yes, that's the song," she replied. "Do you think that blacksmith was your father? He gave us little lanterns that lit up when we sang."

"Maybe. Knight Protector said Daddy sold lanterns in the shop here, but the shop was empty," Ethan's lips turned down, and his heart sank. "Daddy got burnt in the fight last night, and we have to find the Wellspring of Life to make him better.

"I've heard of that, but I always thought it was about the living water we recieve from knowing the Savior," she replied.

"Well . . . Sissy found a snow globe, and it looked like it had a real fountain in it. I think it's water has medicine, and—"

Loud voices outside interrupted him.

The children hopped up and peeked through the bottom of the circular window next to the door. A whole squad of giants was running down the street outside. Ethan recognized Skull Crusher in his black leathers carrying a heavy battle hammer. He seemed to be in charge because he was barking orders at the other giants as they ran down the street.

They must have missed Ethan going into the apartment because they sprinted past the window without looking back.

Ethan let out a sigh. He hadn't put Sarah in danger.

They returned to the bench. "So why did you say I have a light like you 'did'?"

"Well, we have a light burning in the tower at home. But there's so much Darkness that we were going to go to Blooming Glen to light another one. Then Refi'Cul broke it. So we don't have a lantern to put in the tower."

Sarah's eyes got big. "Will that make the Darkness go away everywhere?" she asked.

"I don't know . . ." Ethan looked down at his dirty fingernails, trying to find the right words. "My brother Aiden draws circles and maps and stuff; he would know."

"You can have my light if it will help." She held out the lantern in both hands to him sincerely.

The loud voices came back from the direction they'd gone.

"Oh no!" Ethan whispered. "They must have found my tracks somehow." He held up his palm toward her. "I can't take your lantern. I think you're going to need it to protect your family. Maybe I can find one of the other ones he gave out."

"Many families have fled the city, going north to Blooming Glen," She gestured toward her front window, then the far wall. "Others have gone West to the springs at Bubbling Wine. We stay because my parents feel our mission is here despite the Darkness."

Ethan's heart swelled in his chest. Knowing other Light Bearers were out there gave him confidence. However, he was worried about the giants turning around and needed to go. "Do you have a back door?"

"Yes, through there." She pointed down the hallway behind them.

Ethan stood up. "I'm going to go and draw them away."

The little girl's brow furrowed, and Ethan could tell she was worried.

"Thank you for shining your light." Ethan stared into her eyes. "We'll come back for you with lots of help once we help Daddy and shine the Light in Blooming Glen. I promise."

She nodded silently and turned away. Maybe she thought Ethan had been coming to save her now. Disappointing her deflated him, and he thought about just taking her lantern and shining the Light again for a minute. But Ethan couldn't be sure that would affect the giants the way it did the hell hounds.

Ethan took a deep breath and put his shield on his arm. It reduced to a tiny buckler, and the little girl gasped.

"It's special same as the lantern," Ethan explained. "Where's the back door?"

She showed him to the door and opened it silently. As soon as the door was closed behind him, he put on the speed and zigged and zagged around the alley trash and back up a block, then turned right and blasted out onto the main street.

"Looking for me?" he yelled with all his might.

Skull Crusher's twelve-foot frame loomed over the front door of the girl's house without even using the steps. His head snapped in Ethan's direction. "It's the boy! That's one of Refi'Cul's prizes. Get him!"

Ethan stood for a moment, indecisive. Should he run away to draw them farther up the street from the little girl's house? No, they might find a way to cut him off from the lake. If he could make it there, they wouldn't be able to follow.

He turned and put his buckler up, and ran with all the power the Boots of Peace gave him. His shield lit, and the blinding light caused the giants to shrink back on their knees as he passed.

Ethan poured on the speed and rocketed down the cobblestones. He dared a glance over his shoulder and saw the stunned giants begin to compose themselves and give chase. Two threw spears the size of small trees in his direction, but he was long gone.

He slowed slightly and put his shield on his back, then dug deep for more speed to blast across the lake.

He slowed to a trot once on the other side and carefully walked the last 100 yards through the prairie grass to the cabin. Tye was still asleep on duty. He thought to wake her, but the purple in the eastern sky told Ethan it was close to daylight anyway. Uncle or Mother would be up soon and catch her, and then they could deal with that.

If Sarah was right, there were more Light Bearers out there with lanterns. They just needed to find them. Then, maybe they would know where to find the Wellspring of Life.

"What is the meaning of this nonsense!" Refi'Cul's metallic voice boomed over the giants as they struggled to stand after being stunned by Ethan's blast of light. "Why are you cowering in the street? The way the horn was blowing, I thought an army was attacking."

"Yes, Skull Crusher, why are you and my finest warriors cowering here in this city," scolded the giant's bear hide–cloaked chieftain, Master Warden, as he approached around the corner from the other direction. Two leashed coyotes with studded black leather collars following at his heels.

Skull Crusher straightened and slammed his right fist into his chest in salute. "My Master, it was one of the human children with those accursed weapons."

"What?" Refi'Cul challenged. "What child, what weapon?"

"I cannot say for sure, my Lord. The tracks were small but spread too far for a little child." Skull Crusher pointed to imprints in the dust. "I think it was the one with the shield. The light from it was so bright it was like being battered with a club."

"Battered with a club, you say?" Refi'Cul put his hand to his chin, and a slight screech of metal on metal escaped as his finger rubbed against his cheek. Blooming Glen was supposed to be in a total Darkness area. So even if the children restored their weapons, they should have little power here. Then Refi'Cul looked off to the east and realized that the dawn light was growing, almost unhindered by the Darkness.

It had been over a day since Champion left on his mission to "fix" the weapons. Now a report of children with weapons of the Light attacking the city. Had they managed to destroy the eastern Censer? Where was Champion?

"Forget all this nonsense," Master Warden commanded, and the giants all turned their attention to him. "The gate guards said my daughter captured the humans and brought them to you."

Despite the giant's grey hair and the slight curve of advancing years in his back, his arms were thick as tree trunks. In this space, the giants outnumbered the Steele Brothers two to one. So it wouldn't be wise to provoke him.

"Master Warden," Refi'Cul gave a curt nod of respect, "I have not seen your daughter." He slowly waved his arm around as he continued, "I was given word that she was in the city with prisoners, but they never arrived at the forge."

"Never arrived!" Master Warden slammed his left fist into his right palm. "Then where is she?"

A wave of unease clenched Refi'Cul's stomach. Master Warden's hard-set jaw told him his influence over the giant was waning. He needed to think of something to keep their fragile alliance alive, but what?

The Dark One's Champion was missing, and now a child with a shield, probably the red head he'd captured just days before, came and went from the east. His power over the situation was slipping through his fingers like dry sand.

As the dawn light grew, he noticed some piles of red dust in odd places in the street. It reminded him of the rust dust Last Sister had poured on the ground to scare him before he'd completed the rite of Refi'Cul. One of the soldiers told him the girl's spear could turn a Steele Brother to dust. Were these piles of dust the group he'd sent with Champion? His eyes got big at the thought. Was one of these piles the man himself?

The corner of his mouth turned up at the thought. If the little girl's spear had somehow turned her father to dust— he chuckled to himself—*that would be some bitter irony.*

Something caught his eye . . . or rather, the lack of something caught his eye. A dark haze wafted around the edge of a broken-down trader's stall, darker than the shadows should have been.

He stepped to it and found the corrupted high priestess's wickedly crooked daggers in the dirt. "Master Warden, I believe I know what has happened to your daughter. Somehow the humans overpowered her and the other guards and made off with her."

"What!" Master Warden scowled. "Impossible!"

Refi'Cul held up the daggers, "I gave these to your daughter as a prize for her act of loyalty in the Bjorn Born's village before sending her to capture the humans."

Master Warden's eyes widened as he stared at the blades, "What loyalty? What are you talking about?"

Refi'Cul could tell the whole thing hooked Master Warden. The giant's code kept their loyalties very tight to their own kind. Master Warden was still her father, so casting her out for helping the humans had to have been hard for him. So to make it seem like she'd repented, well, that worked in Refi'Cul's favor now, didn't it? "She captured the youngest one of the group, but others escaped. I gave her the task to capture the rest of them.”

Refi'Cul waited for a beat before continuing. He wanted to gauge the giant's reaction. Master Warden nodded, and his face softened ever so slightly, but Skull Crusher raised an eyebrow. The Steele Lord was going to have to watch that one.

“I believe your daughter was captured by the humans.” A murmur floated through the giants, and they all looked at one another in disbelief.

Master Warden appeared to be just as uncertain, “To what end? Why would they not just kill her? She is a formidable warrior despite being just a girl.”

“Think, Master of Giants,” Refi'Cul tapped his temple with his index finger. It sounded like the tink of a hammer hitting an anvil. “What power would these disreputable humans hope to have over you with your daughter as a hostage?”

The chief's tan cheeks reddened, and he slammed a fist into his palm. “They'll have no such power over me!”

A supportive roar erupted from the crowd of giants. All but Skull Crusher, who took a step back from the group. He looked the area over, ignoring everything else going on around him. Refi'Cul now wondered if Skull Crusher was going to be a problem.

Master Warden continued, “Then we must be off at once!” The giant turned down the street to the east, and his troops fell in behind him.

Refi'Cul clapped his hands together and they rang like two metal pots clanging. “My Master Warden, please do not be so hasty.”

The giant stopped and looked back over his bear fur-clad shoulder.

Refi'Cul continued, "If the little boy has the power to drive your troops to their knees, I do believe it would be wise to gain a defense against it."

Master Warden turned to him, "What power are you speaking of? Those little kitchen knives in your hand?"

Refi'Cul didn't appreciate being provoked, but he merely straightened his shoulders and explained, "There are much more powerful weapons than these. Even now, the lifeblood of the Iron Mountain is making all we'll need."

The assembled giants shifted uneasily, and Master Warden raised his eyebrows, "What do you suggest?"

Refi'Cul held up two fingers. "Send two of your fastest troops to the Iron Mountain. Have them tell the Bishop what has transpired here, and he will send you back with items of power."

"Pah!" Master Warden huffed. "That will take too long. We need to be after them now! Who knows what ill will befall my daughter? The trail will grow cold quickly."

The Steele Lord dropped to a knee next to one of the piles of dust. He picked a handful up and let it drain through his hand. "This . . . this is what befalls a Steele Brother who engages with their weapons. You've seen your own giants cower before it. Only armed with the power of the true light, will you be able to crush your enemy."

A murmur went up from the giants, and Refi'Cul knew he had Master Warden right where he wanted him.

Master Warden pointed at two giants, made a low whistle with a hand gesture, and turned back to Refi'Cul,

"Very well, but they have a head start. How will we catch them?"

Refi'Cul stood and reflexively wiped his hands back and forth against each other to get the dust off. The screeching of metal on metal caused Master Warden to clench his jaw. The Steele Lord took a deep breath, relishing the power he felt he had over the giants. "We know where they are going." He chuckled to himself for just a moment. "They have always been going to Blooming Glen. We will meet them there in force with the power of the Iron Mountain!"

A cry of agreement rose from the half dozen Steele Brothers assembled behind Refi'Cul, and even some of the giants began to join in. But Master Warden raised a hand to quiet them. "Are you sure they'll go there? Won't they realize it's a trap?"

Refi'Cul was just about done placating the giant. He let out an exasperated hough and replied, "Very well, are you not the lord of the Heath? Can you not command the very beasts of the field to do your bidding?" The Steele Lord indicated the two coyotes sitting at Master Warden's feet.

Master Warden stared off toward the lake in the east, "You are wiser than I expected, Lord Refi-Cul." Then, he turned to Skull Crusher. "You brought this conflict to my house. You will harry them and make sure they are driven to the north."

Master Warden pulled a thin wooden whistle from his neck and gave it to Skull Crusher. "My coyotes will dominate the coyotes of the wild. Then, they will drive the humans to their doom."

Skull Crusher gave Refi'Cul a flinty look for the briefest moment, then bowed to the Master Warden, "As you wish! The enemy will find no respite on the plains, while I command the coyote!"

Lauren woke up to sunlight on her face. Warm and bright, it streamed through a hole in the cabin's roof. She couldn't remember the last time she'd woken to pure sunlight. She pulled her knees to her chest to sit in the soothing rays and soaked them in like a kitten.

The cabin looked much worse in the daylight than it had when they stumbled into it exhausted in the middle of the night. The Censer's destruction sent little bits of black metal into the walls and wrecked the cobblestone fireplace at the room's far end. The whole thing was ready to collapse. That made Lauren wonder if that danger was why there was no fire there now.

A groan from Ethan pulled her attention away from the surroundings. "Is it morning already?" He had kicked the blanket off in the night, and the daylight showed just how filthy his khaki pants and button-down shirt had become. She shook her head when she realized her light blue cotton dress wasn't in any better condition after all their adventures.

"Already," Uncle chided as his doeskin-covered form stepped through the doorway. "It's nearly nine o'clock in the a.m. We need to be off pronto." His bushy beard covered up much of his expression, but the hardness of Uncle's eyes told Lauren he was deeply concerned about something.

Then the reality of their situation hit Lauren in the chest like a hammer blow. Was Father OK? Had he made it through the night? She could barely bring herself to ask, "Uncle, how is Father?"

"The geese seem to be keeping him cool, but it's not good. We need to be off to find that thar Wellspring of Life if he's going to have a chance." Uncle shook his head and ran his hand through his unruly blond hair.

Lauren's brown hair had partially fallen over her face, and she wondered if Uncle was giving her a hint. She could feel the dirt in her hair as she pulled it back to glance at the snow globe twinkling next to her grey wool blanket. It was like nothing she'd ever seen. The snow seemed to shoot out of the the three-tier, white stone fountain, almost settle to the bottom, and shoot out again in a rhythm. The sunlight seemed to light it up, a woman appeared to be walking around inside the globe as well. But not like any woman she had ever met. Her features were even more sharp and angular than the Iron Priestesses. So maybe she was made of stone or crystal, rather than metal. Lauren didn't understand what could be powering the scene inside the globe.

Mother walked in the door. "Lauren, Ethan, we must be off." She reached a hand down to help Lauren up. Lauren was taken aback by Mother's appearance. She had deep rings under her eyes, and while her hair was tied back with a leather cord, it was just as much of a mess as Lauren's. Lauren took her hand, and Mother pulled her up into a hug. Mother's leather clothes were surprisingly soft, despite the poof of dust that came from both of them when they embraced. Mother's tight hug helped deaden the dread growing in Lauren's stomach.

Mother let go and put her hands on Lauren's shoulders. "Hurry up and get Ethan moving. We need to be on the road right away."

"Yes, Mother." Lauren nodded, causing her hair to fall back onto her face.

Mother turned and walked out the creaky cabin door, and Uncle followed. Lauren didn't want to keep fighting her hair, so she took a moment to run her fingers through it and bring it all together in a pony tail. Then, she reached down to pull a ribbon out of her pocket to find Meow Meow nestled in there. The kitten opened his eyes, and the sheer cuteness interrupted her worry for just a moment.

She dug around in the pocket, tickling the kitten while she did. He let out an affectionate purr. She finally found the ribbon she'd gotten in Loggerton.

Loggerton.

That had only been a week, maybe ten days ago. Yet, it felt like a lifetime. They had been through so much, and now Father.

The wave of pressure in her chest urged her on, and she tied her hair back in a ponytail. She gathered her blanket and wrapped the snowglobe inside for safekeeping. When she knelt to scoop up the bundle and her spear, Ethan approached.

"Sissy, I have to tell you something," Ethan whispered.

Lauren did a double take. Didn't he see how urgent things were? Mother and Uncle had already left the room, and the sounds outside indicated they were loading up. They didn't have time for secrets.

"OK, but quick, we've got to go" Lauren bent at the waist to let him whisper in her ear.

"Well . . . Meow Meow woke me up last night . . ." He trailed off.

Lauren felt heat rising in her cheeks. They didn't have time for this. "And?"

Ethan's eyes narrowed. "Well, when I went out of the cabin, Tye was asleep."

This statement caught Lauren off guard. On the one hand, the giantess had made a big deal about being fit to guard and then didn't do her job. That could have been disastrous for the family. But, on the other hand, they had all been through a lot, especially Tye—being corrupted by the Darkness. So Lauren couldn't fault her for wanting to show she could contribute to the family.

"Why are you telling me, and what were you doing out?"

"Well, I don't think it's good that Tye was asleep. Somebody needs to give her a talkin' to." Ethan's cheeks reddened.

Lauren looked him in the eyes. "But you don't want to do it because you'd have to tell everyone you were up to something. So what were you up to?"

Ethan's whole face turned red. "Well . . ."

Lauren just knew he was up to no good.

But, before she could find out more, Mother called from outside, "Children, come along now!"

"Coming!" Lauren raced out the door but noticed Ethan didn't have the same enthusiasm as he shuffled out of the cabin, shield and blanket in hand.

Uncle was in the driver's seat of their battered wooden wagon. In the sunlight, the wear from soaking in the river and traveling what felt like hundreds of miles was evident. Even one of the spokes on the back left wheel was broken. Would it hold up the rest of the way to Blooming Glen?

The sun glinted off of the golden breastplate Uncle had put on over his frontiersman leathers. Something about it and the helmet on the seat next to him told Lauren they would find a way to make it to Blooming Glen, no matter what.

Aiden was in the back of the wagon behind Uncle with a breastplate covering his button-down shirt. He was fiddling with a helmet, trying to adjust the straps right to put it on his bushy blond head. For a brief instant, Lauren wondered how long Mother would let the boy's hair grow before she just hacked it off with her dagger. He was going to be as scruffy as Uncle any minute now.

Mother was on the opposite side, similarly armored, and Father lay in the middle. One of Uncle's platinum Geese was standing at his feet, rhythmically beating its wings in a slow, graceful motion.

Mother handed a light brown, leather-covered bundle to Iron Sister and Knight Protector, who stood to the wagon's right. "Get in, children. We need to be off."

"Off where exactly?" Tye questioned from where she stood, leaning against the bark-covered logs that made up the cabin wall. She didn't look ready to hit the road. The rings under her eyes were even darker than Mother's, and the general slump in her shoulders just didn't look like Tye. She seemed—defeated. Maybe Ethan was right, and they should have a talk with Tye about sleeping on watch.

"I know a tale of a grove just south of Blooming Glen that some Parson said was holy in some way. I don't remember the details," Knight Protector offered in an upbeat tone.

Lauren was always surprised by this man. He was easily fifteen years older than Father, and despite weeks of travel, half drowning in the river and being beaten by giants, had a twinkle lit his eye.

Tye looked down her nose at him. "So you think this grove contains the cure you are looking for?"

Lauren gritted her teeth as she handed her bundle up to Ethan, who'd hopped in ahead of her. *Tye, please don't make this difficult. We need to help Father.*

Ethan fumbled the bundle, and the snowglobe fell out.

Her stomach dropped as she lunged to catch the falling object. She scraped her knees on the dirt as she fell, arms out, but managed to catch the globe before it shattered on the ground. Heat filled Lauren's cheeks, "Ethan! You need to be careful!" Her knees smarted, but she was much more concerned about losing their link to the wellspring's healing waters.

Ethan pouted, "I'm sorry sissy."

Lauren exhaled slowly as she awkwardly stood. "Let someone else get it next time."

"OK Sissy" Ethan replied, with a deep frown on his face. Mother put a hand on his shoulder, and Lauren returned her attention back to Tye. There had to be a way to convince her friend to help them. She presented the snow globe to Tye held carefully in both hands, "We found this token. It has to be a sign for us to find the Wellspring of Life, so we can save father."

Suddenly the snow formed an arrow pointing to the northeast. Lauren gasped, and Tye moved closer. Lauren turned the globe as she sat up, but the arrow kept pointing to the northeast as the globe turned just like a compass.

"It looks like we're going that way!" Helmet on, Aiden pointed his arm the same direction.

"I don't have a map, but if my memory serves, that's the way to Blooming Glen," Uncle offered.

"Indeed," Knight Protector nodded as he took a knee next to Lauren. "It may indicate the grove I've heard of."

Lauren knew the snow globe was something special. To have its direction verified by Knight Protector removed the last doubts she might have about that being the right way to go.

"Well, let's get going!" Ethan blurted out from the back of the wagon. "Daddy needs help."

"That way will take us cross-country," Uncle explained while Lauren stood up. "Likely nothing between here and there but open prairie."

Lauren breathed a sigh of relief. After their challenges in Spring Fields, she wanted to avoid places that might harbor giants and Steele Brothers. Lauren held up the snow globe, and Ethan attempted to grab it, but she shook her head and waited for Aiden to take it. He accepted and gently held cradled it to his chest.

Uncle continued, "Not much to worry about other than a mangy coyote here or there and some prairie dogs, but also not a clear path. Even with them special shoes, the horses aren't going to make great time."

"What are you suggesting?" Knight Protector asked.

"Well, we've got the full armor of God now and a giant." Uncle pointed to Tye. "I say we climb back in that boat, pole across the lake, and take the road from Spring Fields to Blooming Glen. Ain't nobody in that town gonna stop us now."

The thought of going back to the city sent a wave of cold dread down Lauren's back. All along, there had been a bit of secrecy in their movement because they were worried about being overwhelmed by the enemy. Why would they abandon that now? She'd seen them fend off her attacks with Censers and corrupt weapons. What was he thinking?

"Absolutely not!" Mother must have been feeling the same way. "My husband—your brother—is in a dire state. I'll not willingly drive him right into the middle of enemy forces! What are you thinking?"

"I'm think'n that's the fastest way to get him help," Uncle retorted with red in his cheeks.

"But, Mama! What about the little girl!" Ethan piped up.

"What girl?" Mother barked. Then took a breath. "I didn't mean to snap. What are you talking about, Ethan?"

"When Daddy was a bad guy, the girl shined her Light in the window, and it saved us. So I told her last night we would help. We have to help her!"

Lauren's eyes went wide at Ethan's proclamation. *How had he gone to see a little girl? She was on the other side of the lake.*

Mother must have been thinking the same thing. "What do you mean *last night*? I thought you raced straight to the water with your father on fire? How did you have time to talk to her?"

Ethan looked down at his feet, "Well . . . you see, Tye was sleeping on guard duty . . ."

Tye gasped and began to open her mouth, but Mother held up a hand in Tye's direction.

"Oh no you don't!" Mother's cheeks went red as she stood and pointed at Ethan. "I asked what YOU did, young man. Don't you try to make this about someone else?"

Lauren hadn't seen Mother that angry since this whole adventure had started. Lauren looked away, because she didn't want to see what happened next. She caught Tye's gaze and could tell by how her head was down that she was embarrassed by the whole thing.

"But, Mama, the light was so shiny, I had to go see it." Ethan whined.

Mother stood up in the wagon. "What did you do?"

"I ran across the lake and talked to the girl," Ethan blurted out.

"You ran across the lake!" Mother's mouth dropped open in unison with Lauren's. She'd seen him run fast the night before, but running across water was amazing.

"Yah, the boots make me really fast. I outran the giants and everything." Ethan pumped his arms like he was running while he talked.

"What giants?" Tye interjected, calling Lauren's attention back to her friend. The giantess had stepped forward and asked, eyes wide, intent on the conversation.

"Well, there were giants on guard, and when I ran by, they chased me. But they couldn't catch me because I'm so fast." Ethan paused to look around. He just had to make sure everyone was paying attention didn't he. Lauren felt a little smile creep into the corner of her mouth. Despite everything, Ethan was still Ethan.

On the other hand, Mother was still Mother. She stood there with her hands on her hips and demanded, "Go on!"

The edge in Mother's voice had only gotten harder. Lauren wondered what consequences would befall her little brother for running off on an adventure.

"Well, I talked to the little girl who shined her Light. She was going to give me her lantern. But I said she should keep it. She said there were people all over with them. Daddy made lots. But then I told her we would come help save her." Ethan held up his hands wide. "We have to save her, Mama!"

From Ethan's earnest plea, Lauren knew this wasn't some tall tale: a little girl in Blooming Glen needed their help.

Iron Sister rested a hand on the wagon's side. "What about my people? They are powerful warriors."

Lauren wondered where she was going with this as the Iron warrior stepped back and held up her sword. "We have enough weapons to arm a whole cadre of Iron Priestesses. The city would easily fall to that."

The suggestion surprised Lauren. Sure, she appreciated the Iron Sister's turn of allegiance, and that she'd helped save Ethan, but was she really trustworthy? They were trying to light the tower in Blooming Glen, not start an all-out war. So, she was taken aback when Knight Protector nodded and agreed, "Yes, that could work."

"But weren't the Iron Priestesses headed south?" Uncle asked. "We're days to the north of the Iron Mountain now. That would only add to the delay; I don't think we have the time."

To emphasize the point, Father groaned, and his pain squeezed Lauren's heart like a clothes wringer. They didn't have time to build an army. He needed help now.

"Wait!" Aiden interrupted. "The arrow points toward Blooming Glen, but that doesn't mean the wellspring is there. I know Knight Protector thinks it's in a grove near Blooming Glen, but what if that's not it?"

All eyes turned to Knight Protector, and the old warrior ran his hand through his beard as he thought for a moment. "Young Aiden may be right. I may just be putting something together that doesn't fit. But, if I'm wrong, and it's somewhere between here and there as the crow flies, we'll miss it, and have to backtrack across the countryside anyway."

"But what if it's beyond Blooming Glen in that direction?" Uncle asked. "Won't we be adding time we don't have to the journey? I still say we could take out anything we run into in the city in no time."

Tye had come closer to the discussion, and Lauren could tell by the set in her jaw the giantess wasn't happy.

Tye's mouth opened, but Mother cut her off, "For the last time, we're NOT taking my wounded husband into a combat zone." Mother stamped her foot. "If it's beyond Blooming Glen, then we have a chance to light the tower there, which gives us more support."

Lauren let out a sigh. Mother was right; they shouldn't be thinking about intentionally fighting, with Father in this state.

Uncle looked up in the air and waved his hands. "Alright, Alright! Cross-country it is. Tye, Iron Sister, lead the way. Make sure there aren't any hazards in the path."

"No!" Tye and Iron Sister said in unison. Uncle's mouth dropped, and the two young women looked at each other with wide eyes.

"After you," Iron Sister deferred to Tye.

"It was your people's 'Darkness' and 'Light' that brought all of this trouble to our land." Tye's flinty gaze could cut Uncle in two. "If you want my help, I'll have no more talk of attacking my people."

Lauren was stunned by this. Tye was cast out of her village based on Skull Crusher's lies. It was so cruel, and her own father had made it clear she was unwanted. So why would Tye feel any loyalty to them? Didn't Tye see this was her family now?

"But—" Uncle's reply was cut short by Mother holding up her hand.

"Tye, you are right. I was there." Mother took a knee next to Father. "Skull Crusher deceived them, and he, in turn, has been deceived by the Bishop. Our fight is with the Bishop and Refi'Cul, not the Heath Wardens."

Iron Sister chimed in, "Which is why I must go a different path."

"What?" Ethan blurted out from the back of the wagon. "No, you need to help us. You're my Iron Sister."

Lauren knew Ethan had become fond of Iron Sister, but she didn't realize how this might just break his heart.

"I will help you, little brother," Iron Sister responded. "I need to gather the Iron Priestesses for battle against Refi'Cul and the Bishop. Their plans for the Iron Mountain must be stopped."

"But will they believe you?" Aiden asked timidly. "I was there when you joined the other side. Won't they think it's a trap?"

Lauren had to agree with Aiden. Yet, tendrils of doubt clouded her mind. Was Tye really on their side, or was this a trick to double-cross them?

"I have to try," Iron Sister held up her sword, and blue flame erupted from it. "We now have the weapons but not the numbers to use them, and the Iron Priestesses would make formidable warriors armed this way.

Lauren stared at the fire for a moment, and it banished her growing doubts. Iron Sister was a Light Bearer for sure.

"I'll go with her," Knight Protector offered. "I'm not the warrior I used to be, but First Sister will recognize me, and I can vouch for the story."

As much as Lauren hated her father's condition, breaking upthe group felt worse. "Is this the only way?"

Everyone looked at each other for a moment. Then Mother broke the silence. "Yes, I think that makes sense. We need an army to defeat the Steele Brothers." Mother began grabbing swords from the weapons crate and leaned them against the wagon's back gate. "My only concern is how to take these weapons to your people."

"We'll take what we can carry, maybe a half dozen, and arm more when we rendezvous at Blooming Glen," Iron Sister replied as she picked up one of the blades. It shrunk to a dagger, the same way Mother's did. "Oh! Well, I guess we'll be able to carry a lot more than that. What about the shields?"

Mother handed Iron Sister a shield, and it shrunk to a dinner plate-sized buckler. Knight Protector picked up some weapons too, joined her, and by the time they were done, they had a half dozen daggers and four bucklers each, the shields on their backs, and full-size swords at their hips.

Lauren cracked an involuntary smile at how ridiculous the two of them looked. She wasn't sure how they would move fast with all that stuff on them, but she was certain they'd find a way.

"That's it for the weapons and shields other than what we're carrying. We have some odds and ends of armor, but I'm not sure that's a help to the Iron Priestesses."

"Agreed," Knight protector offered. "We'll move as quickly as we can. I know where we might be able to borrow horses. We'll meet you in Blooming Glen within a fortnight."

They were really leaving. Lauren put her hands on her face to hide her emotions. Knight Protector had gotten them through so much. Would they truly see him again?

"Iron Sister, hug!" Ethan cried from the back of the wagon. She complied and gave him an awkward hug from the ground beside him.

"Lauren," Mother said softly with one hand on a crate handle. She motioned to Lauren with the other to help. They worked together to drop the two weapons crates over the wagon's side.

Lauren dusted off her hands and saw Iron Sister and Knight Protector begin their journey south. She took a deep breath as she looked down at Father. His skin was a red-blistered mess. They had to find the Wellspring of Life and soon.

Uncle looked back at Tye. "We good?"

"Yes, I will help you find the cure for La'Ren's Father," Tye said with her fist on her chest. "But nothing more."

Uncle yelled, "Yah!" The wagon started across the prairie.

But Lauren couldn't get Tye's words out of her mind. Something about that last line was ominous. Did that mean Tye might leave them when the battle was fiercest?

A coyote's howl in broad daylight shocked Aiden and stole his focus from the problem he was working on. He looked up from his drawing of expected Censer positions on the oak slate, trying to pinpoint the source of the disturbance.

The rock of the wagon and a slight breeze made the prairie grass seem to ebb and flow like a vast sea between the wagon and the lake at Spring Fields.

A shiver went down his spine when he realized the howl had come from the city. *Why would coyotes be in the city?* Then more howls—much closer this time— struck up within the surrounding waves of green. A ball of anxiety built in Aiden's stomach as he felt the world around him go darker. They were back in a Darkness zone.

"Mama, that's not normal." Aiden piped up. "Coyotes don't usually just start howling during the day; they hunt at night."

"Yah, I have a bad feeling about that." Uncle looked over his shoulder from where he sat on the wagon's driver's seat. "That's not natural."

The goose fanning father's burned body let out a loud honk in agreement.

"That may be, but those howls are far from us." Tye walking beside the horses, shielded her eyes with her hand and scanned the horizon. "It may have nothing to do with us."

"Just the same, we need to be on our guard." Uncle placed his hand on top of the golden helmet next to him on the seat, which reflected the sunlight so completely it seemd to almost glow. It reminded Aiden that they all had the Light.

"Why worry about a bunch of coyotes?" Aiden pounded the metal breastplate he was wearing. "We have the full armor of God?"

Howls erupted again across the land, and the horses whinnied and reared. Tye immediately patted the closest one to calm it.

"We might know that, but the horses are just horses." Uncle's knuckles turn white as he pulled back on the reins. "Even these battle-tested Clydesdales' nerves have their limits."

Tye ran around the front of the horses to calm the other with a kind touch.

"What do you think, Tye?" Uncle called to the giantess. "Would we be better off picking up the pace or havin' you take the reins and lead them from the front while this ruckus is going on?"

Father groaned on the floor, and Aiden noticed that the burned skin on his arm was no longer a light pink but a deep red.

Mother bent over and put the back of her hand on his forehead. "In the Darkness, he's burning up. We need to find the wellspring quickly!"

"Yes, we must make haste." Tye nodded. "I can run for some time. Let's hurry."

Uncle put on his helmet. "Find a place to hold on; you're in for a bumpy ride." He snapped the reins, and the horses picked up the pace.

Aiden scrunched down next to Ethan and noticed he held his hands clasped tight and whispered a prayer under his breath. Aiden put an arm around his brother and joined him in silent prayer.

When the coyotes howled again, the horses just kept on running. The knot in Aiden's stomach eased a bit now that they wouldn't have to deal with scared horses breaking away.

However, the geese couldn't keep up their gentle fanning with the wagon bouncing. Mother and the children poured small amounts of water on the blanket covering Father and dabbed his brow with a damp cloth. Aiden could feel the heat on the fabric and his heart ached. They just had to find the wellspring.

They came upon a stream they couldn't cross with the wagon, which took them away from the direction the snow globe pointed. But there was a beaten path along its steep ten foot high bank, so Uncle ssuggested they follow it until they could find a crossing. They kept a fast pace until noon, when Tye finally asked for a break. The howls had subsided, so they thought it would be safe to stop for a quick bite of food and other necessities the next time the bank dipped low enough for them to easily reach the water.

A chill went down Aiden's back when the wagon rolled to a stop. Something wasn't right here. Father's arm had developed some blisters that weren't there before. "Mother, look!"

She gasped; before Mother could say anything, Tye and Uncle began arguing about whether to build a fire.

"Both of you, stop it! We need to move; he's getting much worse!" Mother demanded.

"Mama, I think we're in a double-Darkness zone!" Aiden cried. "Look!" he pointed to his slate. "We were here. After a while, it got dark. Now it's really dark. If we keep going this way, we will run into another Censer."

Mother looked at the slate for a moment with furrowed brows. Then, her eyes got big, and the corner of her lip turned up for just a moment. *Wash she proud of his discovery?* Then father groaned.

"Father is reacting poorly to the Darkness. This double-Darkness zone is literally trying to kill him," Mother said. "We can't stay here."

"But, Mama, look! If we just keep going, we should run into another Censer. If we destroy it, we'll be in the Light, and it won't do that anymore," Aiden said.

"I've been running for hours!" Tye barked. "I vowed to help your husband, but I didn't commit to die from exhaustion in the process."

Mother closed her eyes, set her jaw and growled. "I know, I know."

Aiden desperately wanted to help the situation. But how? With Father laid out in the back of the wagon and the supplies taking up so much room, there just wasn't a good way for Tye to hop in. Plus, she was just huge, half again as tall as Uncle. But he was kind of round in the middle, and she was thin, so maybe not that much more weight. He looked them both over for a second, then had an idea.

"Hey, Uncle, do you think you could carry me on your shoulders for a bit, and then Tye could ride in the wagon? That should balance out the weight the horses are carrying."

A scowl crossed Uncle's face for a moment, then he nodded. "Alright, let's do that."

Tye let out a big sigh and nodded. Uncle hopped off the wagon, and Aiden climbed onto his shoulders. Despite the looming darkness, there was something uplifting about being this high up. Uncle took the reins and began leading the horses when Tye was in place on the seat.

Uncle waded through the tall grass in front of the horses, and Aiden could see the prairie all around them. They were on the high side of the ridge that made up the stream bed, so Aiden had a great view of the prairie in every direction. After carefully squinting and opening his eyes big, Aiden thought he could see where the next Censer might be. It was hard to tell in the haze, but just maybe, he had it pinpointed.

He wanted to keep looking for clues about the Darkness, but he started to feel Uncle slow underneath him. "Do you want me to walk?"

Uncle took a deep breath, then exhaled. "Nah, you can't keep up with my long stride. We'll get there faster this way." So, Uncle continued to blaze the trail in front for another thirty minutes, and Aiden got a better and better idea of how the Censer network lay out around them.

He couldn't tell if it was the feeling of accomplishment from his discovery or a change in the atmosphere, but the weight on his chest and shoulders seemed to subside. *God, are we safe now?* He took a deep breath, and a chill went down his back. They were through the worst of it. Aiden patted Uncle on the top of his head to get his attention. "I think we're safe."

Uncle let out a deep sigh. "Good thing. I was about to have to put you down Darkness or no Darkness." Uncle pulled the horses to a stop and set him down in the back of the wagon. Aiden's heart leapt to see the blisters on Father's wounds recede as the Geese fanned him.

Tye set to making a fire, while Uncle gathered water from the stream and tended to the horses. Finally, Mother and the children got out to stretch, and Aiden brought the slate.

"Hey, Sissy, can you hand me the snow globe?" Aiden asked as he sat down criss-cross applesauce in the grass.

"I've got it!" Ethan offered as he raced back to the wagon.

"Oh no you don't!" Lauren scolded. "That is our hope to save Father. I wouldn't want your butterfingers to drop it off the wagon again."

"Hey!" Ethan protested. Aiden gritted his teeth. She was probably right, but that sure was a mean way to say it.

Before he could stand up for Ethan, Mother interjected. "Lauren, that wasn't very kind. But she is right, Ethan; we need to be very careful with it. So why don't you let Lauren get it."

"Yes, Mama," Ethan whined through his nose.

Lauren got the snow globe and brought it to Aiden. "So why do you need this?"

Aiden took it and shook it. Then turned it a bit to the left, then back to the right until an arrow appeared. He wanted to see how their path to the wellspring might align with the Censer positons.

He was worried the arrow might disappear while working with the slate, so he set the snowglobe down on the ground and folded some grass over to point in the same direction.

"The Darkness is bad for Father," Aiden explained. "The double Darkness, doubly so. So we need to keep him out of it if we can."

Ethan and Lauren were on their knees on either side of the slate, and the others stood behind him as he pointed to a circle he'd filled in with white chalk in one corner of the slate. That circle intersected three other circles.

"So we started here in the Light zone." He used his pinky to slowly erase a path through the white circle, and the residue on his finger began to draw a path through the dark ring next to it. "So when we traveled this direction, eventually we came to the double-Darkness zone." His pinky stopped at a point where the circles he hadn't filled intersected. "It took us a long time to go through that zone, so we went through the long way, not the short way."

He used his index finger and thumb to compare the long axis of the oval made by the intersection versus the short axis. "So that means if we keep going, we'll run into a Censer." He picked up the trail with his pinky again and quickly dragged it through the intersection and to the center of the next ring.

"That sounds about right." Uncle looked off in the distance and stroked his beard. "Your Pa will be real proud of all that figurin' you just did."

"Yes, Aiden, I am proud too," Mother patted him on the shoulder. "But I'm not sure how this helps us."

"The double-Darkness zones are everywhere." Aiden pointed to multiple intersecting circles along their path to Blooming Glen. "It looks like our path will keep running us through them."

"That's not good!" Lauren blurted out. Her eyes were wide. Aiden could hear the pain in her voice. He felt it, too, but he couldn't let the thought of Father's condition prevent him from explaining the plan.

"Sissy, let me finish. What makes a double-Darkness zone double is two Censers," Aiden continued. "If we keep going, we can break the one in front of us just like the one in the cabin yesterday. So that will put us in the light for a long time."

"Oh, I get it," Lauren chimed in, "but then we're back in double Darkness before finding the next one."

Uncle pointed with his sword tip at the center of a ring to the left of their path. "Not if we split up,"

Aiden had to bite his tongue. He was just about to say the same thing, and Uncle stole his thunder.

Before he could come up with more to say, Mother interrupted, "What?"

"Look, the boy has a solid map here." Uncle tousled Aiden's hair and continued to point with his sword. "If a group of us starts out early, we could knock this one out."

Uncle paused and looked at Mother. Her furrowed brows and set jaw told Aiden she didn't approve. But Uncle was right; it was the only way to keep Father out of the double-Darkness zones. So he piped up to support Uncle. "If the wagon can keep going and skirt the edge of this to keep oriented, then we can all meet up at the next Censer."

Mother took a deep breath about to respond, but Tye interrupted, "I will do this." The sharp edge in her voice sent a ripple of concern through Aiden. He'd seen her under the influence of the Darkness. Going after a Censer on her own wouldn't be good.

Uncle began to protest, "Well, sure, and some of us will come with you. We just—"

"No! These are my people's lands. I am their Warden. This is how I will help save La'Ren's Father." She put her hand to her chest.

"Tye—" Mother began, but the giantess cut her off.

"I am faster than all of you. I am the only one who can go and destroy the Censer and allow you to move at speed along your path." She put her hands on her hips. "I will destroy that Censer and any others I find."

She was right about the speed. Aiden looked at Lauren to gauge her thoughts. The wrinkles in Lauren's forehead told him all he needed to know. She didn't think Tye should be on her own, either.

Uncle turned to Mother. "I don't like it, but it makes sense. What do you think?"

Mother let out a sigh. "Her words are wise."

"But, Mother . . ." Lauren began with a quiver in her voice.

"I will do this . . . without delay," Tye said with a cold snap in her voice. Aiden couldn't tell if she was mad at them for some reason, or if she was being cold because she didn't really want to leave them.

Regardless, the giantess turned to the general direction of the Censer Uncle indicated on the slate. Aiden agreed it was the right thing to do, but something felt . . . off. Was his map correct? A slight miscalculation here could put her way off course. "Wait, Tye! You'll have a better direction if you wait until we destroy the next Censer."

She paused for a moment, staring off in the distance, standing stone cold, still as a statue.

Lauren ran to her and grabbed her hand. "Maybe we can find horses or something between here and there, so you don't have to go alone."

The way Lauren was pleading with Tye, told Aiden his sister hadn't completely bought into the plan to send Tye off on her own. However, a groan from Father punctuated the urgency for action. They were going to have to find a way to destroy that other Censer, or Father wouldn't make it to the Wellspring of Life. Would they find a way to send someone with Tye or risk her going it alone?

As the sun started its descent into the west, they crested a rise to find a ramshackle structure sitting in the middle of a flat, bare earth depression on the other side. Rocky sand and scattered gnarly sun-bleached driftwood bits formed a ring around the depression, and in its center, it looked like someone had thrown the remains of a boat dock, a couple of rowboats, a canoe, and a stack of driftwood into a big pile. The black smoke of a Censer spewed out from under the debris.

Looking more closely, Lauren realized they were standing on what had been the sandy shore of a lake, and off to the west, the dam had washed away. A thin stream of water ran from east to west through and under the large pile of debris. The water going into the structure looked clean, but what was coming out was black and putrid.

Lauren's heart sank into the pit of her stomach as she remembered how dark water had almost killed Ethan's pet Sparkle Frog. This was bad for everything downstream.

"We have to destroy it!" she said. "Who knows what creatures are being affected by that putrid sludge?"

A sudden coyote howl in the distance behind them punctuated the point. They hadn't heard the canines for hours, and now that howl sounded close. Tye drew her sword at the sound and took up a battle stance on the balls of her feet as she scanned the perimeter.

"Hold up," Uncle reined in the horses. "This is a dried lake bed, but it's hard telling how long it's been like this. I don't want the wagon to get stuck if all we're seein' here is a dry surface with a foot of mud underneath."

The tension in Lauren's shoulders tightened. The last thing they needed was further delay because the wagon got stuck. Father was so red, and his breathing was so shallow. "Are you sure?" Lauren asked.

"Yes, your Uncle is wise in this. We will scout it out." Tye seemed to set her sword in the wagon's bed absentmindedly as she started to look at the ground around the wagon.

Lauren cocked her head and called, "Shouldn't you go armed?"

Tye picked up a six-foot piece of driftwood as thick as Lauren's arm, then grabbed it in two hands and took up a combat stance. She raised an eyebrow at Lauren and smirked.

"OK, point taken." Lauren chuckled.

Uncle stepped off the wagon and set his helmet on the seat.

Ethan piped up, "Uncle, don't leave your helmet. You don't want to get conked in the wonkus, do you?"

"Not much likelihood of that here, little guy," Uncle replied. "Besides, I need to see all around to make sure I don't miss any sinkholes." He stepped to the back of the wagon and tousled Ethan's hair. "Thanks for thinking of me."

Tye must have been thinking the same thing because she added, "Good point," and removed her helmet as well, setting it next to Uncle's.

Lauren let out a chuckle, and the tension in her neck eased a little. Uncle was trying to move as fast as he could. He was a good tracker and knew all the dangers on the frontier. He'd find a way through this.

Like Tye, Uncle picked up a piece of driftwood, albeit much smaller, and the two began poking at the ground as they crossed to the dried lake bed. They slowly marked a path they thought the wagon could take as they went.

Lauren moved up to the wagon seat to find a better view, and the boys came with her. It became apparent quickly that Uncle's intuition was correct. The top of the depression was a thin layer of dried clay, but when he pushed the driftwood in at a certain point, it broke through the surface. When he pulled it out, soupy mud dripped off the end.

A sudden breeze kicked up, wafting the rotten Censer smell up her nose, and the whole sight reminded her of one of Ethan's dirty diapers when he was a baby.

The boys must have thought the same thing because they both groaned, "Ewwww."

Uncle misjudged a spot at about the midpoint and fell with one leg into the mud. Lauren's breath caught in her throat, but Tye managed to grab him before he fell all the way in.

"Uncle!" the three children cried in unison and stood.

"Wait," Mother barked from the back of the wagon. Lauren turned and saw she was diligently holding a wet cloth on Father's head while the geese and Daddy Duck took turns fanning him.

After a minute of tugging, Tye managed to pull Uncle free, but he lost a boot in the process. Uncle seemed to shake the whole thing off and went right back to finding a good path. The children sat down with a collective sigh of relief.

The hard ground led Uncle and Tye ever closer to the debris pile. Two figures appeared on top when they got within ten feet of it. Lauren realized that Tye and Uncle couldn't see the people from where they were. She opened her mouth to warn them, but the figures cut her off by screaming a battle cry as they threw objects over the side of the pile.

Tye looked up to see the danger and caught a melon-sized rock squarely on her chin. She dropped like a sack of potatoes.

"No! Tye!" Lauren cried as she stood up, knocking Tye's helmet off the wagon.

"I told them they needed their helmets!" Ethan blurted out as he stood with Aiden.

Uncle dodged the first big rock and began blocking others with his make-shift staff, but a lucky throw hit his bare foot, causing Uncle to hop around. He landed in one of the muddy spots with his good foot and quickly sank to his knee. It was all he could do to keep from sinking further while blocking the larger rocks raining down on him.

"Ethan! They need your shield." Aiden called while he hopped in the back of the wagon to pick up Tye's sword.

"Yes, they need all of us!" Lauren urged.

"But what about Father?" Ethan asked with a quiver on his lips.

"He's too far for them to reach with their rocks." Mother looked around the area. "The birds will protect him, right?"

The geese replied with vigorous honks, and Daddy Duck gave a loud quack. Lauren wondered if it would be better if they tried to tell the birds to attack the Censer. But the way the smoke was leaking from the pile made getting a clear "shot" at the Censer impossible.

Mother broke Lauren's musings. "Children, put your helmets on!"

They donned their helmets and raced down the center of the path Uncle and Tye had marked in the dirt. When they were fifty yards out, the rocks stopped raining down on Uncle, and he struggled to pull free of the sucking mud.

Then a cry came up from on top of the pile. "Ha ha! We got them no-good egg-stealin' varmints! I tell you, my boy. Ain't no egg stealers gettin' in our chicken coop!"

"That's right, gramps!" A young boy's voice called.

Lauren was puzzled by this exchange. They had run into Censers guarded by corrupted animals and evil machines, but a grandpa and his boy? That didn't make any sense. Why would any grandfather put his grandchild in that situation?

Before she came to a conclusion, the old man hollered, "What's that over there? More egg-stealin' no-good varmints. Get yer rocks ready, boyo."

"Ethan, take the front, shield up!" Mother commanded, "Lauren, look for an opening with your spear."

Ethan ran forward and held his arm up with the shield attached. It grew wider and taller. As it did, the Light showed all around. Lauren could almost feel the power of the Light throbbing off Ethan's shield. Her spear sprang to life in her hand, surrounded by blue, glowing liquid.

When they closed within a few yards of the structure, the attackers started throwing rocks. The first couple fell short, then the old man managed to make range to Ethan.

He deflected the blow with his shield, but his step faltered, and he went down on one knee.

Lauren shot past him and out of the shield's protective bubble. Before she could change direction, she got pelted by a couple of smaller rocks on the helmet. It didn't hurt her at all, but the sudden ringing noise caused her to waver. There was so much going on, and the ringing from the rock blows was a distraction.

She backpedaled into the protective shield and took a deep breath to try to find a better approach. There was no good shot at this angle, and moving to a better position was going to involve taking lots of hits from those rocks.

"Gramps, they're getting close. There's too many of them," the boy called.

"Ahhh! I got something gonna give them varmints the what for!" The old man pulled a dagger from his belt and waved it victoriously overhead.

Lauren had a line on the old man for a brief instant, while the old man's arm was in the air. She pulled back to throw, but he finished the sweep of his arm with the dagger, and fell back out of view.

A loud *ka-chunk* came from the debris pile, and a mass of silver blasted into the air and then broke apart over them. The little strings of metal fluttered down, and the old man opened up in a cackle of laughter.

The family paused and just watched the metal bits fall. Lauren raised her eyebrow as she looked at Aiden. The streamers were harmless bits of foil—nothing to be concerned about, right?

He just shrugged back at her as the silver coils floated down, covering everyone in little strings.

The old man's display did manage to completely break their momentum. Lauren realized the time spent looking at the pretty strings should have been used to pull Uncle out instead.

Then, eyes appeared in all the little nooks and crannies of the debris pile. A chill ran down Lauren's spine. What new threat was this? The eyes seemed to grow out of the pile into wicked black beaks, as hundreds of crows made their presence known with a thunder of caws.

"Get them egg-stealin' varmints!" the old man cried. "They've got yer pretties!"

As one, a caw that almost sounded like the word *pretties* came up from the birds, and they took to the air.

The birds darted toward the family, creating absolute chaos. The wings and talons of hundreds of birds descended on the family. The cacophony of cawing birds drowned out any chance of coordinating actions.

Mother's and Aiden's flaming swords repelled the birds wherever they swung. However, the the birds darted around to peck at them from behind. Their sharp beaks focused on dislodging the glittering streamers, which had landed all over Lauren and her family, getting caught in the cracks of their armor.

The crows assaulted Lauren with abandon, and she fell to her knees trying to avoid their incessant pecks, and managed to drive them back by twirling her spear. But she couldn't keep that up and stand again. So she slowly edged toward Ethan, where he'd taken cover behind his shield. The protective glow around it seemed to be working.

"Just go on, you egg-stealin' varmints!" the oldster called. "Them crows'll pick yer bones clean if you don't get out of here."

Just then, Daddy Duck and the geese arrived. There was a flurry of feathers in the air over where Uncle struggled in the mud. The blessed birds managed to intimidate the crows into leaving Uncle and Tye alone, but otherwise merely stood their ground.

Mother and Aiden managed to move back-to-back, creating a circle of flaming swords around them, holding the crows at bay. They, too, joined Ethan and Lauren huddled behind the shield.

Mother pointed toward the debris pile. "Lauren if we can move a little closer, do you think you can hit the old man with your spear?"

"I don't think that's going to work." Lauren shook her head. Her ears were still ringing a little from the earlier encounter with the rocks. "As soon as I find a good position, they move to a better one and ring my bell."

"I can't get much closer either. The shield makes the rocks bounce off, but it hurts!" Ethan whined. "I don't understand! The Light is keeping back the birds, why not the rocks?"

Lauren felt helpless. She thought having the Armor of God would make her invincible. But maybe it was only protection from the Darkness, and not so much physical things.

Aiden must have been thinking the same thing because he offered, "Maybe because the rocks are just rocks and not of the Darkness." He thumped his chest with his fist. "So we have to count on the armor just doing its job."

A sudden honking and quacking called their attention. A group of crows broke off to harass the geese, pulling them away from Tye, while another group dove for her.

"Go on, you varmints! Get!" the old man called from the debris pile. "My birds is tougher than you!"

The geese and crows whirled around each other in a dizzying dance of beaks and feathers. Aiden's jerky motions pulled Lauren's attention away from the birds. He was actively picking streamers off his armor. When he caught Lauren's eye, he explained, "We just need to pull the strings off of us, and they'll leave us alone."

Lauren planted the butt of her spear in the ground to follow Aiden's lead. But a loud "Quack!" from Daddy Duck caused her to look up. The crows intensified their efforts driving Tye's protectors away. A crow took the opening and began pecking at the giantess.

Lauren gasped and surged toward her friend, determined to help her, but Mother grabbed her arm. Lauren whirled, eyes squinted, about to rebuke Mother for stopping her, but she was cut off.

"We'll help her together!" Mother said.

Lauren nodded in agreement, then Mother continued, "Ethan, keep the bubble at our backs, Aiden and I will clear the way. Lauren, if you get a line on a target, take the shot."

Crouched behind the shield, Ethan gripped it with both hands, and carefully kept them covered in the Light as best he could.

It was tricky for Lauren to stay in the Light and find a target at the same time. The attackers on the mound were keeping low, just letting the birds do their job for them. So she turned her focus to the crows, looking for an opportunity to scare them away with her spear.

However, Mother's and Aiden's swords were blazing the trail to Tye, and it was hard to line up a target through their fiery arcs.

Lauren was so focused on trying to spear the birds, she didn't notice that the path around the mud holes had driven them closer to the debris pile. A small rock pinged her helmet, warning her of a much larger one falling towards her. She managed to dodge just in time, but it took her slightly outside the protective bubble. Her quick movement bumped Aiden, and he stumbled off the marked path and into a sinkhole.

"No!" Lauren reached for him, but he slipped through her grasp. Her heart sank, as the sucking sound of the mud began to slurp Aiden up. He flung his arms wide to catch the firm ground, but lost hold of his sword. Its flames guttered out as it flew toward an opening in the debris pile.

Before Lauren could act, the birds used this opportunity to intensify their assault, further separating her from the protective bubble and forcing her to twirl her spear to keep the crows at bay. Mother was holding her own, surrounding herself with arcs of blue flame, while Ethan tried to grip the shield and give Aiden a hand out of the mud.

"Now I got you!" The old man lifted a watermelon-sized rock with both arms and threw it at Ethan.

It hit the shield with a loud gong, knocking Ethan to the ground. He lost his hold on the shield, and its pale bubble of protective light winked out.

Terror squeezed Lauren's chest, and the added tension slowed her spear. There was just too much going on to know what to do. *God! Please help!*

The birds must have seen Ethan as an easier target, because the group attacking Lauren let up and darted for her brother. Lauren turned to help him and caught the old man throwing up his arms in the air from the corner of her eye.

"Now we got them!" the oldster yelled.

This gave Lauren the chance she needed, and she flung her spear with all her might, catching the old man in the forehead, knocking him out of view.

The little boy cried, "Gramps!" and dropped down behind the edge of the debris pile.

However, Lauren was so distracted by the chaos around her, that she'd forgotten the spear would *pop* back in her hand. So, as it re-materialized, it slipped through her fingers and thumped to the ground. "No!" she barely croaked as dread gripped her throat.

The birds were on her in an instant. Lauren's stomach glenched as she was englufled in a flurry of wings and talons. *God, please help!* She whirled and dodged in an attempt to flee their pecking beaks. In confusion, she tripped over driftwood embedded in the mud, stumbled through a hole in the debris pile, and slammed onto the ground on her back. She hit so hard that her helmet popped off and rolled toward the deep red glow of the Censer in the center of the room.

Lauren wheezed, trying to catch her breath. Her vision blurred, and black dots she didn't think were from the Censer's smoke clouded her vision.

"C'mon, Lauren, you've got it together!" she told herself. Another deep breath, and the black dots disappeared, so she quickly stood and thought to grab her helmet. However, it was so dim in here that she wasn't sure she could see with it on. She heard stamping feet and a snort somewhere behind the Censer, but the smoke blocked out whatever it was. A horse? If so, Lauren hoped it was tied up. She was in no shape to fight an angry horse.

She took a couple of wobbly steps on the uneven ground to get her bearings. She stood in the light just under a ladder that went up to the top of the shack. Should she try to capture the boy? Would that make the birds stop?

She looked out the hole she had fallen through to see the swirl of the battle. Ethan had regained his shield, but her family remained stuck under the onslaught of the birds. She could see her spear, but there was no way to grab it without being overwhelmed by the birds. She stared at it for a moment, trying to will it into her hand. She let out a frustrated sigh. Despite weeks in her hands, she still didn't really know how the spear worked. She wished Father could tell her more about it. FATHER! Was he still OK, or were there birds attacking his defenseless body?

Before acting on her fear, she felt a presence above her. "Don't you move, you no-good egg-stealin' varmint!" Came the voice of the little boy from the top of the ladder. "You hurt Gramps. Now you just put your hands on your head, and get down on your knees. If I even see a hint you're tryin' something tricky, I'm a gonna clobber you."

Her heart fell deep in her stomach. If only she'd grabbed the helmet before looking around. What was she going to do?

"Do it now, er, I'll just clobber you all the same," the boy called.

She slowly lifted her hands as a puff of wind threw a metal streamer into the shack, and it lazily fell to the ground. Something about its path mesmerized her for just a second. She followed it to the ground until it landed ever so gently on the pommel of Uncle's sword.

In an instant, she threw herself to the floor in a summersault. This caught the boy off guard, because the rock he threw landed just short of Lauren, and she came up with the sword in her hand. It burst into flames. The boy gasped. Lauren didn't dare look up the hole to see what he was doing for fear he might just throw rocks at her. She side-stepped the ladder and then carefully navigated the room, looking for places where the ceiling was the most solid.

With the crows keeping Daddy Duck and the geese busy, the only way they would destroy the Censer was if she did it. Every time they'd done that, it had made a big explosion. If she hit it with the sword, would she be hurt too?

She heard scrambling around above and noticed light suddenly coming through in a new place.

"I'll find you, you no-good egg-stealin' varmint." Came the muffled voice of the boy. If she was going to destroy the Censer, she needed to stall so she could grab her helmet.

"We didn't steal your eggs!" she called, hoping talking might slow him down.

"That's not what Gramps says! I'm gonna find you." A new place opened up in the roof, illuminating her helmet.

Oh no! There's no way I'll be able to put my helmet on without getting clobbered first.

Would the breast plate alone be enough to protect her from the explosion?

The boy ripped a hole in the ceiling just three feet from her. "I'm gonna find you!"

If she didn't act quickly, he would find her, and that would be that. Unfortunately, he was under the power of the Darkness, and without her spear, she couldn't knock some sense into him.

The ceiling above her opened up. She dashed for the Censer, holding the sword in both hands in front of her. God, please protect me.

The sword connected with the Censer, and it exploded!

6.   Interlude - Lord of the Prairie

Refi'Cul reveled as his royal chariot carried him toward Blooming Glen. The horse-drawn, black-lacquered, two-wheeled buggy glided over the gravel path to Blooming Glen more smoothly than any he'd ever ridden. At the speed they were traveling, the Censer on the back trailed its dark vapors over all his troops, giving them the drive to keep pace to the horse's trot. It also had the added benefit of ensuring the Steele brothers wouldn't freeze up as they went.

Deep down, he knew the Bishop would disapprove of him taking a Censer from the network. But the band of Steele Brothers and giants following him, assured him that whatever punishment the old man might try to inflict would be met with swift resistance from his entourage.

The Master Warden was still a problem. The giant had held his troops back when Refi'Cul ordered a homestead burned to "warm up the troops" in front of the cowering women and children that lived there, before sending them running off into the night. He had no intention of hurting the helpless people, only leaving them with a clear message that there was a new Lord of the Prairie. But he needed a way to be rid of Master Warden without losing the might of the giants.

While Refi'Cul was lost in thought, Master Warden closed the gap between them and spoke. "Refi'Cul, it appears this Censer you carry has enlivened not just your Steele Brothers but the Wardens of the Heath as well. I've never seen them move with such speed, even the moose benefit."

Refi'Cul raised his eyebrows. Respect? Admiration? These were the last things he expected from Master Warden. If he played this right, he might be able to turn the giant to his will after all. "As I have said all along, Master Warden, the Censers bear the one true light. That is what has enlivened your Wardens and their moose."

The giant nodded, "Yes, yes, of course, but it does seem to leave us in a precarious position, having only one of these Censers." He waved a hand toward it. "A broken wheel or a lame horse, and we'd quickly lose its power, no?"

Refi'Cul furrowed his brows. Was the giant trying to take control of the Censer? The Steele Lord took a measured breath as he tried to work through a dozen different scenarios before he answered. Then, off to the southeast, he noticed a patch of slightly darker sky. "I share your concerns, mighty Master of the Heath. One Censer is vulnerable, but two are unstoppable." Refi'Cul paused to gauge the giant's reaction.

Master Warden's face was a blank slate, until a very tiny curve grew on the corner of his lip. The slow reaction told Refi'Cul that his initial assessment that the giant wanted to take the Censer was correct. The Steele Lord pointed to the southeast. "There is another Censer, hidden under a rock outcropping in the prairie in that direction. See the darker sky; that is your guide."

Master Warden turned to scan the horizon, "I see. So you think we should go there next?"

"Oh, no, Master Warden, my mission is too time-sensitive to redirect." Refi'Cul shook his head. "My Steele Brothers on foot are much too slow across the wild prairie.

We'd lose a whole day going there and back to the main road as a group."

Master Waden gave Refi'Cul a flinty stare. "So what are you suggesting."

"If you were to take a dozen of your fastest troops, you could retrieve it and rejoin us just as we reach Blooming Glen." The Steele Lord indicated Master Warden's moose with his right hand. "Your moose powered by a second Censer's vapors could easily carry you across the prairie in half the time these horses and my men could travel."

"Why should I not take all the Wardens with me?" The Giant challenged.

Refi'Cul closed his eyes for a brief moment. This was it; he had the Master Warden where he wanted him. The giant needed the power of the true light. Now, he just needed to cement the alliance. "That is your right; you are their Master." The giant's face softened ever so slightly. "But I'll offer a piece of advice my mentor, the Bishop, told me. Keep your friends close and your enemies closer." Master Warden's eyes got big at that. Refi'Cul smiled. "I know you still question whether I am friend or foe. So you might want to leave someone you trust to . . . keep me close."

Master Warden suddenly let out a laugh. "My young Refi'Cul, you are far wiser than you appear." The giant turned in his saddle, whistled, and waved toward one of the giants behind him, who sped up his moose to close the gap. When he arrived, the Master Warden began, "I'm taking a journey of Wardens with me to gather another Censer." The giant pointed toward the smoking device in the buggy. "You and the rest of the Wardens will accompany Lord

Refi'Cul as his defenders until I return. In my absence, Lord Refi'Cul is your master. However, if he orders you to violate the code of the heath, you are to withdraw immediately. Understood?"

The other giant nodded. "Yes, Master Warden."

"You are the Journey Leader; guide the Wardens well." Master Warden nodded toward the giant and turned his moose with a whistle to join the Wardens behind them.

Refi'Cul felt his cheeks might crack from the broad smile on his face. If Master Warden really wanted the true light for himself, he would be a powerful ally. However, he'd also left a younger, hopefully more ambitious, Warden in his place. Refi'Cul had time now on the road to gain his confidence and solidify his power over the Wardens once and for all.

A loud *tha-wump* came from inside the debris pile, shaking the ground. There must have been a bit of a concussion in the air as well, because the crows scattered. Even the geese wobbled in the air for a moment before circling down to land next to Uncle, where he was desperately trying to free himself from the muddy sinkhole.

A big puff of black smoke followed the blast, pouring out all the cracks and crevices in the disorganized jumble of boats and buildings. But then there was no more smoke, and the sky over the shack began to clear.

"Lauren!" Mother called as she raced into the shack. Ethan wanted to follow. Sissy might need Sparkle Frog.

But Aiden called, "E! Help me out of here."

Aiden was stuck in the mud up to his knee, and it didn't seem like he had the leverage to get himself out. Ethan wasn't sure he'd be much help and thought it might be better to go help Lauren first. But Aiden looked so pitiful he had to try.

Ethan grabbed Aiden's arm in both hands and leaned back to pull as hard as he could. There was a very satisfying slurping sound, and Aiden came free. Ethan didn't expect him to pop out of the mud so suddenly and fell hard on his bottom, bringing Aiden on top of him.

Both boys broke out into laughter. This was the most normal thing that had happened since Father had gone missing. "Daddy!" He turned to see the horse and wagon was still right where they had left it. So maybe he was fine. "Aiden, do you think Daddy is OK? Did the birds attack him?"

Aiden got up off of Ethan, sat on his bottom, and began wiping the slimy dark brown mud off his leg with his hands. "I tried to keep the wagon in the corner of my eye." Aiden grimaced as he whipped his hand around, trying to fling off the mud. "I didn't see any crows go that way."

Ethan caught a whiff of the mud and grimaced. The mud must have had dark water in it. "If the birds didn't get him, then I should check on sissy. That was a big boom!" Ethan hopped up and put his shield on his arm. It lit up with a faint blue glow. It warmed Ethan's heart that his little Light still shone.

"Yeah, I'll help Uncle and Tye," Aiden said as he abandoned trying to clean his leg and stood as well.

Ethan rushed to the shack to see how he could help Lauren but quickly slowed when he came to the uneven ground just inside the door. His shield lit the way into the dark room that was otherwise only brightened by little beams of sunlight reaching through holes in the ramshackle ceiling.

Mother sat on the floor, holding Lauren with her ear next to Lauren's mouth and nose. Tears began to well up in Ethan's eyes. Was she dead? No, not Sissy! "Mama, is she OK?"

"Yes, I think she's just knocked out," Mother nodded softly. She lay Lauren's head on her lap. Dust motes danced in the beam of light, illuminating Lauren's face.

Ethan followed them up to the hole in the ceiling and then remembered their attackers. "Did you find the boy?"

"Boy?" Mother raised an eyebrow.

"Yah, the little boy who was throwing rocks." Ethan pointed at a large stone on the floor. If he was still up there, then both Mother and Lauren were still in danger.

"No, he's not down here. Maybe he's on top." Mother pointed to the ladder. "I suspect the blast must have hit him hard too."

Ethan moved toward the ladder.

"Oh no, you don't." She waved a finger at him

"But, Mama, he could be hurt. We should help," Ethan whined.

"There's no telling what trouble is up there. You wait for your Uncle." Mother scolded. "Actually, to stay out of trouble, go grab some water. Maybe I can use that to wake Lauren up."

"Not water, Mama." Ethan waved in the direction of the wagon. "Meow Meow. He's the best waker-upper in the whole Heathlands. Does she have a head egg? I can grab Sparkle Frog too."

Mother raised an eyebrow then focused on Lauren, inspecting her head. "I'm not sure, but if you think her kitten can help, it's worth a try."

Ethan picked his way over the uneven floor in the shack and then raced off to the wagon. He heard a loud honk to his left. The sight made Ethan pause for a moment in amazement. Uncle was still stuck in the mud, holding the staff of Lauren's spear in his hands, shoulder-width apart. Aiden was pulling in the middle, and the geese were pulling on either end. Ethan was about to go help when Uncle pulled free. So he turned and ran to the wagon, hoping Aiden was right, that the birds had left Father alone.

When he got to the wagon, he climbed up onto the front seat. Meow Meow was sitting there sunning himself like they hadn't just been through a big battle with rocks raining down and birds pecking at them. The little kitten looked like he thought he was the king of the world. It made Ethan chuckle.

His smile faded when he noticed Father's unconscious form. With the Censer gone, Father was bathed in clear sunlight. His skin looked light pink rather than the burning red it had been. So Aiden was right about the Darkness making it worse.

"Meow, meow," the kitten cried as it rubbed its body against Ethan's leg and purred. The kitten must've known Lauren was in trouble. Why didn't it just pop on over to her? The kitten hopped off the seat onto Sparkle Frog's wooden bucket. Maybe the kitten knew she had a head egg after all.

Ethan picked up Meow Meow and set him back on the seat. Then he took the lid off Sparkle Frog's bucket. The frog let out a throaty "Croak" and hopped up on Ethan's curly red heair. Ethan laughed as he cradled Meow Meow in his arms and jumped off the wagon. He ran back to the debris pile at full tilt.

Uncle was on a knee, getting ready to pour a waterskin on Tye. Ethan realized he was trying to wake her up. "Let me try," Ethan called.

Sparkle Frog hopped off Ethan and onto Tye's bruised chin. The bruise disappeared, and the frog jumped back onto Ethan's head. Then he set Meow Meow down beside her, and the kitten licked Tye's ear.

The giantess' eyes fluttered open, and she caught Ethan's gaze. "I will have to listen to you the next time you say I need a helmet." She rubbed her chin, and Uncle helped her stand. Ethan's face beamed with a huge smile at that.

He scooped up Meow Meow and ran for the debris pile where Aiden was leading a pony, tied with a rotten grey rope, out of the opening. Ethan grimaced as it came out. It was the dirtiest pony Ethan had ever seen. With every step it took, grey dust poofed off its legs, and the rotten garbage smell from the mud got stronger as the pony got closer. That poor animal really needed a bath.

When they broke through the entrance of the shack, Sparkle Frog leapt onto Lauren's forehead. Ethan held Meow Meow out at arm's length in both hands as he ran to Mother. The kitten wriggled and whined in his hands, unhappy with the treatment. Mother gently took the kitten from Ethan.

"So now what?" Mother asked, eyebrow upraised.

"Just put him on her belly. He'll do the rest." Ethan pointed. Sparkle Frog hopped off Lauren and back onto Ethan's head.

Mother let out an unexpected chuckle. "That Frog sure likes to make a nest in your red hair," which made Ethan wonder what it was about his noggin that Sparkle Frog liked so much.

Mother set the kitten on Lauren's stomach, and then he gently padded up and licked her nose. When he bumped noses with Lauren, she groaned, then lifted a hand to pet Meow Meow's back.

Ethan's heart warmed to see Lauren's eyes open. He was so glad everyone was going to be OK.

"Lauren, are you hurt badly?" Mother asked

Her eyes flutter open. "My back hurts a bit, but I'll be OK." Meow Meow licked her nose again. "Good kitty." Ethan knelt down next to Lauren and gave her a hug. She leaned into him and smiled.

Uncle ducked in through the opening, his bottom half caked in mud and missing a boot. "Everybody alright in here?"

"Lauren was knocked out by the Censer's destruction, but I think she's OK now." Mother looked down at Lauren, her furrowed eyebrows full of concern.

"She's OK, Mama. Sparkle Frog, fixed her head egg." Ethan patted the frog. "Right, Sissy?"

"I'm OK," Lauren nodded and set Meow Meow on the ground. "But next time, I'm making sure my chin strap is tighter, so I don't lose my helmet. That explosion packed a wallop."

"Yeah, I bet." Uncle nodded and scanned the room, "So where's the kid and the old man?"

"I think they're still up on top," Lauren offered.

Ethan had nearly forgotten about the boy. He wasn't sure, but he thought their little attacker was his age. Maybe now, with the Censer gone, they could be friends.

Uncle looked up at the ceiling, "With the Censer done for, do you think they're still up for a fight?"

"No, the boy was just scared." Lauren shook her head.

Ethan felt his eyes scrunch up. "Did you say something mean to him, Sissy?"

"No!" Lauren scrunched up her nose and pursed her lips, "I knocked out his grandpa with my spear. Wouldn't that make you a bit scared?"

"Oh." Ethan looked down at his feet. He sure hoped the boy would forgive them for that so they could be friends. "I see. Do you think you hurt him badly?"

"No, I think the old man should be OK," She paused and looked up the ladder. "He might just be a bit disoriented with the Darkness knocked out of him."

"Alright, I'll go check it out." Uncle made for the ladder.

"Wait, you might need this one." Lauren picked up Meow Meow and put him in Uncle's pouch. Uncle raised his hands and shrugged in confusion. "He'll know how to wake up the grandpa."

"Alright then." Uncle climbed the ladder and disappeared. Sparkle Frog jumped up through the hole in the cieling after him.

Mother scanned the room. "What is this place?"

Without the Censer's haze, sunbeams lit the room through holes in the ceiling. A broken wooden trough sat in the right rear corner. That must have been where they kept the pony. The whole area looked more like a hog woller than a stable. Ethan grimaced. No wonder the poor animal was so dirty.

Next to the trough, there were a couple of ratty wool blankets laid out on a hodgepodge of uneven wooden pallets surrounded by crates, glass canning jars, and grain sacks.

A flurry of flapping wings stole Ethan's attention, as crows flew through the bigger holes in the ceiling and began roosting in the broken-down remains of a chicken coop to the left.

"Hey, Gramps is coming down," Uncle called, "Can someone give him a hand?"

Did that mean the boy was OK too? Ethan moved to the ladder to try to see, but Mother gently led him out of the way and reached up to help the old man as he shakily navigated the ladder.

When Gramps reached the bottom, he whirled on Mother pointing a finger at her, "You ain't no dirty egg-stealin' varmints are you?" He wobbled for just a second and had to grab the ladder to stay upright.

Mother was small for a woman, and Gramps was maybe just a couple of inches taller, but his back was hunched. His suspenders pulled filthy blue jeans up to his chest, leaving his ankles showing, so he looked like a little boy trying to give his Mama a-talkin' to rather than her elder. It was all Ethan could do to hold in a laugh.

"No, we didn't come here to steal your eggs." Mother held her hands up palms forward. "Although, this is the first I've heard of keeping crows for eggs."

"Crows? What do you mean, crows?" the old man balled his fists.

Mother gestured to the broken chicken coop.

Gramps turned to look, and his mouth dropped. He stood stupefied for a moment. Ethan's mirth died in his chest. The way the old man's face drooped was the saddest thing he'd ever seen. A tear formed in Gramps's eye, and Ethan very much wanted to give him a hug.

"Is everything OK?" Mother pulled a blue paisley handkerchief from a pocket in her doeskin-leather shirt and offered it to him.

The old man ignored Mother's offer and instead fell to his knees and wept. The family stood in silence for a moment. Ethan couldn't come up with good words for the old man, and nobody else must have had them either.

The awkward silence was broken by Uncle. "Boy's comin' down. He's a bit shaky too."

Ethan's eyes brightened as he stepped to the ladder to look up. He really wanted to make a new friend.

Mother helped the boy down. Ethan was ready to put out his hand to shake hello to his new friend.

But when the boy got to the bottom, he cried out, "Gramps!" then ran to him and wrapped an arm around him.

Ethan gritted his teeth and scrunched up his eyes. He wanted to be friends, and the boy ignored him entirely. As Ethan was trying to figure out what was next, more crows returned, filling in the rest of the roosts. They were all carrying bits of metal in their beaks and began incorporating them into their nests.

Gramps looked up to the ceiling and lifted his arms, "My poor, poor chickens."

Why did he keep going on about chickens?

Before Ethan could ask, Mother said softly, "Can you tell us what happened here? Do you remember?"

Gramps wiped his eyes on the shoulder of his tattered white shirt, which smeared dust and dirt across his face. "I'm not entirely certain. We lived on the upriver levee that separated the upper lake from the lower." He waved his right hand absently in the direction of the pony's stall. "We had chickens, fished the lake, and tended the flood gate to keep it all in order. I'd lived pretty much the same way since before this one's Pa was born. God rest his soul." He gave the boy a one-armed hug. "The pox done got him, my wife, and the boy's mum."

Ethan's heart hurt for them. He knew what it was like to lose his Daddy. Even now, that could still happen at any minute. They should be moving on, not listening to storytime.

Gramps cleared his throat. "Then one day, as twilight had fallen, a giant, shrouded in smoke and flame, appeared on the levee. He had a hammer, the biggest I ever saw!"

"Skull Crusher!" the kids blurted out. Ethan's heart raced at the mention of their worst enemy.

"Yeah, that's what he called himself. He said, 'Oldster, I am the Crusher of Skulls. There'd be no honor in crushing an old man and a boy's skull, so I'll not waste the effort. Be gone!'"

Ethan stamped his foot. "That's so mean!" The memory of the giant hanging him out over the river made his blood boil.

"We'd just come in off the fishin' boat, so I had nothin' to put up a fight save the walleye I'd just caught." Gramps stared off in silence for a long moment.

Uncle stepped up and waved a hand in front of Gramp's face, "Hey, oldster, you alright?"

"No, I'm not alright!" Gramps slammed his left fist into his right hand. "That there was the biggest durn walleye I ever did catch. I was gonna hang it on the wall."

He waved his arms as he stood up, red beginning to show through the dirt on his face. "That no-good giant done stoled it right out of my hand and then destroyed the levee and our house with it."

Ethan clenched his teeth. "If I ever find that Skull Crusher again, I'm gonna conk him in the wonkus!"

"Ethan!" Mother snapped her finger at him. "Please let the man finish."

Ethan's lips made a pout, and he looked down at his feet as Gramps continued, "Next mornin' both the upper and lower lakes were drained. This here pile of debris was what was left of our home, boats, dock, everything we had. It was all just washed here, and dark black smoke was rising from the pile."

The boy interrupted, "I told him to not to go into the pile, but he did." Ethan looked up to see that the boy had stood and now had his hands on his hips. "Gramps just fell down unconscious. I tried to wake him up, and I guess I passed out too. That's the last I can remember."

"It was a Censer of Darkness." Lauren pointed to the crater in the center of the room, "I destroyed it, and its hold over you is gone."

A wave of sadness passed over Ethan as he remembered his friend Nicolas telling him about losing his memory. The Darkness took these poor people the same way it had taken Nicolas.

"Well, I thank you kindly for that, but now what?" Gramps motioned to all that was left of his belongings.

"We are on a mission of great need to save my husband. He's been burned very badly and needs to get to the Wellspring of Life quickly." Mother looked out the shack's entrance and seemed to lean in that direction like she was already on her way out the door, but her feet were stuck talking to Gramps.

Ethan knew how she felt. They really needed to be moving on to save Father.

"You don't say." Gramps asked. "Do you know the way?"

"We kind of have a general direction we're headed." Aiden pointed to the crow coops.

"That general direction huh." Gramps got to his feet and tried to dust off his hands on his pants, but just kicked up more dust and coughed before continuing, "Well there's this grove of the high and mighty or some such in that general direction."

Mother raised an eyebrow and looked at Uncle, who just shrugged. Ethan wasn't sure what to think. Was the old man talking about the same grove Knight Protector mentioned? Could he know the way to the Wellspring of Life?

Gramps continued, "Trees don't grow up in the prairie without lots of fresh water, so that's go to be the place yer lookin' fer."

Ethan's heart sang at the the thought that they had a guide. "Really, you know the way?"

"Sure thing, youngster." Gramps nodded. "I know the bestest way there. Especially with the whole valley in a mess from the lakes bein' drained."

"So you'll guide us to this grove?" Mother asked with raised eyebrows.

Gramps stroked his scraggly white beard for a moment. Ethan's heart skipped a beat, waiting for the answer.

Finally the old man took a big breath, "Well, now that all depends. This here is all we have left, and this is no place to raise a boy."

Mother nodded, but didn't interrupt. Ethan had to agree, this place was gross.

"How about a trade? I show you to the high and mighty grove, and you take us on to Blooming Glen where the boy's aunty lives?" Gramps squinted an eye like he was weighing out his trade. "You all look armed to deal with anything that might come our way."

"We're packed tight as it is; not sure we can take more weight." Uncle looked at Mother.

Gramps squinted with one eye, "I see how you are; you want to bargain. I'll help you and give you my pony as payment. Wait, where's my pony? You all aren't no-good horse theieves is ya?"

There he goes with that thief talk again! Ethan's cheeks turned hot. They were Light Bearers, they wouldn't steal anything! What was wrong with him?

"No, no, we didn't steal your pony. He's outside." Mother answered. "and we won't need the pony as payment. It will be worth it if you can help us find the quickest path to the wellspring."

"Deal!" gramps spit in his hand and held it out to shake.

Ethan wrinkled up his nose. Eww gross.

Uncle did the same, and they shook hands. "We need ya to pack up quickly, Old timer, my brother's in a bad way."

Well if Uncle did it, maybe it wasn't so gross. Maybe it was manly. He caught the boy's gaze. "My name's Ethan. Want to be friends?" Then spit in his own hand and offered it to the boy.

The boy raised an eyebrow, then followed Ethan's example. "I'm Jesse, and I could use a friend." They shook, and Ethan's heart lifted a little. He was glad to have a new friend, and the hope that Gramps might help them bring Father to the wellspring in time.

Uncle helped Gramps climb up into the driver's seat of the box wagon that was now stuffed with the newcomer's supplies and the children. Gramp's pony was tied to the wagon's rear by a spare black leather bridle Uncle had pulled from their supplies. A breeze kicked up, sending the lingering smell of hot garbage over the wagon. But that wasn't what turned Lauren's lips down. The poor pony's mane was so dirty the wind didn't even ruffle it.

She wished she could give it a bath and a good combing, but there was no time. Father was still unconscious from his burns. The battle and its aftermath had cost them precious time to find a cure.

The sound of Tye sheathing her sword caught Lauren's attention, "I am off to destroy the Censer. I will meet you at the next one."

Lauren had completely forgotten about the need to prevent Father from entering a double-Darkness zone. Her frown deepened at the thought of her friend going off on her own.

Mother stood in the back of the wagon and held up a hand. "Tye are you sure you're good to do this on your own? We could find another way."

Tye held up her hand palm out, "Enough! Mother of La'Ren, there is no other way." The words seemed to shake Mother like a blow. Tye softened her tone as she continued, "I saw how the Darkness affected your husband. Even in the pure light of day, he looks like he may not make it."

That statement rocked Lauren to her core. She hoped he was improving, but Tye knew more about medicine than

Lauren did. He must be in worse shape than she thought. They had to prevent Father from being in a double-Darkness zone again. They just had to. But Tye needed help, she couldn't do this on her own. "I'm going with her." Lauren blurted out

Aiden held up his slate from the back of the wagon. "She has to move faster than us to make this work Lauren. There's no way for you to keep up."

"I can ride the pony." Lauren pointed with less confidence than she felt. The way it's head drooped made her think to take back her statement. But she was committed to helping Tye.

"Lauren! That's not our pony to be using any way we want." Mother put her hands on her hips, red growing in her cheeks. "Besides, I'm not letting you out of my sight."

Gramps interjected over his shoulder, "Well, now I did offer you all the pony fer yer help. What is she askin'?"

That offered Lauren a hint of relief, and the tension in her neck eased just a bit.

Aiden pointed to the slate like he was teaching school, "We know the Censers are laid out in a network where they overlap is very dangerous. We destroyed this one"—he pointed to where the debris pile would be on his map—"but as we go this way, there's a place where two Censers' smoke overlaps. We need to destroy one of them, so we are only passing through partial Darkness."

Gramps rubbed his beard, "Ah I see. Well, that sounds pretty important to the mission. The lass can use my pony if it will help."

Lauren's heart leapt. She wouldn't leave Tye to fight on her own.

Mother put her hands on her hips. "We don't need that kind of help." Her brows furrowed and lips pursed to give Gramps her "Mother look." "Lauren will be staying with us."

No! Tye can't go alone. God give me the words to help Mother understand.

"Mother, then you need to go." Lauren pointed a finger at her. "'Two are better than one; because they have a good reward for their labor. For if they fall, the one will lift up his fellow: but woe to him that is alone when he falleth; for he hath not another to help him up.'"

Mother did a double take and was speechless for a moment.

Lauren pressed on. "Uncle's too big for the pony, and this isn't Gramps's fight. It's got to be you or me if we're going to save Father." A tear broke through Lauren's bravado and rolled down her cheek.

"La'Ren you should listen to your Mother." Tye stared into Lauren's eyes. "I can handle this on my own. Don't you trust me?"

The hurt in Tye's eyes was painful to see. But it wasn't that she didn't trust the giantess, she just didn't want her friend to be all alone in this fight.

"I trust you with my life, but you might need help." Lauren pointed to Gramps and Jesse. "These two and their birds were almost the end of us. Who knows what might be waiting at the next Censer."

Lauren looked at Mother and saw she was staring at Father, tears rolling down her cheeks. "He would never want you to sacrifice yourself for him. If I let you do this and something happens to you, he'll never forgive me."

Lauren squeezed past Jesse who looked up at her with an eyebrow raised. She could tell he had no idea what was going on. But he had Ethan for a friend, just like she had Tye. She put a hand on Mother's arm. "Tye and I survived on our own together. We took out an angry Darkness-turned brown bear." Lauren tapped the lantern image on her breastplate. "The Light is with us. Surely we can handle whatever is at the next Censer."

Tye nodded and turned to Mother. "Your daughter is strong and a good fighter. We will prevail together if you allow it."

"This doesn't feel right to me, either, but she's right." Uncle waved his hand at the others. "No one else is small enough to ride the pony and keep up with Tye at a good clip. I've seen Lauren in action; you have too. She can handle herself."

"Alright." Mother sniffled up her tears and wiped her face. "I don't like it, but it must be done." Mother pulled Lauren close for an awkward hug as they were both armored. "At the first sign that it's too much, you cut and run. We'll find another way."

"Yes, Mother." Lauren hugged her back and lingered for a moment. Did she want to go off without her family? Would they make it? They had the Light, and God would help them find a way through.

Ethan held up Lauren's helmet. "Don't take this off, Sissy, you need protection in case you get conked in the wonkus."

Uncle pulled Meow Meow out of his pouch and handed the kitten to Lauren. "Here's your watch kitty. He'll be sure you stay safe at night."

Aiden called up into the air, "Daddy Duck, can you go help Lauren be safe?"

The duck quacked and banked into a gentle circle over them all.

"I won't be gone long." Lauren hugged her brothers in turn. "If Aiden's map is right, we'll meet up tomorrow evening. Hopefully, you'll find the wellspring before then."

"God willing," Mother said a tear reforming in the corner of her eye. "Now go! Before I change my mind."

"She'll be safe with me, " Tye assured her, and then they were off.

The wagon rattled to a stop next to a well in a clearing with a cobblestone firepit of uneven white rocks. They were at the hard-packed earth crossroads of what used to be the lakeside trail and the path across the dam. The prairie grass around the crossroads was cut short from animals grazing here recently.

Ethan heaved a sigh of relief at being done bouncing around in the wagon for the day. However, it was cut short by the pained look on Mother's face.

The absence of the Darkness had allowed Father's skin to take on a very light pink color in a few places, and his breathing seemed better. So Ethan didn't understand why she looked so worried.

"Mama, Daddy looks better. Do you think he'll wake up soon?"

She put her hand on his brow, "No he's still burning up. I hope this grove is the answer. He needs help soon."

"Don't you worry, young missy." Gramps encouraged, as Uncle helped him off the wagon's seat. "That spring's just beyond the upper lakebed. Why if'n we take off at first light, we'll be there 'efore noon, I tell yah."

Ethan looked at Aiden for confirmation, thinking his map held the answer, but Aiden merely shrugged. Ethan's brow furrowed. *If Aiden wasn't sure about the wellspring, did he really know the path Lauren and Tye should take?*

"Do you think Sissy's OK?" Ethan whispered.

"She's with Tye and Daddy Duck. Nobody's going to mess with them." Aiden added with pride.

Ethan hoped Aiden was right. Sissy had her helmet so the bad guys weren't going to conk her in the wonkus, but he was still worried. "What about Skull Crusher? He was sneaky, and he caught Sissy and me and almost threw Tye in the river."

Aiden hopped over the side of the wagon and landed on his feet with a thump, then looked up at Ethan. "Don't worry, Daddy Duck's on scout. He'll warn them . . . and Meow Meow will wake them up if there's danger."

Ethan thought about it for a moment, and the tension in his belly subsided a little. That kitten did make sure nobody snuck up on them when they were sleeping, "I sure hope you're right."

Uncle grabbed Ethan under the arms and picked him up, then looked him in the eye. "That sister of yours is strong with the Light, and with the Armor of God. I don't think she's got anything to worry about from that knuckleheaded giant."

Ethan cracked a big grin and laughed. "Knuckle Head. That's what we should call him."

Uncle smiled a toothy grin behind his bushy beard as he set Ethan down and tousled his hair. "Yah, I'd say that's about right." Then Uncle turned to help Jesse down as well.

"Well, we ain't gots to worry about no giant around here," Gramps piped up. "Just them no-good egg-stealin' prairie dogs. Right, Jesse?"

"Yah, Gramps. They're the worst." Jesse pounded a fist into his hand.

Gramps scowled. "Best keep the supplies up in the wagon as much as possible and keep a solid guard on them.

Them prairie dogs will rob you blind if you give them half a chance."

"Really?" Uncle raised an eyebrow. "I never heard such a thing."

Ethan hadn't heard that either. He knew they liked to dig big holes in the ground and their caves could be really large, but stealing things?

"Ever since the Darkness came, them prairie dogs are out in the night stealin' everything what's not locked down." Gramps caught Ethan's eye to make sure he was listening, "Sometimes the crows will catch them in the act and save a trinket or two, but for the most part, they're wily varmints."

To emphasize the point, two crows landed at Gramps's feet. One placed a large navy blue button, likely from a winter coat, and the other a large black metal bolt. Ethan was surprised at how big it was for the size of the bird.

Uncle slowly stroked his beard. "Well I never."

"I told you them prairie dogs are theiv'n varmints. You gotta sleep with one eye open." He picked up the button and pocketed it. Then turned the bolt over in his hands to inspect it on all sides before nodding. "This is worth a pretty penny." He presented it to Mother. "Fer savin' me and the boy from that dark place. It's not much, but maybe it'll be useful."

Mother held up her palm. "There's no need for that. Really"

Ethan couldn't tell if Mother wasn't accepting it because it was kind of a weird gift for a lady, or if she really didn't think it was necessary.

"Ma'am you'd deny an old man what gratitude he has to give." Gramps frowned.

"Of course not. You're welcome." She accepted the bolt and tucked it in her belt pouch. "Let's set up camp."

"Uncle, can I help with the horses?" Aiden asked from where he was gently petting the right horse's black mane. Both of them had a slight bit of a lather, and Ethan was sure they had to be tired.

"Sure, but I think we'll just feed and water them where they are." Uncle pulled a sack of grain from the back of the wagon and set it at Aiden's feet. "Normally, I'd unhitch them to give them some room to graze and sleep better, but it sounds like if we move quickly at first light we might have a cure fer yer pa before midday.

Aiden took a double handful of white whole oats from the sack and held it under the right horse's nose. The way the horse licked at Aiden's hand made Ethan think it was a happy horse. So he picked up a handful to feed the other.

"Are you sure that's wise?" Mother asked. "These horses have been through a lot. Would they be better rested and move a little faster if we took the time to let them loose."

"I think it's better to be prepared for a quick get away," Gramps added. "It's possible there's more than egg stealin' prairie dogs in the area." A coyote's howl in the distance punctuated the sentence.

"Fair enough. We'll be ready to travel quickly." Mother replied.

More howls rang out, and the horse chuffed in Ethan's face, its eyes wide. Ethan's stomach clenched as a chill went down his back. He jerked his head to try to determine where the howls were coming from and dropped the last of the oats from his hand. "Mama, can I sleep in the wagon?"

Something about the gentle rhythm of the pony lifted Lauren's spirits. It helped that they were in the clear sunshine of the late afternoon, and the warm prairie wind was crisp and clean. But she just liked the little guy.

Gramps called him Sad Sack for some reason, which irritated her. He could use a good bath and a brush down. Cleary Gramps wasn't caring for the poor thing, which is probably why he looked so sad around Gramps.

But she thought the little pony was sweet. He bobbed his head in the cutest way when she approached with food and always stood very still when she mounted and dismounted.

He also had excellent stamina for a pony. Tye could jog for a couple of miles before she got winded and had to slow to a brisk walk. The pony kept rhythm with her just fine, so they were a good match. A fully grown horse would have outpaced Tye, but as it was, they were moving quickly. She was proud of her new trusty steed. The way he seemed to be holding his muzzle high despite the run, led her to believe he was happy to be out on the plains.

Based on Aiden's map, they would make it a little more than halfway before dark and would be at the next Censer by noon if they got up at first light. Lauren was glad she was partnered with Tye on this mission, because already they had to back-track and wind around some obstacles that Lauren wasn't sure she would have been able to re-orient herself past to stay on target. However, Tye took it all in stride.

Lauren tried to drum up conversation with Tye during the walking periods, but she waved Lauren off. It wasn't clear if it was just Tye trying to conserve her breath, or if there was something more. Being under the control of the Darkness must have been horrible. Was she remembering it's dark influence, or maybe she was hurting for being shunned by her people?

They were traveling north and west, and the sky began to turn orange as the sun set. Finally, Tye called them to a halt on top of a rise. "La'Ren, can you stand on my shoulders and look around to see if there's water nearby?"

"Sure, I guess I can try."

Tye took the pony by the reins.

Lauren thought she should give him a pep talk before she tried to stand on his back. She patted his shoulder, "Hey, big guy, I need to climb on you, is that OK?"

He unexpectedly nodded. "You seem to be happy to have the chance to go on this mission. I think that's what I'll call you, Chance." He bobbed his head again, which made Lauren smile. Then she carefully brought her feet up on the saddle and pulled her knees up to move into a squatting position.

Tye turned her back to Lauren and stood next to the pony with the reins held tight. Lauren could put her hands on Tye's shoulder but couldn't quite just put a knee on them, so keeping her hands in place she squatted down and launched herself up, pushing down hard with her hands on Tye's shoulders. Tye grunted under the pressure, but Lauren kept going and got her knees on Tye's shoulders.

"Sorry," Lauren said as her knee dug in.

"Not to worry, I asked you to do this. Please stand." Tye let go of Chance's reins and reached her arms up to give Lauren some support. Lauren grabbed Tye's hands and moved to a standing position on her shoulders. She must have been no more than four years old the last time she did this on Father's shoulders. Pain gripped her heart at the thought of Father. Their mission had to succeed; he wouldn't survive another trip through a double-Darkness zone.

A slight breeze kicked up, drawing her attention to the sea of prairie grass all around. It was amazing to be up so high. It was a good thing, too, because while they were on a rise, the land around them ebbed and flowed. She scanned to the limits of how far she could see, both to the left and right, and didn't see any open water anywhere. "Tye, I don't see any streams, lakes, or ponds nearby."

"What about trees? Do you see clumps of trees and brush anywhere?" Tye asked

"Just beyond the hill to the left, maybe a mile away and in the wrong direction."

Tye turned her body in that direction. "I see just a little clump of leaves that way, I can't make it out."

"Yes, definitely a few trees there. I can't tell from here in the failing light, maybe oak trees," Lauren replied.

"Very well, you can come down," Tye replied.

Lauren carefully lowered herself back to her knees on Tye's shoulders, and Tye picked her up under her armpits, then sat her back on Chance. Lauren giggled. "That was kind of fun."

Tye smiled. "I bet it was. I haven't done such things since I was a little girl." Her smile quickly faded, and she scrunched up her eyebrows.

Lauren wondered if Tye was having her own memories of better days with her Father. Would she open up now that they were alone?

"Tye, what is it?" Lauren implored.

"Nothing . . . we can talk later. We need to find water before dark, or your pony won't make the run tomorrow." Tye took off in the direction of the trees. It took Lauren a minute to get back in the saddle, and she had to gallop Chance to catch up with Tye. The sprint didn't last long, and then she was able to pull Chance back to the speedy trot they'd used most of the day.

They came to the trees as the sun was setting. The low spot was filled with tall rocks, patches of sand, and clumps of twisted trees with roots trailing across the exposed bedrock into a pool in the center. The place just seemed a little weird compared to the surrounding rolling prairie. It made the hair stand up on her neck in the failing light.

"Tye, have you seen anything like this before?" Lauren asked as she dismounted Chance by the pool.

"Not exactly. But, fires are common on the prairie, so it's rare for trees to grow. But, the rock, sand, and water have made a place that works for these trees. This water is connected to the blood of the prairie."

Chance bent to lap at the pool.

"Blood? No, Chance, don't!" Lauren grabbed the pony's reins.

"No, La'Ren, not human or animal blood, but like the lifeblood. There is a great underground river that goes through the prairie. This place is low enough to have it come to the surface."

Lauren let out a sigh of relief and patted Chance on the shoulder. "Go on, boy. I'm sorry."

"My father told me your people dig wells, and when they find water, they are just finding access to this river," Tye explained as she knelt next to the pool.

Chance bent his nose to the water, and suddenly, Tye grabbed his mane and pulled him. He whinnied fiercely.

"Tye! Why'd you do that?" Lauren protested.

"Dark water!" Tye pulled her sword out and put the tip in the pool, then lifted black muck for Lauren to see. It smelled terrible. "Your Darkness now pollutes the lifeblood of the prairie." Tye's flinty stare scared Lauren. Why did she blame Lauren for all these troubles? It wasn't "her" Darkness. *God what can I say that will make a difference?*

Tye shook her head, stood and took Chance by the reins. She lead him to a depression in the rock that appeared to be full of clear rainwater.

"Tye . . . " Lauren began.

"Not now." The giantess snapped. "We need to make camp before we lose all the light." Without a word she untied the straps on Chance's saddlebags and then threw them over her shoulder. This reminded Lauren just how different they were. Tye was a giantess. Those bags would have crushed Lauren if she'd tried that.

"Tend to the pony while I make a fire." Tye ordered flatly.

"Sure." She patted Chance's mane, and a poof of dust came out. Maybe she should have named him Dusty. "Is there any chance we brought a brush for this poor pony?"

Tye rolled her eyes and huffed. "No."

She laid their supplies near a depression in the bedrock a few feet from the rain water pool Chance was lapping from. Lauren moved to the pony's side and started working on removing the saddle.

Tye got up and started gathering loose sticks and branches. "That will be the best place for us to camp. With our back to the pool, nothing can sneak up on us from behind, and those sandy spots are a good place for the pony and us to sleep."

Lauren hated the ice in Tye's words. Where had her friend gone? Regardless, the light was failing fast. So she joined Tye in silence as they put the camp together. They got a cheery fire going just in time for total darkness to set in. That wasn't exactly right because the moon was out, and there were so many stars in the sky. It was always so nice to look at the stars when the Darkness wasn't present.

They both sat by the fire, munching hardtack. Lauren thought now might be a good time to talk to Tye about earlier. "Hey, when I was on your back, you got really sad suddenly, and I noticed a couple of times when your Father seemed to come up in conversation, you got a very sharp tone. Are you OK?" Lauren tried to put an arm around her friend, but Tye stood up.

"No, I am not as you say *OK*, La'Ren of the Tower," Tye responded.

Lauren was so taken aback by the force of Tye's response she dropped her biscuit. "Can we talk about it?'

"What is there to talk about?" Tye snapped. "I am a Warden far from my home and real responsibility. Disowned by my father and fighting a battle that, from what I can tell, only helps your people. What about the Wardens? How does any of this help us?"

"Tye, I'm not sure—"

"Enough of your explanations! Your Light may have helped me save my brother, but since then, it has done nothing but create trouble."

"What do you mean? You were under the control of the Darkness, we saved YOU with the Light," Lauren protested.

"Did you?" Tye's hard look told Lauren they were on treacherous ground. "To what end? Never-ending servitude to humans and their Light? Never to see my family or the woodlands of my youth again?"

Lauren was at a loss for words. How could she explain? The Savior said they might lose family and friends to embrace the Light. That the eternal blessings would outweigh the loss. But out here alone in the endless prairie, how could she help Tye see the Savior's glory?

Lauren's loss of words left an opening, which Tye filled. "You have no answers. If I had taken you and your family to Lord Refi'Cul, I know my Father would have taken me back. It would have shown atonement for—"

"Atonement for what?" Now Lauren was angry. Tye's father had taken Skull Crusher's word over Tye's. What kind of Father did that? "You didn't have anything to atone for. You found your brother and returned him to the family. If we'd gotten there before Skull Crusher, I don't think they would have believed him, and you'd be home with them. You can't blame the Light and us for Skull Crusher."

"Can't I?" Tye asked. "This overlord, the Bishop, isn't he human? Isn't he the one who brought the Darkness to this area? How is this not just another human problem?"

"Well, he might be human, but not all humans are like him. That's why we're fighting so hard for the Light. If the Darkness wins here, there will be nothing left but desolation." Didn't Tye see that? Didn't she remember all the burned-out farms on the way to Spring Fields, or was she so under the control of the Darkness she didn't remember?

"But isn't that exactly what the bishop is trying to do, make all humans follow his Darkness? Isn't that what the Censers are about?" Tye retorted.

"Well, that may be his idea, but we don't want a part of it, you know that. You've seen what they've done to the Bjorn Born and the bears." Lauren stood up and started pacing.

"You just made my point. Humans don't care what their plots and plans do to the rest of our lands and people." Tye pointed an accusing finger at Lauren. "We were at peace with all around us—including the bears. It was your Bishop corrupting the bears that led to my brother's capture in the first place."

Lauren balled up her fist. "But . . ."

"But nothing, La'ren. You helped me save my brother, and I am in YOUR debt, not another human, and not for this war that seems to be brewing with my people. I will help you in this task to save your father." She turned her back on Lauren. "But when that is done, so am I. I'll have no more part in this human battle of the Darkness and the

Light. I need to return to my people and repair things with my father."

Lauren took a deep breath. "Well, if that's how you feel about it . . ."

Tye whirled on Lauren, the giantess's eyes flaring. "That *is* how I feel about it."

"Then we'll just break the Censer tomorrow, and once I'm back with my family, you can go your own way." Lauren did everything she could to hold back her tears. Tye was her friend; how could she be like this? "I won't try to stop you."

"You couldn't if you tried," Tye said, with a cold finality that broke Lauren's heart.

Lauren turned and hung her head. She couldn't hold back the tears any longer. What had happened to Tye? Tye's voice was resolute and clear. When she was affected by the Darkness, she sounded weird and trancelike. This was different, Tye really meant it.

"I will scout the edge of this clearing and take the first watch. Go to sleep," Tye ordered as she stalked off into the twilight.

The last part was so final. She spoke to Lauren like an adult scolding a child and sending them to bed. Despite their nearness in age, Lauren found herself reflexively saying, "Yes, Ma'am."

She made sure Chance was comfortable and tied him where he could nibble some grass and drink from the rainwater, but not the corrupted pool. He sniffed Lauren, then nudged her shoulder. It was almost like he was trying to give her a hug. That was what she needed right now—a hug. How could her friend turn on her, again?

As they settled in for the night, tucked in tightly in the back of the box wwagon, Ethan dug the snow globe out of the satchel and shook it. Mother and Aiden had already fallen asleep under their grey wool blankets on either side of Father, exhausted from the day's battle. Ethan lay at his feet, heart hurting for his daddy, who occasionally moaned in his sleep.

Ethan used the distraction of the snow globe to take his mind off Father's condition. It's internal illumination was so amazing, he just stared in wonder at the device. The arrow pointed to the north, letting off a faint glow. He wondered if Jesse might want to see it.

The boy and his grandfather were sleeping in between the wagon and the cobblestone fire pit. Ethan was torn about the decision to sleep in the wagon. He knew Jesse would be warmer in the deep of the night next to the fire. Uncle was up, sipping water from a tin dipper out of the wooden well bucket. But his rigid stance told Ethan he was keeping a careful eye out for danger.

Gramp's snoring pulled Ethan's attention back toward the fire pit, and he noticed Jesse was just staring up at the stars.

"Jesse?" Ethan hissed.

The boy on the ground looked up.

"Wanna see something neat?"

"Sure" Jesse hopped up and stood at the foot of the wagon.

Ethan held the snow globe over the edge. It added a faint white glow to the red light coming from the fire.

"Ohh pretty." Jesse cooed. He stood up and held up his hands to take it from Ethan. "Can I look at it?"

A small knot formed in Ethan's stomach as he remembered how angry Lauren was when he dropped it earlier. He'd sure hate to upset her again or lose the way to save Father. But Jesse was his friend and it was so pretty. Surely Jesse wouldn't hurt it. "Be careful. It shows the way to the Wellspring of Life."

When Jesse had it in both hands, Ethan was still reluctant to let it go, but Jesse's eyes lit up so much Ethan finally let go.

"That fountain almost looks alive," Jesse responded.

"Yah, sometimes I think I see a person walk through there for just a second," Ethan explained. "Just on the edge there, it's almost like we have a spyglass, looking at something far away."

"Yah, I see that too." Jesse nodded.

"Hey, you two, get to bed. It's going to be an early mornin,'" Uncle ordered in hushed tones.

"Can I look at it some more," Jesse whispered.

"OK, but just keep it safe." Ethan turned back into the wagon to snuggle down into his blanket.

Jesse returned to his bedroll with the snowglobe in hand and a million bad things suddenly poured into Ethan's mind. Gramps was always talking about the No-good egg-stealin' prairie dogs. Could they really steal something as big as the snow globe…or worse?

***

The howl of coyotes broke through the night. Ethan sat up with a start to see glowing eyes ringing the camp. Uncle was helping Gramps up with one hand, while holding his flaming sword in the other. Its light illuminated a half dozen snarling coyotes just outside the reach of the fiery blade.

Ethan struggled to free himself from his blankets, eager to help. Mother stood on the left side of the wagon, flaming sword in hand, illuminating another group of coyotes on her side of the wagon. Aiden stood with his little hammer and a confused look on his face. The tiny tack hammer glinted in the flames of Mother's sword, but otherwise didn't seem to be of much use. Ethan wondered if he missed his sword. It was too bad Tye had taken hers back.

Ethan raised his shield, and a bubble of light formed all around the wagon. The coyotes let out deafening howls.

"Everyone, get in the wagon! hurry!" Mother called.

Ethan stood in the back of the wagon, and the light-bubble extended to where Uncle was protecting Gramps and Jesse.

"Coo Coo, jump in!" Ethan called. Uncle, Jesse, and Gramps moved into the light.

The horses screamed in terror, and Ethan's heart jumped into his throat. Then, his attention snapped to the front of the wagon, where glowing yellow eyes seemed to be closing in on the horses from all sides. That wasn't natural; they had to be Darkness coyotes.

"E! The horses aren't protected. You need to move toward the front," Aiden cried as he dropped his hammer and jumped for where the reins lay on the seat.

A coyote struck the left horse in its flank, and it reared, shaking Ethan's balance. The other horse was struck, and they both took off at speed. Ethan's balance was already off, and he toppled out of the wagon, shield and all.

Ethan rolled when he hit the ground and managed to see Mother wobble and fall into the wagon next to Father, but she lost her sword in the process. It clattered off the side of the wagon and into the night.

Ethan heaved a deep breath, trying to hold back the fear threatening to overwhelm him. Would Mother and Aiden be OK? *God please help us!* They needed his shield to keep the coyotes away. He had to stand.

Gritting his teeth, he rose on one knee and planted his shield into the ground, illuminating the clearing. He peered over the top, looking for their attackers. The coyotes were gone! Maybe they thought the horses would be tastier?

"Is everyone alright?" Uncle called from behind him.

"I'm OK." Ethan's voice barely croaked out. He was shaking from the encounter. He tried to breathe deep to calm himself, but how could he be calm when coyotes were chasing down his family?

"Not a scratch." Jesse put a hand on Ethan's back. Ethan looked up at his friend, and something in Jesse's eye told him he knew what Ethan was feeling. Jesse held out a hand to help Ethan up, and he took it. It was so good to have a friend in this dark time.

"The only thing I don't like more than them no-good, egg-stealin' prairie dogs is coyotes. Never seen anything like this though, not that many in one group." Gramps shook his head. "They must have been after something."

"I suspect they were tainted by the Darkness," Uncle replied. "We ran into a corrupted cougar. It attacked us despite the fire, very unnatural."

"What do we do now? Shouldn't we go help Mama and Aiden?" Ethan asked.

"Those spooked horses surely outran the coyotes in short order. So I'm not too worried about them," Uncle said. "But we've got a mess right now." He pointed his sword at the overturned supplies and camp gear scattered around. The coyotes had overrun everything except the fire pit, and all their things were in disarray.

"Hey, Jesse, where's the snow globe?" Ethan asked.

Jesse scanned around. "It was next to my bedroll. I don't see it."

The tension of the battle intensified into a deep sense of dread in the pit of Ethan's stomach. They needed the snow globe to find the wellspring. They had to find it. "Maybe something's covering it. It's really bright. We should be able to see it," Ethan replied.

He left the shield planted in the ground, and it continued to shine the bubble of light around the camp. The boys looked through all of the gear and couldn't find the globe.

"It's gone. We've looked everywhere," Jesse cried in frustration.

Ethan's jaw set hard. He was so mad at himself for letting Jesse have the snow globe. If he hadn't, it would be safely in the wagon. But was that even a safe place now?

"Now hold on. What are you sayin'?" Uncle put his hands on his hips.

The way Uncle's brows were furrowed made Ethan really not want to answer that question. Uncle must have figured that out because he demanded, "Well go on, out with it."

Ethan took a deep breath and explained, "I let Jesse have the snow globe as a little light to help him sleep. But it looks like the coyotes took it."

"Nope, not the coyotes." Gramps slammed his right fist into his left palm. "Them no-good egg-stealin' prairie dogs done took it."

Ethan raised his eyebrows. "What?"

"Lookie here, mixed amongst our tracks and the coyotes'—prairie-dog prints." Gramps pointed in the dust. "Are you sure those weren't here before?" Uncle asked.

"There's way too many of them." Gramps waved around the clearing. "I think them there coyotes sent in the prairie dogs to steal our stuff. Then made a ruckus so's we'd hightail it out, and they wouldn't know."

Ethan didn't like Gramps and Uncle arguing. It was doing nothing to reduce the knot in his stomach. He scanned the dirt, but he couldn't distinguish which tracks were which. He wished Aiden were here, he'd be able to settle this.

"Now I ain't heard tell of such a thing. Prairie dogs an' coyotes working together," Uncle protested.

"Well then how else would you explain our gear missin' and all these prairie dog tracks, young whipper snapper?" Gramps complained.

Uncle stood speechless for a moment, just stroking his beard with one hand. The tension in Ethan's neck reduced a little now that Uncle seemed to at least be listening to Gramps.

The big man squatted near some tracks right in front of the pulsing light blue glow of the shield. "I gotta say, you probably are right, Gramps." He pointed to the pawprints.

"Them there prairie dogs are the smartest I've ever seen. Lookie here."

Gramps groaned as he took a knee next to Uncle. "These here tracks look like a prairie dog's walkin' on two feet, a couple of them. Then there's this flat depression with a lot of two-feet prints. Then just a foot or two farther, it looks to be on all fours with somethin' dragging between."

Ethan's eyes went wide as he tried to take everything in. He stepped next to the path Uncle indicated, and now he could make out the tiny prairie dog prints amongst the coyote tracks.

"I told you them no-good egg-stealin' prairie dogs is smart," Gramps added.

Ethan could see where they must have been dragging a pack between two of them. "Uncle we have to go find the snow globe! If we're going to save Daddy and the little girl, we have to!"

"I know, I know." Uncle sighed as he stood up, then helped Gramps to his feet. After scanning the sky, he made eye contact with Ethan. "It's just past mid of night. We've had some long days lately, and I think tomorrow will be the longest yet." Uncle paused for just a moment and it seemed like he was holding something back, then a big old yawn came out of his mouth, "I'm not prone to go chasing them prairie dogs without at least a couple hours of shut eye."

Ethan could feel the sleep creeping into his eyes. Uncle was right. "OK, Uncle." Ethan's lower lip pouted out. He knew he was too tired to keep going, but Father needed the wellspring, and who knew what happened to Mother and Aiden.

Jesse put an arm around Ethan's shoulder, "It'll be OK Ethan, we'll find those no-good prairie dogs in the morning."

Ethan leaned into his friend and felt just a tiny nugget of peace dislodge the knot in his stomach. They would figure it all out. God would help them.

"You whipper snappers get bedded down. I'll stoke up the fire and take first watch," Gramps offered.

Uncle opened his mouth like he might protest, but then just nodded. "Hopefully, they'll send them coyotes off on a big run and circle back by mornin'. If not, we'll see how long the wagon and the prairie dogs stay on the same path. Come on, boys. Let's gather everything up as close to the fire as possible."

They quickly regathered their scattered things while Gramps stoked up the fire. As the firelight rose, Ethan's shield slowly faded. By the time their bedrolls were all in place and their meager supplies stored by the fire, the shield was only reflecting firelight.

"I think we're safe for now," Ethan offered as he retrieved his shield. "The light's gone out—the bad stuff must be far away."

Gramps patted his head. "That's good to hear. Now you just bed down and rest. You too, Jesse."

"Yes, sir." The boys responded in unison.

Ethan snuggled down in Uncle's cloak, since his bedroll was still in the wagon. He pulled his shield on top of himself just in case. He sure hoped Mother and Aiden would return by morning. What would they do if the wagon didn't come back?

Aiden leapt from the back of the bouncing box wagon onto the driver's seat, reaching for the reins. His fingers barely connected with the smooth black leather before they bounced off the bench and out of reach. The horse's screams of terror sent ice down his back. He felt the minor bumps of the trail turn into jarring bounces across the uneven prairie, as the coyotes forced the horses off the beaten path.

He was sprawled across the driver's seat, hanging on for dear life. The rough wood under the seat bit into his fingers with every bounce. The horses' shoes took on an unearthly blue-white glow as they raced away, which intensified as they ran faster. The cart bounced Aiden mercilessly, and it was all he could do to hold on and hope the horses could outrun the coyotes.

He managed to look over his shoulder to see Mother wasn't in much better shape as she tried to hold on, while sheltering father from the bouncing gear on the back of the wagon.

"Are you OK?" Aiden managed to squeak out between bounces.

"Just hold—" Mother was cut off by a bounce that nearly threw both of them out of the wagon. "Ooff." She grunted as she came back down.

God please help us! Aiden struggled to maintain his grip and eye contact with Mother, so he focused on the horses and tried to find a better grip.

After what felt like hours of relentless pounding, the horses jerked suddenly to one side; Aiden felt it but couldn't see it. There was a thump and a scratching sound underneath the wagon for just a second, then a loud smack followed by wood cracking. His stomach lurched as the back of the wagon started to tilt down on the far side, then both sides fell to the ground with a thump. Aiden managed a peek at the wagon's rear, and he thought he saw the back wheels sitting still on the ground. But, unfortunately, the image was lost in the dark of night.

With the whole back of the wagon dragging on the ground, the horses slowed to barely a walk.

"Quick, we need to control the horses," Mother called.

Aiden shakily eased himself back into the wagon's bed, picked up his hammer where it had fallen under the driver's seat, and tucked it into his belt. It gave off just enough light for him to see his surroundings.

The wagon was a mess, a couple of burlap sacks of grain had fallen partially on Father. That must have hurt. But it might also be a good thing, because he was pinned in place and not sliding down to the gate.

He couldn't help Father if they didn't stop the horses. So he took a deep breath, hopped off the wagon's side, and landed a little off balance. He let the fall take him into a roll to keep from falling flat on his face. *All those summersaults down the hill with E were good for something.* Being separated from his brother again pained him, so he gritted his teeth as he rose and sprinted to catch up to the horses.

Mother gently tugged and reeled in the reins of the left side horse as she closed with it. Aiden followed her example and patted his horse gently to calm it to a stop.

Aiden pulled out his hammer and held it like a torch. He let out a deep sigh when he concluded there was no sign of pursuit. The wagon was a wreck; the rear wheels were somewhere in the dark behind them. It wasn't going anywhere any time soon. The horses had outrun the coyotes . . . but for how long?

Meow Meow's tongue was gritty on Lauren's nose as she woke in the middle of the night. Her back hurt from sleeping on the hard rock next to the corrupted pool Tye called the blood of the prairie. She started to let out a groan that was cut short by a large hand roughly covering her mouth. Lauren jolted under the pressure, eyes wide before realizing it was Tye.

The giantess whispered in her ear, "Wake up very quietly. Trouble's coming."

Unfortunately, Tye's warning was too late. A coyote howl split the night very close to the camp. Then, more coyote voices took up the call all around the camp. Ice ran through Lauren's veins. It was just the two of them, if it was a whole pack of coyotes, could they defend themselves?

Dusty whinnied and stamped. It was clear he knew there was danger afoot. All around them, at least a dozen pairs of yellow eyes stalked toward them from the prairie. Lauren inhaled deeply and said a silent prayer for courage to clear the fear trying to crush her chest.

"Quickly, stoke up the fire!" Tye commanded as she donned her helmet.

Lauren rushed to the coals and began blowing on them, while she added smaller pieces of wood to the pile. Some of the kindling caught fire and blazed brightly.

This did not stop the coyotes' advance. It was just too small of a fire. A familiar quack caught Lauren's attention.

Daddy Duck flew out of the pool, spraying a fine mist as he soared to the top of the tallest tree in the thicket. Once he was there, a light beam blasted across the sky and connected with the white spot on his crown. It bounced down spotlighting the whole camp. Inside the beam, it felt like a bright sunny day.

The corrupt pool began to bubble, and a bright mist covered the water. A gust of wind blew the mist away, revealing clear liquid. But, corruption kept leaking in from the north side of the pool. Lauren didn't know what that meant, but at least if they got pushed into the pool, they wouldn't be standing in dark water.

Lauren's heart leapt. "Way to go, Daddy Duck!"

The howling intensified briefly, and Lauren was scared they would attack despite the light. Their slavering jaws looked intent on doing them some harm. However, anything scary about the situation quickly turned to annoyance because the coyotes weren't daring to cross the beam of light, rather, they stomped around the perimeter, taking turns howling in frustration.

They were smart enough to stay out of Tye's reach as they circled, so there was little Lauren and the giantess could do to reduce the odds against them. Then Lauren remembered her spear. She took it out and blasted the closest coyote. It yelped and fell as the spear returned to her hand.

Chance huffed at this, and it almost sounded like he said, "YES!"

The rest of the coyotes in view yipped and shrank back from the edge of the light. Then howls came one after the other from two coyotes out of sight. The canines closest to Lauren responded to the cry by racing forward and snapping its jaws at the edge of the light. The rest followed, almost jumping through the shielding light.

Tye closed her eyes for a moment like she might be trying to pick her words carefully, "La'Ren, this is your Darkness at work. Coyotes are a family, not a pack. For the alpha couple to drive their family at us despite the fire and your light is unnatural."

Lauren cocked her head, "Alpha couple? Can you pick them out from the others? Maybe if I hit them with the spear the pack will break up."

"I can't tell, but maybe if you drop another, they will reveal themselves. Wait a moment." Tye went to the fire, grabbed the unburnt end of a three-inch wide branch, and held the eighteen-inch log up as a torch. Then she threw it underhand to a spot of open sand in the midst of the coyotes. "Now!"

The area beyond their protecting light was now better lit, and Lauren could see they were up against nearly two dozen coyotes. They could easily be overwhelmed by that amount. She said a brief prayer of thanks for protection as she got ready to attack another coyote but froze in shock to see the first one she'd dropped begin to stand again.

Something is odd. Nothing just gets right back up after being hit by this spear. What is going on here?

Her musings were cut short by a coyote leaping to where Tye stood on the edge of the light. She threw with all her might. It hit the coyote between the eyes, and the animal fell with a thump just outside the circle of light. Again the coyotes retreated, and the alphas urged them back.

"I see them! They are behind that rock." Tye pointed off to the left of the torch in the sand.

"I don't see." Lauren moved back and forth, careful to stay within the circle of light.

"Quick, give me the spear. I have a shot," Tye said

Maybe Tye decided it wasn't just Lauren's Light after all.

Lauren threw the blue, glowing spear to her friend. When it landed in Tye's hand, its Light disappeared.

"No! Tye, don't throw it!" Lauren exclaimed.

Tye wasn't listening and threw the spear that was no more than a staff. Her aim was true, but the coyote turned at just the last second, and the staff glanced off its hindquarter. It yelped, but didn't go down. However, the spear bounced off and landed, leaning against one of the big rocks rather than returning to Tye's hand.

"I don't understand." Tye exhaled.

"Well, you said it was 'MY' Light and 'MY' Darkness. You have to believe to put on the Armor of God. After all we've seen and done, how can you not believe?"

"I . . ." Tye faltered.

"Well now we're in a fine mess." Lauren felt the heat in her cheeks, "How are we going to retrieve it?"

Tye just hung her head and looked at her feet.

Chance whinnied and pawed the ground. It looked like he might just leap out of their protective bubble.

Lauren grabbed his mane. "Whoa little guy. There are dozens of coyotes out there."

The little pony nodded and stamped his front hooves.

"No it was . . . my error. I need to do it." Tye stammered.

Lauren realized her words hurt Tye. She was still angry, but berating Tye wouldn't make things any better. "It's not your fault, Tye. It worked before." Lauren consoled. "I think Chance is right, but we'll have to work together."

"How so?" Tye asked.

"They aren't behind us on the poolside. You were right to put it to our back. They don't want to swim across it." Lauren pointed behind. "But it's barely up to your knees. So you could wade across it slowly. That should draw them away from this side. I'll act like I'm going to ride Chance through the pool, then when things clear out enough, we'll race for it."

Tye took in a deep breath and stood up a little straighter. "That is a sound plan."

She helped Lauren saddle Chance, then picked her up and put her on Chance's back. Tye picking her up was mechanical and lacked the warm feelings from earlier. Was their friendship gone? There was no time to dwell on that now; they needed to go.

Tye waded into the pool, and the yips from the coyotes grew as they began to race around the light to the other side.

Finally, a path cleared to where the spear lay, and Lauren cried, "Charge, Chance!" The pony took off at top speed.

As they crossed through the Light barrier, Lauren saw the second coyote she'd hit rising from the ground.

"Go, Chance. Go!" Lauren dug her knees into the horse.

The little pony picked up speed, but the coyotes howled and charged after them. The alphas let out a furious cry, and the whole pack changed direction.

"No!" Tye yelled, "La'Ren return to the light."

"We've got this!" Lauren cried back.

Then Chance screamed in pain and slowed for an instant. Lauren turned to see the coyote trailing, but a welt on the pony's hindquarter showed it had made its mark.

"C'mon, Chance we can do this," Lauren's heart ached for the poor pony, but she knew they had to get her spear back. Lauren snuck a glance over her shoulder, and the coyote closed to take another bite.

Lauren pulled on the reins to change direction slightly and yelled, "Kick!"

Chance's gait slowed, and his left rear foot slammed into the attacking coyote's snout. The beast yelped as it catapulted away head over heels.

"Good job!" Lauren cried as she returned her attention to the front; four glowing yellow eyes appeared at the edge of her vision. Chance raced toward the eyes, revealing the shapes of two coyotes, larger than the rest, bearing down on them.

They let out a howl, and Lauren risked a glance behind to see the whole pack swarming toward them in hot pursuit.

"C'mon, Chance! Faster!" Lauren urged the pony on with her knees. She could feel Chance pour more energy into his pounding hooves. They were going to make it, now she just had to grab the spear.

She didn't think they could risk stopping, or they would be overwhelmed by the coyotes from behind. So she put the reins in her right hand, and reached out with her left as they approached the spear.

She could feel the warm wave of power from the spear before it slapped into her palm. She curled her fingers around it, and the spear tip materialized. She tilted the spear under her armpit and clamped down hard with her arm just in time to ram the spear into the coyote on her left as it jumped to attack.

It let out a howl and dropped like a rock. Lauren jerked on the reins, and Chance skidded to the left as the other coyote pounced. It fell short, and Lauren quickly twisted the spear up to her left and dropped the reins, as she grabbed the shaft with her right hand. Then, she thrust it down into the crown of the second coyote. It, too, yelped and dropped.

Lauren retrieved the reins and wheeled Chance around, expecting to engage the pack. However, howls erupted from the group, and they scattered into the tall grass.

Tye ran toward Lauren. "You did it! You are safe!"

"Yes, thanks to Chance." Lauren patted the pony's mane. However, the poor pony let out a moan instead of a satisfying whinny.

"Oh! You poor thing!" Lauren jumped down and inspected the wound by the light of her spear. The coyote's teeth made a set of slashes through the skin about two inches wide. Not deep enough to need stitches but painful just the same.

"Let's bring him into the light, and I will see what I can do." Tye held out a hand.

"What about these two?" Lauren pointed the glowing spear toward the downed animals. Tye patted Chance on the nose, and he chuffed at her, then moaned as she passed.

Tye squatted down and looked the nearest coyote over, then bent very low and sniffed.

"What are you doing?" Lauren asked.

"This animal has been deep in the Darkness," Tye offered. She moved to the other and did the same thing. "As has this one." Tye began to poke and prod the coyotes as if trying to verify her claim. "I do not believe this family of coyotes was all affected—just the alpha couple."

"I see," Lauren looked up and scrunched her eyes. "Is that maybe why the other coyotes were able to rise so quickly? They weren't under the Darkness' control?"

"Could be. When we downed the bear, it slept a deep sleep," Tye responded.

"Yah, that's how every other person or animal affected by the Darkness worked." Lauren nodded. "Do you think they'll attack when they wake up?"

"No, coyotes avoid humans whenever possible, and Wardens can only approach them if they are in distress." She held up the male's back leg between her finger and thumb. Lauren could barely make out a lump in the bone where Tye held it. "This appears to have been broken. Only a Warden could have set this without the mate attacking. But that's not the big sign. They have leather collars with Iron Wood in them." She dropped the leg and indicated the mate. "I suspect while the Warden was healing this one, both stayed in the vapors of a Censer." Tye spat as she stood up.

"Do you think it was Skull Crusher?" Lauren asked.

"I do not know—the Censers are everywhere." Tye waved her arm toward the open prairie. "It would have been easy enough to be accidentally exposed."

"I see." Lauren suddenly felt something wriggling around in her dress pocket. "Meow Meow! I'd forgotten all about you! I hope I didn't squish you on my wild ride!"

She tucked her spear under her armpit, pulled the kitten out of her pocket, and held him up with both hands to look him in the eye. The kitten squinted at her and meowed accusingly.

"I'm so sorry." She pet him gently, and the kitten quickly began to purr.

"Should we have Meow Meow try to wake them up?" Lauren asked.

"Go ahead. They will likely just run," Tye replied. "I'll tend to Chance's wound." Tye grabbed Chance's reins and gently tugged him toward the campfire. Once he was in the fire's glow she returned to Lauren. Daddy Duck no longer shone his bright light on the camp and was paddling in the pool.

Lauren set Meow Meow next to the female coyote and he licked the canine's nose. Then she pulled the kitten away, not wanting to risk the poor thing getting eaten. The creature's eyes fluttered open, and it let out a low growl. Then it spied its downed mate in the spear light and slunk over to it and whined.

Lauren carefully put Meow Meow next to the other coyote, despite the low growl from its mate. As its eyes fluttered open, Lauren snatched Meow Meow from it.

Lauren let out a deep breath. "That was a close one, little guy." She looked the kitten in the eyes. "If our new friend Chance hadn't been so brave, we might have been stuck here, surrounded by those coyotes." The kitten's eyes got big. She wondered if he understood her or was waking up all the way. She petted the kitten's back and put him in her pocket with his nose and paws sticking out as she stepped away from the coyotes.

Tye sat on her knees, hand up, palm out, facing the canines as the second got up shakily on all fours. The coyotes bumped noses with the other. Then they turned to Lauren, growled, and sidestepped away from her. This took them closer to Tye and the light. They turned to the giantess and bowed to her.

"These are my father's coyotes!" Tye exclaimed. "There's a mark on their ears. Do you see?"

Lauren inspected them in the firelight, which made their eyes glitter menacingly. She had to pull her attention away from their threatening eyes to look at their ears. Tye was right; there was an irregular arrow-shaped scar on each of their left ears.

"I have known them since I was young. They would never have attacked me, if it weren't for this human Darkness." Tye spat.

"Tye—"

"Don't! I don't want to hear any more about your Darkness and Light." Tye snapped. She pulled some jerky from her leather belt pouch and tossed a piece to each animal. They snapped it out of the air and began chewing loudly.

Tye stood up, "These two will no longer be a threat. They will be a help guarding us." She pointed back toward the camp. "Go check to see if any others are still down from your attacks or lurking in the grass. They'll join these two to protect us. I'll tend to Chance."

Lauren thought to object since her spear was no longer lit up. But it might be best not to argue right now with Tye's emotions so high. So Lauren searched the grass for coyotes, while the giantess led Chance back to the camp.

After ten minutes of searching, she'd covered the immediate area and hadn't found any, so she returned to the firelight, where Tye was mixing water with some moss in a depression in the bedrock.

The giantess looked up. "I thought we weren't going to have a way to protect the wound. The open prairie can be a hard place to find medicines." She began to squish the moss in the water with a stone the size of Lauren's fist.

"However, this peat moss was growing under the lip of the rock there. It is a good way to pack a wound to keep infection out." Tye dipped her fingers in the goop she'd just made and then stood and pressed it into the wounds on Chance's flank. The pony moaned and stamped his front feet.

Lauren rushed to the pony and stroked its nose and mane. "I'm so sorry Chance," The pony leaned into her, and she could tell he was grinding his teeth. She continued to pet the pony until Tye was done.

"There is no good way to bandage this wound." Tye began. "We just don't have the supplies. This poultice will dry and flake off as we travel. So we'll have to make more. There wasn't a lot of moss, but I can make it stretch."

Tye squatted down and carefully picked up the remaining moss and set it by the fire. "Drying it out some will help it keep until we need it."

Lauren gently pulled on Chance's reins and guided him back to the water, where he drank with gusto. "Good boy."

With a knot in her stomach, Lauren asked, "Tye can we please talk about what happened?"

Tye let out a deep sigh. "La'Ren, it has been a long night; morning is just a few hours away. I'll not waste precious rest on talk of your people's Light and Darkness. It is your turn for the watch. I am going to sleep."

With that, Tye turned her back on Lauren and proceeded to bed down for the rest of the night. The coyotes joined her in overwatch of the giantess.

Dread welled up in Lauren's heart. They'd barely survived this battle; what if a greater force of the Darkness was at the Censer? Would Tye even be able to fight it, or worse, would she change sides . . .again?

Aiden woke to the sound of a groan coming from Father. He rose from the wet, bristly praire grass next to the wagon, and a shiver took him as he let the grey wool blanket fall to the ground.

Mother was kneeling in the back of the wagon, trying to cool Father with a damp cloth. With the wheels missing from the back of the wagon, the bed slanted at an odd angle. In the night Mother adjusted the grain sacks that had held him in place on his back to put him in a slightly less awkward position, while preventing him from sliding down.

While Father's face lacked the burns covering the rest of his body, the slightly green pallor of his cheeks and forehead told Aiden the bouncing ride hadn't been good for him. Moreover, he wondered what it had done to the burns on his back.

Mother seemed to be thinking the same thing because she tried to gently pull father into a sitting position. "Do you need help, Mother?" Aiden asked.

"Yes, please keep him from slipping while I look at his back," Mother said.

The two of them carefully sat Father up, despite the awkward angle of the wagon. Then Mother opened up the white linen shirt they had put on him, backward for just this reason.

It was damp and smelled awful. Aiden turned away. He didn't want to know just how bad it was. Mother let out a few hisses and sympathetic groans as Father cried out from some of her probing. For a second, it looked as if Father was waking up, then his head slumped, and Mother hurried to lay him back down. She held her ear to his mouth and, after a moment of holding her breath, let out a sigh.

She looked up at the reddening sky. "At least we're not in the Darkness. The burns on the front are healing better, but his back is … horrible. It's putting stress on his body. We need to take him to the wellspring, but I'm at a loss as to how we can do that quickly with the wagon in this state."

"I could make a litter, and the horses could drag him," Aiden offered. "It shouldn't take too long."

"Maybe," Mother just stared at him for an uncomfortably long time. Aiden put a hand on her shoulder, and she shook her head, "I think the only thing less smooth than this bouncing wagon would be a litter, but would we even be able to move faster than a walk?"

"Yah, you're right, Mother, but the wagon seems absolutely broken." Aiden scowled.

"Your Father believes you are a great builder. I think he made that hammer just for you." Mother pointed to Aiden's belt. "If anyone can repair this wagon and get us back to the others quickly, you can."

Aiden's chest swelled with pride at Mother's confidence, then deflated as he thought about Ethan, Uncle and their new friends stranded somewhere far behind them. Were they OK? Did coyotes hurt them in the night? His confidence faltered under the weight of the responsibility.

Mother must have sensed this because she knelt in front of him. Tears brimming in her eyes, she said, "Aiden let's pray."

He closed his eyes and clasped his hands together, holding back his own tears.

Mother continued, "Father God, please give us wisdom beyond our understanding to reunite our family, and take us swiftly to the Wellspring of Life. Amen."

"Amen," Aiden repeated and gave Mother a mournful embrace. They sat there in the quiet for a moment, letting their tears come. Then Aiden slowly let go.

Mother wiped the tears from under his eyes. "You can do this, son."

He nodded. There had to be a way to save Father; he just had to think. He stared off into the prairie, lost in thought, then the wagon wheels came into view. He was surprised at how far the horses had dragged the broken wagon.

"I'm going to go check out the wheels and see what I can do." Aiden turned back to Mother and noticed all the supplies still in the wagon's bed. A brief sense of family pride came over Aiden, reducing the tension in his shoulders. Uncle sure knew how to tie things down, he would take just as good care of Ethan. "Can you move heavy supplies to the front of the wagon? Maybe on top of the seat and put the rest on the ground?"

Mother raised an eyebrow. "Yes, but why? I need to tend to your Father."

"If the wagon wheels aren't too broken, we'll need a way to lever the box up high enough to put them back under the wagon." He pointed to the front wheels. "The more weight we put in front of the front wheels, the easier that will be."

"Yes, of course," Mother tousled his hair.

Aiden looked up at her with furrowed brows. "Mama, I'm not little anymore!"

She let out a chuckle. "You have grown up some haven't you." She took him by the shoulders. "Now go, mighty builder; we must return to the others and be off to the Wellspring of Life."

Aiden took off in a jog, determined to fix the wagon despite his heavy heart. He reflexively looked to the sky for his friend Daddy Duck and was quickly reminded that he'd sent the duck to help Lauren and Tye, because the only birds in the sky were crows.

Dozens of crows circled and wheeled in the air between the wagon and the wheels. Aiden wondered if there was some big dead animal nearby. He sniffed and didn't smell anything off. However, the area was mostly tall prairie grass with occasional rocks, some as high as his waist jutting up from the ground. In the distance, there were some trees, and he guessed there might be water there.

He returned his attention to the wagon wheels, and his eyes went wide at the sight of a dozen crows sitting on the axel and top of the wheels. Aiden skidded to a stop and pulled out his hammer. The last thing he wanted was another battle with the crows. They stayed where they were, almost like they were guarding the wheels. Then a crow flew up from behind a pointy rock nearly as big as Ethan. That must have been what broke the wagon. The jerk he'd felt the night before was the horses trying to avoid it, but the wagon whipped, and the rock ended up under the carriage. The smashed grass behind the rocks confirmed Aiden's intuition.

A crow approached Aiden with something large in its beak. His reflex was to flinch away and put up his hands, but the bird just stopped for a moment, flapping its wings mid-air. Finally, he relaxed, and the crow landed on his shoulder. It bent its neck back and forth, offering what it had in its beak. It was a unique crow amongst the group, as it had a white spot on each wing.

Aiden held up his cupped hands, and the bird dropped a large carriage bolt for him. He recognized it as the kind of bolt father used to secure the axel to the wagon's base.

"Thank you, my new feathered friend," Aiden said, wishing he had a treat for the crow. Then he realized he didn't know what a crow would think was a treat. He thought they were carrion birds, so that might be tricky as he wasn't planning to carry dead things around in his pocket.

The bird flew off and landed on the rock. Aiden decided he should investigate. When he got there, he found splintered wood on the backside of the rock and embedded in the cracks of the stone. Its top was sheared off. Aiden could see its tip on the ground, and the flat top of the rock was a lighter color than the outside. In addition, there was a very slight chip, just below the lip of the flat spot on the back of the rock. He put the head of the carriage bolt into the chip, and it fit perfectly.

The rock gave Aiden a pretty good idea of what had happened. He approached the axel, and the crows flew up and began milling around behind it. *I guess they were guarding it for us.* When he got to the axel, the broken wood told the tale. The right wheel had slammed into the rock and caught the bolt, which ripped through the axel mount. The wagon bumped up, and with one side broken and stuck on the rock, the momentum pulled the other side free.

The axel itself was generally intact but weakened by this. But if he could find the carriage bolt for the other side or something similar, he'd just need some wood to strengthen things, and they'd be in business. He cast about the area, looking for the other carriage bolt, and didn't see it in the vicinity.

He held up the bolt. "Hey, crows, have you seen another one of these?"

A thunderous response of caws came from the birds on the axel and the one still on his shoulder. Then they all flew up and dove, skimming just above the prairie grass around the broken wheels. Finally, they returned to their perch after five minutes, including the white-spotted one, which landed on his shoulder. It looked Aiden in the eye and cocked its head. Aiden assumed that had to mean they couldn't find it.

"Well, OK then, I'll figure something out." Then, on a whim, Aiden asked, "Any chance you all could help me push this to the wagon?"

In answer, the birds flew into the air and circled. He wondered how they were going to help him push the wheels. *Time's a wasting.* He struggled to push the wheel by the rock through the deep prairie grass around in a circle to line up with the wagon. Sweat broke out on his brow at the exertion, and he couldn't tell if his shirt was wet from sweat or the last of the morning dew from the grass.

He took a moment to catch his breath, then moved to the center of the axel to push. The whole thing was cumbersome, and the clumps of prairie grass were making it hard to keep both sides moving at the same time. He was merely rocking it back and forth without any forward movement.

Suddenly there was a flurry of wings, and four crows flew in unison, one to each wheel and one to the axel on either side of Aiden. They gave a tiny push as they swooped by, and four more hit the same spots just a few seconds later. At first, they rocked it like he had, but Aiden timed a shove with their next touch, and it started to roll. He stood flat-footed for a second, hardly believing what he saw, and the wheels stopped in the tall grass, despite the crows continuing their pushes.

The crow with the white spots cawed in his ear, jolting him into action to push again. His timing was off on the first shove, but he recovered, and soon the wheels were rolling and kept rolling. Slogging through the grass, pushing the wheels was hard, and sweat soon soaked his shirt. It was hard to keep going and keep the sweat out of his eyes. So he centered his direction on the wagon and squeezed them shut as he pushed as fast as he could.

"Aiden, that's amazing! Let me help," Mother called. Sweat stining his eyes, he looked up to see he was now only twenty yards or so from the wagon. The birds scattered, but the grass had been flattened here, by the wagon dragging on the ground, so Aiden could keep it going on his own.

Mother joined him for the last ten yards, then they just let it bump into the wagon to stop. Aiden pulled his shirt up and wiped the sweat out of his eyes. He looked at Mother, and she stared at him with upraised eyebrows.

Heat rose in his cheeks, realizing that probably wasn't the "proper" thing to do. "Mother, I know, I know, but I lost my handkerchief somewhere between Quinn's ferry and the Iron Mountain, OK?"

Mother laughed and gave him a side-armed hug. "I'm sorry, son. Old habits die hard. The wilds are no place for worrying about the proper use of a handkerchief."

He looked up at her. "I think I can put this all together if I find some wood." He pulled the carriage bolt out of his pouch. "But, I'm going to have to find something to replace one of these."

"Would this work?" Mother took a bolt out of her own pouch.

A big smile broke Aiden's mouth. "Where did you get that?"

"A little bird." Mother winked, and the crow on Aiden's shoulder cawed.

Aiden compared the two bolts, the one she had was longer and thinner, but it had a hole for a cotter pin near the bottom. Uncle had packed some baling wire, so Aiden was sure he could rig up something. "This will work great."

"We need to gently pull your father out of the wagon and onto his stomach so I can better tend his back." She pointed to the bedrolls. "That should also help with the weight when you try to raise the back of the wagon. But I'm not sure the two of us can do this. He's so much bigger than the both of us."

Aiden looked things over, and she was right. How would they lift Father, let alone carry him where Mother wanted to lay him down? He thought about it for a minute, and the circling crows began to take turns resting on the wagon's side.

"I think the only thing we can do is have him splat down," Aiden offered.

"Splat down? That doesn't sound … better," Mother replied with crinkled eyebrows.

"We should put the bedrolls at the foot of the wagon." Aiden indicated the spot. "Then just stand him up and let him fall forward onto them."

Mother gasped. "That's likely to cause damage on its own."

"Well, maybe if we put a blanket in front of him, we can help him fall gracefully." The white-spotted crow landed on his shoulder. "The crows can help."

Mother took a deep breath. "OK, let's do this." Mother took one grey wool bedroll and laid it out at the foot of the wagon. Then she placed the other on top of Father, keeping his face clear.

They both worked together to roll the edges of the blanket under father into the bedroll. He looked like a catapillar in a cocoon. They both grabbed the fabric near his chest and pulled. Two crows flapped down and helped. Once he was sitting up, more crows came and grabbed the fabric, and they all toppled Father forward out of the back of the wagon. It wasn't exactly a gentle landing on the bedroll, but it wasn't a *splat* either.

"Well done!" Mother exclaimed as she worked to position him better.

"Thank you, crows!" Aiden exclaimed. "Mother, they have been great helpers. What should I give them for a treat, since they did such a good job? I don't have any dead animals."

"Crows have a reputation for being carrion animals, but they eat just about anything we do." Mother responded while she unrolled the blanket from Father's back. "Why don't you feed and water the horses and throw out some of their grain? We'll need their help getting Father back into the wagon later, and we wouldn't want them working on an empty stomach."

"OK, Mother." Aiden grimaced as she opened Father's shirt. The sight turned his stomach. He quickly got to his chore of feeding and watering the horses. When he was done, he scattered grain in the flat grass behind the wagon, and the crows flocked to it.

Mother was done tending Father's wounds but left his back open to the air. It looked like raw meat in places. Aiden was used to butchering things on the farm, but something about seeing Father in this condition made him gag a little bit.

"Aiden! Look at me." Mother caught his attention. "These wounds are nothing like I've seen before. It's almost like there's little flecks of darkness pooling under his skin." Aiden's gaze was drawn back to Father's back and he could see what seemed like little swirls of darkness moving just under Father's skin."

Mother put a hand on Aiden's chin and turned him back to her, "I'm going to try to carefully draw that out so it might heal more naturally and maybe the darkness zones won't have so much of an effect on him."

There was moisture pooling in the bottom of Mother's eyes. It broke Aiden's heart to see her like this. He despirately wanted to help make things better. "Can I help?"

"Yes, but not with this." She shook her head,"You need to fix the wagon quickly so we can take him to the wellspring that's our best hope."

Aiden looked away and took a deep breath. Of course, she was right, but now he was at the hard part. He had to find a way to raise the wagon off the ground and repair the axel. He was going to need some wood, but the few wooden boxes they had were thin pine, more meant to collect things than handle a heavyweight. He wished they'd kept the armor crates. They were made of sturdier stuff. Then, he remembered the woods off in the distance. If he could find a downed tree branch, that might do it.

"Mother, I'm going to go find some wood." He pointed in that direction.

"OK, hurry back, and be safe," Mother replied.

It wasn't far. Hopefully, the crows would follow—in case he needed help. But all he had to find were a couple of thick pieces of wood, so how much help would they be?

Morning came, and Ethan crawled out from underneath his shield next to the cobblestone well in the clearing. The dew made everything around him wet, and he shivered. Uncle and Gramps were up, already tending the fire and making some breakfast. Ethan stood and stretched, causing himself to shiver more.

"Well, lookie who decided to finally wake up," Uncle chided with a smile so big Ethan could see it through the big man's bushy beard.

Ethan looked around a minute and realized it was barely past dawn. "It's not that late." Ethan's teeth chattered.

"Come over here and dry yerself off by the fire." Uncle held out his hand.

Ethan complied and sat criss-cross applesauce by the fire. "So Mama and Aiden haven't come back yet?"

"No sign of them," Uncle responded.

"I'd say if them there no-good, mangy coyotes done scared them horses good, they could be halfway to Blooming Glen by now," Gramps offered.

Ethan's mouth dropped. "But we need to take Daddy to the Wellspring of Life!"

Uncle put up a hand in Ethan's direction and scowled at Gramps. "What I think the old-timer is sayin,' is after runnin' away from them coyotes, the horses might be a bit tired, and it will take them a while to make it back."

Gramps huffed. "Yah, I guess that's what I was sayin'."

"Well, you know I can run REALLY fast. I should go check on them!" Ethan put a hand down on the ground and turned to stand up.

"Hold on!" Uncle snapped. "I know you can run really fast, but yer Ma would be might angry with me if something happened to you while yer running really fast and I wasn't there to help you out."

"Hey what's all the yelling about!" Jesse called from his bedroll.

"Oh nothin' you need to worry about, sleepy head." Gramps crabbed. "Get yerself up and out of bed. Food'll be done in a minute."

"But, Coo Coo," Ethan tried his pet naming, hoping that might help.

"Cuckoo, now that there is a rightful name for this one." Gramps slapped his knee and laughed. "With that wild hair, he definitely could be a crazy one."

Uncle's face turned red, and Ethan noticed just how out of sorts he was. Ethan never really thought of Uncle as a wild frontiersman, but the way Gramps said it gave Ethan an uncomfortable feeling in his tummy—like it was something mean.

"Watch it, old timer," Uncle snapped, giving Gramps a flinty stare before pointing an accusing finger at Ethan. "You ain't goin' running off on my watch."

"Yes, sir," Ethan replied through his nose. He didn't see why he couldn't just go run and see Mama and Aiden. He was so fast, the giants couldn't catch him, so what could hurt him on the prairie?

Some crows landed next to Gramps, showing him little prizes. Ethan remembered the fight with the crows, that would have been bad without the whole family. So maybe Uncle was right. What else was out there that the Darkness made horrible?

"The boy might have a point, though," Gramps offered. "If they just ran on down the path, they might have just kept a goin'."

Uncle raised an eyebrow. "What do you mean?"

Gramps pointed down the path. "Well, we was headed on the path to the wellspring Y'all are lookin' fer. So what if they just kept goin' till they found it?"

Uncle sat there for a minute, stroking his beard, then nodded. "Yah, that does make a bit of sense." Uncle turned to Ethan. "As much as yer Ma might worry about you, yer Pa was in pretty bad shape. I think we could expect she'd be in a hurry to take care of him and figure we could take care of ourselves for a bit."

Ethan's heart hurt at that. He wanted Daddy to be better but didn't like being left alone in the wild. Well, he wasn't exactly alone. There were friends around the fire right now, and that was better than being locked in a cave with a bear that was supposed to eat him, but still, he missed his family.

"Here, have some vittles." Uncle offered a plate with jerky gravy-covered hardtack. Not exactly Ethan's favorite food in the world, but better than nothing.

Jesse joined them, and Uncle dished him out a plate as well. Ethan was about to take a bite and then stopped himself. "We need to pray!"

"Well, I guess we have a thing er two to be thankful for," Gramps said, spoon halfway to his mouth.

"Alright, I'll give it a try," Uncle said dropping the spoon back in the gravy before filling his own plate. He stood over the fire and clasped his hands.

"God in heaven, watch over the family spread out across this prairie. Keep them safe and bring them back to us soon. Bless this food. Amen." Uncle stood there for a minute, more like he might be saying his own prayer and then started spooning up food for himself.

The prayer brought a smile to Ethan's face. Uncle had seen the Light in their travels. Ethan remembered praying over their first fireside meal fondly.

They all dug in and quickly cleared their plates. As unremarkable as the food was, its warmth in Ethan's belly drove the last of the shivers away.

"So, what's the plan now?" Ethan asked.

"Yeah, are we going to go after them or staying put?" Jesse asked.

"A little of both if Gramps is up to it," Uncle responded.

"You don't need to worry about me; with a belly full of gravy, I'm fit as a fiddle." Gramps patted his stomach, and Ethan giggled. "What did you have in mind big man?"

"Other than the water barrel, we should be able to lash together the supplies into some backpacks and start followin' them prairie dog tracks." Uncle pointed up the trail. "Right now, they follow the path we were going to take anyway, and it looks like the wagon went that way too."

"Yah, that looks to be about right," Gramps replied. "I bet we find them no-good, egg-stealin' prairie dogs 'efore we run into the wellspring."

"That's what I'm thinkin' too," Uncle replied. "Even if we don't, it will save the wagon time backtrackin' to pick us up."

This sounded pretty good to Ethan, but then he wondered, "What if the prairie dogs go a different way?"

"Well, we'll figure that out when we get there," Uncle replied unconvincingly.

Ethan was worried too. Gramps said he knew where the wellspring was, but was it really the Wellspring of Life the snow globe was pointing to? Without the snow globe, they would never know.

Aiden waded through the chest-high prairie grass, leaving Mother, Father, and the wagon behind. He pushed hard to the small clump of trees that would surely have the wood he needed to fix the wagon.

The crows didn't follow, seeming to be more interested in finding the last bits of grain he'd thrown out than helping him. He shrugged it off. He only needed a couple of pieces of wood the correct size. What help could they give?

As he approached the grove, he saw a dozen large rocks, almost boulders, scattered about its edge. He changed course slightly to pass by the largest one and caught sight of water inside the tree line. *There must be some kind of stream or pond over there.*

WHACK!

A sharp pain blossomed in Aiden's forehead as something wooden slammed into it. He fell hard on his bottom and sat dazed for a moment with blurry vision. When his vision cleared, he was looking at the very sharp point of a gleaming spear. Behind the spear tip stood a boy Aiden's age, with curly blond hair, dressed in denim overalls and a white cotton shirt—just like Aiden's—with a leather tool belt around his waist and a spyglass on a strap over his shoulder.

Aiden couldn't tell if the boy was a minion of Darkness. Regardless Aiden's brain was so foggy from the blow that the only thing he could think to do was hold up his arms, "I surrender, I surrender. I'm not your enemy!"

"So you say." The boy just glared at Aiden, spear at the ready. "Lots of people coming through these days saying they're friends. But they're wolves in sheep's clothing." He menaced Aiden with the spear.

"Please, my father is burned badly." Aiden waved toward the wagon.

A pinch of concern crossed the assailant's eyes for just a second, then the hard look returned. "Yah, I bet he is, an that's 'cause you're them Darkness folk. What was he tarred and feathered and set alight to get you out of town?"

Aiden took a deep breath and paused. The story was too complicated, and the boy wouldn't understand Father being Refi'Cul's champion. So what would the honest answer be?

"My Father got burned while we saved him from the Darkness people," Aiden pleaded. "We were on our way to the Wellspring of Life to heal him, and coyotes attacked."

The stranger cocked his head. "Coyotes, you say?"

"Yes, we think the Darkness people have corrupted the coyotes to attack us." Aiden waved back toward the horses. "Our horses were faster because they have the Armor of God, you know, the shoes of the gospel of peace, but as horse shoes."

"Well, I haven't heard of anything like that before." He squinted at Aiden. "How do I know you aren't just making up stories to stall me until more of you come?"

Aiden closed his eyes and tried to relax. What would make this boy see the light? "How about I very slowly and carefully give you my hammer. Then you'll know I'm no threat."

The boy took a deep breath, then moved the spear to a one-handed combat grip with the butt end clamped in his armpit. He reached out his other hand. "Nice and slow now, or I'll stick you just the same."

Aiden slowly lowered his arms and reached across his middle to put his hand on the top of the hammer. It took on a faint blue glow that illuminated his midsection at his touch.

The stranger gasped and took a step back. "What devilry is this?"

"No devilry, it's from the Light." Aiden pulled it from his belt, holding onto the head of the tack hammer with the handle between two fingers. He held the handle out to his captor. "Go on. You can take it."

The boy tentatively reached for it with his free hand like he was worried it would bite him. When his fingers wrapped around it, Aiden let go. The light went out, except for the faintest glow around the head. *Could this boy be a Light Bearer?*

"Wait, where'd the light go?" The boy protested as he examined the hammer. He let the spear slowly turn vertically and finally set it with the butt on the ground as he stared at the designs on the the hammer.

Aiden relaxed just a bit, but the pain in his head and bottom from the hard fall, still distracted him. He moved positions on the ground to lean back against the boulder. "I don't know. It kind of chooses when to be powerful."

The stranger squatted for a second, laying his spear behind him, and turned the hammer over in his hands, shaking and tapping on it in different places as if he was trying to turn it on. "What do you mean it chooses? It's a hammer. How can it choose anything?"

From Aiden's new position, he could vaguely make out the horses and wagon. However, the sea of prairie grass waving in the slight breeze blocked out any sight of Mother or the crows, who must still be eating seeds from the ground. There was no help coming from that direction, but Father needed to be on his way. Now!

"Look, I can't explain it, but my father can. He's hurt badly, and we need to take him to the healing waters quickly. Can you please let me go?" Aiden held his hands together as he pleaded.

"Go and do what?" the boy ran his thumb over the emblem of the lantern embossed where the handle met the head. His eyes widened a bit, almost like he recognized it. Then, he stared Aiden with upraised brows. Aiden knew he wanted an explanation, but he wasn't sure he had words this boy would accept. His attacker tucked the hammer into a belt loop on his left hip, opposite the hatchet on his right. Then, he retrieved his spear and took it in both hands across his body—not at the ready. "Well, go on. What are you doing here?"

"Well, I need two pieces of wood about this big." Aiden motioned with his hands to a shape about the size of two loaves of bread end to end. "and a thick branch maybe eight or ten feet long to use as a lever."

"Stand up," the stranger ordered.

Aiden complied.

"Slowly show me what's in that pouch."

Aiden carefully opened the pouch and pulled out string, a couple of tin soldiers, some jerky, and nuts to show him.

"There's more in there, I can tell. Show me."

The carriage bolts had fallen to the bottom of the pouch, and he couldn't hold everything in his hands simultaneously. He didn't want to put his food in the dirt to show him. "I have the carriage bolts to fix the wagon, but that's it."

The stranger stepped up to Aiden, put his hand in the pouch, and took the carriage bolts. "What were you thinking, you might catch me unaware and hit me upside the noggin with these?"

"No!" Aiden huffed. "I was hoping if I gave you the bright glowing hammer, you might believe that I'm a Light Bearer, and you should help me save my father!" Aiden felt heat rise in his cheeks.

The other boy took a step back at the force of Aiden's words and dropped the bolts in the dust as a concerned look crinkled his eyes. The boy side-stepped to Aiden's left, closer to the big rock, and leaned his spear against it. Then he took the hatchet and hammer out of his belt, one in each hand. He held them toward Aiden, blunt side of the hatchet up. It had the same symbol embossed in it as his hammer. "My Pa's good friend gave him this hatchet, made it himself. Did you steal this hammer?"

Aiden's mouth dropped. "Of course, I didn't steal it." Aiden paused. "My Father made it for me!"

"Well, I guess that means your Pa and mine are friends then, doesn't it?" The boy flipped the hammer in the air and caught it by the head, offering it, handle first, to Aiden.

Despite the throbbing behind his eyes, Aiden let out a sigh of relief as he stuffed his supplies back into the pouch. He reached up and grabbed the hammer, but the other boy didn't let go, so he used it to lever himself up. Then the boy released it and knelt to pick up the carriage bolts. He offered them to Aiden, who returned them to his pouch.

Then despite his frustration with the boy, he put his hammer in his belt and held out his right hand. "Let's start over, I'm Aiden"

The stranger stared at him for just a second and tentatively put his hatchet away before extending his hand. "My name's Logan"

"Nice to meet you, Logan," Aiden responded with a little more politeness than he wanted to show the boy. "So where is your Father? Is he out here with you too?"

"No, he's at the homestead." Logan motioned off to the west, but Aiden could barely make out the top of a distant barn, obscured by the prairie grass.

It was Aiden's turn to be suspicious. "That seems far away."

"About two hours by horse, but mine got scared away by a snake this morning." The boy looked at the ground as he shook his head.

They seemed to be the same age. Before this adventure, Aiden couldn't imagine exploring that far from home without Father. Something was wrong here. "Why are you here on your own?"

Logan looked up, grabbed his spear from the side of the rock, and motioned toward the trees. "People have been flooding through this land for weeks now. At first, you might see one or two in the distance, traveling light. Then, from time to time, whole families in wagons."

As Logan talked, he and Aiden weaved through a few big rocks before they came to the edge of the tiny grove. "We stopped some of them and found out that the giants and some metal men were creating trouble to the south and that the Darkness was going everywhere. So we offered to put people up, but they all had places to go."

He pointed to a downed limb. Aiden nodded, and they moved to inspect it. "One of the things that kept coming up was how the Darkness was getting into the water."

Aiden gasped, "I destroyed a Darkness-machine making dark water near my house."

"Yah, there was a lot of talk about stuff like that." Logan pulled out his hatchet and whacked a couple thin limbs at the branch's top. "Will this work for your long one?"

"Yes, can you help me carry it back?" Aiden asked.

"Well, I came out to watch the pool to make sure you weren't going to fill it with Darkness." He looked back at it and frowned. "But it looks as if something underground is already filling it with Darkness." He pointed to the corner of the pond, where water bubbled up with streams of black goo in it.

"That's horrible," Aiden responded. "Once we get my father the help he needs, we're going to light a tower that will push the Darkness out of the land for good."

"Really?" Logan picked up the lighter end of the branch in one hand and his spear in the other. "Well then we need to help your father right away."

Aiden picked up the heavier end in both hands. It was a pretty stout branch and would be good for the lever to pick up the wagon. But they still needed some pieces to fix the axel.

"So, do you water your animals here or something?" Aiden asked.

"No, Pa says this watering hole is a low spot in the rock around here and exposes an aquifer. I'm not sure what that means," Logan admitted.

"I don't know either," Aiden replied.

"Anyway, he said if the bad ones polluted this spot, then all the wells and other water in the area would go bad." Logan began to huff with the exertion of carrying the branch through the tall grass.

Aiden was feeling it, too, and it was making his head throb. "So your father sent you out to guard it?"

"Not exactly . . ." Logan trailed off.

Aiden paused for a few minutes as they waded back through the tall prairie toward the wagon. "So what then?"

"Well, Pa said it was important, and he seemed worried about it." Logan stopped and set his end on the ground to catch his breath. "But he decided to store water around home, rather than try to stop the bad guys from ruining it. We've been digging cisterns next to the house and barn to hold rain water and carrying buckets of water from our pond for a couple of hours every day to fill them up for a couple of weeks now."

Aiden let his end down, mopped his brow on his shoulder, and winced from the bump on his head. "I'm not following. If you had water, why did you care about this pool then?"

"When the people started streaming in, I thought the giants would be here any minute. I wanted to fight them. I didn't want to run away. This is my home," Logan said.

"I get that. I felt the same way about my home," Aiden replied. His mind flashed back to building a trap for Knight

Protector in the Tower of Light. He would have done anything to protect their farm.

"Pa had an old trunk in the barn attic with a spyglass, armor, and a sword. He was a Mighty Mercenary before I was born. He had a book on fighting. You know stances and exercises, so I made my spear and started practicing when he wasn't looking."

Logan nodded toward the branch, and Aiden picked up his end. They returned to carrying it as Logan kept talking. "Then, late yesterday, everything got bright around here. We had sunlight like we hadn't seen in months. Pa was sure something big had happened and that the Darkness must have been defeated."

"We destroyed the Censer for this area yesterday," Aiden offered.

"You did what?" Logan asked, and he slowed as if he might stop and turn around.

Aiden kept his pace, hoping to keep Logan moving "Keep going. We have to hurry." Logan picked up his pace again as Aiden continued, "It's a long story, but my family destroyed the Darkness-machine controlling this area yesterday. But if you all thought things were good, why were you out here today?"

"I didn't trust it," Logan admitted. "It's been months of scary things going on, and I didn't believe it would just go poof. I thought it might be a trick."

Aiden blew out a deep breath. At this point, he could understand that sentiment. It was pretty easy not to want to believe the Darkness would stay away. "OK, so what happened next?"

"Every morning at sunup, I've been watching the watering hole with the old spyglass from the loft, before I milk the cows." When I looked out today, I noticed the wagon and horses. Being a few miles away, I could barely tell what it was, but I knew it had to be no good.

"So what did your pa say about it?" Aiden asked.

"Well, I didn't exactly say anything to Pa about it," Logan replied.

Aiden's eyes got big at that. The forces of Darkness were potentially attacking their water supply, and Logan hadn't told his father.

Logan must have read Aiden's mind. "Pa said we wouldn't get involved. He said he was done with fighting. He'd pack us up and go to Blooming Glen, like other families, before going back to war."

"I see," Aiden replied with disappointment leaking into his voice. He was glad to have the help carrying the wood, but Aiden wished Logan told his Father where he was going before running off into danger.

Logan continued, "Anyway, I thought if I snuck down here, I could spy out whatever was going on and do something about it, and that's how you got that whack on your noggin."

They broke through a thick patch of prairie grass to find a clear view of Mother and the makeshift camp. The crows took to the air in a flurry of wings and caws. Mother turned and reached reflexively for the sword that was not at her hip.

"Mother! It's OK. This is Logan. He's a friend," Aiden called. She seemed to relax for just a moment and then waded through the grass toward them.

The gap closed quickly, and Mother said, "Thank you for your help, Logan." As she reached out a hand in greeting, the white-spotted crow landed on the branch, grabbed it, and began beating its wings—a dozen more crows connected with the limb and lifted it out of the boy's hands.

Logan's mouth dropped at sight, and he limply offered his now-free hand to Mother. "You all are Light Bearers, aren't you?"

"I'm sure there's a story here," Mother said as she shook Logan's hand. "However time is short. Aiden's father is in desperate need of medical help." She pointed toward where he lay on the bedroll.

"Yes, ma'am," Logan replied. "He told me."

"Aiden, is that all you need?" Mother asked.

"Not quite. Can you guide the birds to put that by the front and unhitch the horses, and we'll run back and find the other pieces?" Aiden replied.

"Yes, go quickly now," Mother said as she waved the birds in the direction of the wagon and started walking there.

"Let's go, Logan!" Aiden raced back toward the woods.

Logan just stood there dumbfounded for a moment, watching the birds carry the branch.

Aiden called, "C'mon, slowcoach! Last one, there is a rotten egg."

That snapped Logan out of it, and he grabbed his spear in both hands and raced after Aiden.

They were able to follow the path they had beaten through the tall grass, and without the weight of the tree limb, they crossed the field in no time. When they reached the trees, Aiden quickly scanned for another limb that might be the correct size. He promptly eliminated everything on the ground. "I don't see anything."

"I don't see anything either," Logan replied. "Should we cut something down?" He pulled his hatchet from his belt.

"I don't think that would be good." Aiden shook his head. "We really need dry wood."

"Could we lift the wagon with the other log and break it up?" Logan asked.

"I might be able to do that for one side, but it thins out too fast. I'm not sure it would hold," Aiden said.

"We might be stuck then," Logan replied. "Other than this stump, I don't see anything dry. I guess I could go home and see if Pa could come help."

"But I thought your house was miles away."

Logan nodded.

Aiden frowned. "That will take hours. We need to get going right away. We have to think of another way."

The sun glinted off the design in Logan's hatchet. "Can I see that?" Aiden asked.

"Sure." Logan handed it over, handle first.

It was a small hatchet, like the one Aiden's family used in the kitchen to split kindling.

"I have an idea." Aiden pulled the hammer out of his belt.

"OK?" Logan replied with a raised eyebrow.

Aiden walked over to the knee-high stump. It looked clean-cut maybe two or three years earlier. It was dried out but hadn't started to crack deeply yet.

Aiden rubbed his hand over the top of the stump and found a spot that felt "right." "Hold the hatchet right here." He handed it back to Logan.

"What are you doing?" Logan took the hatchet in both hands.

"You'll see." Aiden raised the tack hammer high, and Light showed all around it as he brought it down on the hatchet. The symbol on the hatchet lit the whole head of the tool, and the log split cleanly to the ground.

"Wow!" Logan cried. "I don't think Pa could have split that with a heavy maul in one hit!"

Aiden ran his free hand over the surface of the log. "I don't know if Father made them as a pair, but it sure seems like they go together like butter and jam, right?"

"Yeah, like peas and carrots." Logan smiled.

Aiden looked at the stump and concentrated for a second. Something guided him to draw his finger across the stump ending next to the split. "Place it here and make a *T* on the cut."

Logan followed his instructions, and Aiden hit it again. There was a crack, but they couldn't see how deep it went because of the location.

Next, Aiden put his hand on the stump with his thumb next to the first cut. He drew a line with his finger down the pinky side of his hand. Logan set the blade there, and Aiden pulled back his hand, then whacked the hatchet with the hammer again. The stump split down to the base of the tree, wrapping around a root to where the first cut was. Aiden measured the other side of the cut and did the same thing.

This time the hatchet went deep into the trunk and popped out two different pieces of wood, each about the size of a loaf of bread. "Perfect!" Aiden exclaimed.

"WOW! That was amazing," Logan replied, then offered the hatchet to Aiden. "These should go together."

Aiden held up his right hand palm out. "No, you keep yours. It takes a team."

"So we're a team?" Logan asked, eyebrows raised.

"Yah, like the Good Book says, 'as iron sharpens iron, one man sharpens another.'"

"That sounds good to me." Logan put his hatchet in his belt and picked up a log. Aiden did likewise, and they both ran back to the wagon. As they jogged up the beaten path, Aiden noticed how high the sun had gotten, it was nearly noon already, and they hadn't even started repairing the wagon. *Would they be able to repair the wagon fast enough to save Father?*

Ethan was surprised at how fast they packed the food, cooking gear, and bedrolls. They had cleaned up the clearing by the cobblestone well as best they could. Uncle admonished them to leave no trace. But that was pretty hard, considering all the human, coyote, and prairie dog tracks in the area.

Uncle was serious enough about it that he took the bulk of the load on his back in a ramshackle bundle wrapped in rope, with the cooking pot bouncing around at the bottom. It didn't look comfortable, but there wasn't another way to split the load with only two young boys and a grandpa.

"Alright, everybody." Uncle held out a tin cup. "Drink as many of these as you can stomach, cause I'm not sure how far it will be to water, and we can't carry much on us."

Ethan hadn't thought of that. The path seemed to be taking them away from the stream they had been following the day before. Water was essential, and they each just had a small water skin. But, it got hot out on the prairie. It was barely past sun up, and it was warm enough to dry the dew from his clothes.

Ethan took his turn drinking, and he was sure to drink two whole cups, which cooled him off just a bit. A breeze came up to finish the job. A smile broke out on his face as his hope for the day blossomed. Uncle was wise, so he'd make sure they didn't run out of water.

Ethan's smile turned upside down in less than an hour. The weight of his pack added to his shield made the straps dig into his shoulders. He didn't want to complain, but it was a lot for him to carry. He wanted to see if there was a way to trade some of the load with Jesse, but the concentration on his friend's face said he wasn't fairing any better.

On the other hand, Gramps was just whistling away as they went along, as if he didn't have a care in the world. It surprised Ethan because he thought Gramps would start being grumpy by now.

Uncle must have been thinking the same thing because he asked, "Hey Gramps, what's got you in such a fine mood?"

"The sun on my face, the sun on my face," he responded. "We'd been locked under that cloud of Darkness for months now. Isn't that right Jesse?"

"Yes, sir," Jesse whined, not sharing Gramps's upbeat attitude.

Gramps must have picked up on that. "C'mon now, boy, we're in the sun, bellies full of gravy!" He adjusted his pack. "Sure, we've got everything we own on our backs, but we're in the sun." Gramps looked up to the sky, and a broad smile cracked his face.

It made Ethan forget his pack and let out a little giggle. It was good to be in the sun and out of the Darkness. The warm thoughts carried Ethan through the morning.

Uncle broke the silence as the sun reached its peak, "Hey, old-timer, I think we have a problem." Uncle stopped and got down on a knee, which looked awkward with the giant pack on his back.

"What's that, big man?" Gramps stopped next to him.

"Well, it looks like the prairie dogs go off to the left here." Uncle pointed to a series of tiny tracks between the tall grass. "But if you look about fifty feet up, the wagon turned to the right. See that big the rock jutting out of the ground? Rather than veering left to stay on the path it took a hard right into the prairie." Uncle stood back up.

"Yah, that seems about right," Gramps agreed.

That wasn't good. It meant Mother hadn't gone to the wellspring like they'd hoped. Maybe they were lost, or worse, the coyotes hurt them. Ethan's lower lip started to quiver.

"Hey now, no reason to get too excited." Uncle put a hand on Ethan's shoulder. "We thought this might happen, so now we just have to deal with it."

Uncle's hand on his shoulder felt reassuring, but he still didn't feel settled. "I know. I can go run really fast and see if they are OK!" Ethan blurted out.

"You keep saying that," Jesse interjected, "How fast?"

Ethan dropped his shield and pack and held up his foot, "My boots make me go so fast, I can run on water like a skipping stone."

"No way!" Jesse said, shaking his head.

"Yah huh!" Ethan said back. "I'll show you."

Uncle held up his hands in protest. "Hold on, hold on."

"But Uncle, I can run fast and find Aiden and Mama!" Ethan pointed down the path.

Uncle put his hands on his hips. "I know, but what did I tell you the last time you said you could do that?"

Ethan let out a long sigh. "That you couldn't let me do that because if anything happened to me, you'd be in trouble with Mama."

"Well, that's not exactly what I said." Uncle looked at Gramps as if he wanted some help.

"Well, we are in kind of pickle, big man," Gramps replied.

That made Ethan smile. Gramps might be pretty cranky most of the time, but now he seemed to be on Ethan's side.

Gramps continued, "As I see it, we can track down them no-good, egg-stealin' prairie dogs and retrieve our stuff, but possibly miss the wagon if it comes back this way." Gramps pointed off in the direction of the wagon tracks. "Or we can follow the path they took, hopin' to catch up to them. Of course, if they took a different path back to the wellspring, we'll miss them again, and they can move a lot faster than we can."

Uncle groaned. It was clear he felt stuck by the situation. He set down his pack, stretched, and let out a sigh. "What are you sayin', old timer?"

"Well, as I sees it, if this one can run as fast as he says, why not send him off up the trail to see where his ma is?" Gramps pointed at Ethan's boots.

"If he can run that fast," Jesse chided.

"I can so!" Ethan protested.

"Now, Jesse, don't provoke the boy," Gramps corrected. "We've seen them do some amazing stuff now. If he says he can run fast, I suspect he can."

Ethan squinted his eyes and stuck out his tongue.

"Hey!" Uncle barked. "Don't be makin' this a tussle, Ethan."

"Yes. sir!" Ethan's face fell

Uncle continued, "Gramps, I see what you're saying, but I can't just let a little boy run off in the wild undefended."

"As far as I saw, that shield of his was pretty handy against the crows and them coyotes." Gramps motioned toward Ethan's shield, covered beneath his pack. "If anybody's going to be undefended, it's us!"

Ethan's chest puffed up, and a smile cracked his face. Gramps was right, he was the one protecting them from the coyotes. So he would be just fine.

Uncle's eyes took on a thoughtful look as he stroked his beard. "Alright, I guess you have a point." Uncle stepped to Ethan and took a knee.

"Can you do exactly what I say, no exceptions?" Uncle stared into Ethan's eyes.

Ethan was intimidated by the big man's presence and the intensity of that stare. "Yes, sir."

"Alright then, you can go run up that path through the prairie grass." Uncle pointed to where the wagon had veered off course. "You follow it as long as you can till you either lose the wagon tracks, or you find your Ma."

Ethan nodded.

"If you lose the tracks, you come right back. You got it?" Uncle asked.

"Yes if I lose the tracks, I'll come right back," Ethan echoed. He wasn't going to lose the tracks. He was going to find his family.

"If you find your Ma, you stay with her and let her know where we're waiting." Uncle paused for Ethan's response.

"Yes, sir!" Ethan saluted.

"I'm going to send one of my geese to try to keep up with you. If you find yer Ma, he'll come back, and I'll know you're safe."

"That's pretty smart, if he's that fast." Jesse quipped.

That made Ethan's blood boil. "Can I go already?" Ethan demanded.

Uncle let go of Ethan's shoulders. "Alright then."

Ethan bent and retrieved his shield from underneath the pack and put it on his back. Then he side-stepped Uncle and made to run off at full speed.

But he didn't. He ran at his normal speed. There was no power in his shoes. A wave of uncertainty washed over his body. Why wasn't he fast?

"Not lookin' so fast," Jesse chided as he started to run after Ethan, keeping pace if not slightly catching up. As Ethan cleared the fifty yards to the path through the grass, he finally gave up.

"I don't get it. I don't have any power." Ethan whined wide-eyed.

"I knew you were just making that up," Jesse said as he stopped next to Ethan.

"I was not!" Ethan protested. "Really, I've run so fast. I don't understand."

"Yah, I'm sure you're really fast." Jesse smarted off.

"Hey!" Uncle hollered. "No need for teasin'. Ethan, you got any idea what's goin' on?"

"No, sir," Ethan replied, crestfallen.

A coyote's howl in the distance punctuated Ethan's response. Followed by the barks of a dozen or more—much closer.

"I think we might have found the answer," Gramps said as the bottom dropped out of Ethan's stomach. He couldn't run off to find Mother when there were coyotes about to strike!

Lauren woke up stiff and sore from sleeping on the bedrock that surrounded the pool. A wet tongue on her cheek pulled her from her slumber.

"Meow Meow, stop!"

She tried to bat away what she thought was her kitten, only to find it was Chance licking her cheek. He jerked his head, and his eye drooped pitifully.

"OH! I'm sorry, Chance." She scrambled up and out from under the coarse wool blanket. From her knees, she patted his nose and inspected the poultice on his flank. It was dried and cracked, showing a bit of the wound. In the sunlight, it looked much worse than the night before, making her wince. She wished she had an apple or some other treat for the brave pony. They would have been lost the night before without him.

"Finally," Tye said curtly, pointing to the orange in the eastern sky. "If I hadn't set the pony on you, I do believe you would have slept until noon."

"Tye, I—"

Tye held up Meow Meow, dwarfed in the giantess' hand. "No need to apologize. I fell asleep on watch. This one was the savior of us both, I believe."

Lauren chuckled at that. "It is his special ability. I don't know how he does it."

"We can ponder this on the trail." Tye set the kitten on Lauren's shoulder. "I will refill the water, and you saddle the pony. We can eat biscuits while we travel."

Lauren sighed as she took the kitten off her shoulder and put him in her dress pocket. For just a second, she felt her friend was back; now, they were off to business again. She frowned and almost grabbed Tye's arm to talk about the night before, but the sun was rising fast, and they didn't have much time to destroy the Censer. So instead, she took a deep breath and promised herself she would reconnect with Tye on the trail.

Lauren led Chance to water to make sure he was ready for their ride. Then she proceeded to load him back up with the saddle and meager supplies. Within fifteen minutes, they took care of their necessities and were off toward the Censer.

The pair of coyotes followed them at a discrete distance. One was always there; the other would occasionally dart off into the grass. There would be a yip or a howl, and it would return with another coyote to join their pack. Lauren wondered if they would have a coyote army by the time they got back to Mother.

A wave of dread fell over her at the thought. Were they able to keep Father out of the Darkness? Had they run into their own coyote troubles. *God, please help Father.*

The depression they slept in shielded them from the rest of the vast prairie, so they didn't see just how isolated they'd become until they cleared the next rise. All Lauren could see off to the north and east was a vast ocean of waving grass, topped here and there with a seafoam of flowers. Far off to the east and a bit north there seemed to be some tended ground and a maybe a farm house but at this distance she couldn't tell for sure. Regardless they were miles and miles from civilization, or even just people. It might have been a beautiful sight if it didn't suddenly make her feel very alone.

Other than the brief greeting at wake up, Tye had said nothing, save an occasional warning about possibly treacherous ground, and she seemed immune to any attempts at conversation. They had eaten their hardtack biscuits in silence.

Lauren could see how being under the influence of the Darkness daggers must be a heavy weight, and her friend had good reason to be resentful of being Refi'Cul's pawn. But that wasn't Lauren's fault . . . or was it?

Lauren's contemplation was broken by Tye's exclamation, "There!" She pointed to the left of their current path. "See the smoke plume?"

Lauren squinted to see more clearly what Tye was pointing at. "I think so?" The whole sky had the haze a Censer puts in the air. *Oh wait, we're back in a Darkness zone. Maybe that's why Tye is so tight-lipped. Could it be affecting her again?* Lauren's stomach took on a tight knot.

"It's moving!" Tye said barely above a whisper.

Was she shocked, or was she in awe of it? Lauren couldn't see Tye's face to know one way or the other. "Are you sure?"

Tye let out a sigh, "Yes, it is definitely moving."

"What direction?" Lauren still couldn't quite make out what was happening on the horizon.

"To the east." Tye kicked the prairie grass at her feet and dislodged a large chunk, leaving a small patch of loose dirt exposed. She knelt and drew in it with her fingers. It looked a bit like the map and circles Aiden had made.

"It's moving due east. If it started where we were planning to find it, going east in that direction will cause it to eventually cover the southern half of the zone everyone else is traveling in. Shortly, the lower half of that zone will be a double-Darkness zone!"

"No!" Lauren cried. Chance whinnied in support. "We've got to do something! Catch whoever is carrying that."

"Yes! Yes, of course." Tye stood and stamped out the makeshift map. She pointed off to the northeast of their position. "If we make for that settlement with speed, we might be able to beat them there."

Lauren pulled on Chance's reins, steering him in that direction. "C'mon big guy, we need all you've got!" She nudged him with her heels.

Chance took off like an arrow, and Tye kept pace as they raced across the prairie. Lauren's doubts about Tye nagged at her, but there was nothing she could do about it. Father would die for sure if the whole zone was covered in a double layer of Darkness. They had to intercept that Censer.

Master Warden sat tall on the back of his albino moose, surveying the rocky outcropping topped by a marker of a dozen neatly stacked, blackened stones. It was just as Refi'Cul had described.

He hated following the Steele Lord's suggestion to gain "power" for himself. Was he not already the Master Warden of the Heathlands? He had Wardens, moose, and all the animals of the prairie. What more power did he need? So why was obtaining the Censer so enticing?

Something about these Censers and their smoke was elusive. Being in their presence made him feel he must embrace the human's "power," or be overwhelmed by it. But the way to that power was now blocked by potentially deadly plants.

A field of giant sickly green parsnips surrounded the Censer's hiding place. Instead of the cheery yellow blossoms, they had the hue of infected pus. Normal parsnip pollen was an annoyance to avoid, but the size and color of these told him they must be deadly.

Something else was off. When they approached the Censer Lord Refi'Cul had removed from its shrine, it was billowing dark smoke into the air that was visible from a distance. If this was the right location, the Censer was either gone or destroyed.

"Master Warden, come look!" His advance scout waved him over. The leader nodded and whistled his moose to follow. He raised his hand in a closed fist to have the rest of the two dozen giants in his honor guard stay put ten yards from the parsnips.

A bison herd drew Master Warden's attention away from the scout on the ridge above them. He couldn't remember the last time he'd seen bison. Yet now, they looked down at him as if they were waiting for something. Were they here to follow him? He put his hand to the ancient bison horn hanging on his chest.

The scout cleared his throat and pointed out a path crudely stomped through the parsnips. From his vantage point, high on the moose's back, he could more clearly see the black soot-covered rock overhang surrounded by the remains of animals killed by the parsnips.

The scout cocked his head, "Should I inspect it, sir?"

An uneasy feeling filled Master Warden, and he shook his head. "No, I'll not risk my best scout in this corrupted field." He paused to inspect the area around the rock. "The trail goes in toward the stone here, and I don't see another out from it. So whoever took the Censer went in and came back out the same way."

"It was a Warden, sir"—the scout pointed to the outline of footprints muted by the broken-down grass, which made Master Warden's eyes widen—"and a moose." He indicated some parsnip stalks near the rock outcropping. "Look there. Those were cleanly cut near the blossom. Who would collect this vile weed?"

"Something tells me this is the work of Skull Crusher." Master Warden slammed a fist into his palm. "He was to drive the enemy to us in Blooming Glen, not come up with some scheme to take the human's power for himself. I'm beginning to wonder if he truly serves our people."

"Sir?" the scout asked.

"Never mind." Master Warden frowned as he pointed to the tracks on the ground. "How old are these?"

The scout squatted down, careful not to touch the standing parsnips. "Hours or less, sir."

"Then, I must be off. No time to waste." Master Warden circled his hand in the air, giving the signal to move out.

"But, sir, won't this delay us rejoining Lord Refi'Cul for his assault on Blooming Glen?" the scout asked.

"No, you will lead the troops to 'Lord Refi'Cul.' He sent me off to gain the same power he has. I will retrieve it from that traitor Skull Crusher myself."

The scout's eyes went wide. "But, my lord! If he has the human's power, won't that put you at risk?"

Master Warden lifted the horn from around his neck and blew. The bison on the hill began a purposeful march toward the giant. "I have the power of the prairie. If he has betrayed us, he'll not stand against me. The truth will come to light, soon enough. Now go!"

A chill went down Ethan's back as the Coyote howls got louder. "Uncle! What do we do?"

"We fight!" Uncle pointed at the boulder that separated the beaten path from where the wagon had gone off into the prairie. "We're too exposed here, and we can't see them comin' through the grass. The only thing that might protect our back is that rock."

Ethan looked around and realized just how right Uncle was. Except for the two paths, Ethan was dwarfed by the surrounding prairie grass. They'd have no idea that a coyote was about to strike until it was right on them.

"So, what do you have in mind?" Gramps raised an eyebrow.

"There's a rise going off the direction of the prairie dogs." Uncle drew his sword, and it burst into flame.

The coyotes must be close. Ethan gritted his teeth in a vain attempt to force the anxiety out of his body. His shield should keep them away, but what if it didn't work this time—the way his boots failed him.

Uncle continued, "If we can top the rise, we'll be able to see them comin', and if there's a sharp drop off, we can put that to our back."

"Well, let's get to it," Gramps said.

"Wait! What about Mama?" Ethan asked. "If we just run off down that path, how will she find us?

"Can't worry about that now; we need to find a safe spot." Uncle picked up Ethan's pack in his free hand. "Ready your shield, and let's go!"

Ethan's face fell. He didn't want to lose this connection to his family. However, he knew there was no changing Uncle's mind.

"I know!" Jesse blurted out. "Mark the path with your sword. Cut arrows in the ground to show the way."

"With this grass bein' so dry, I'm afraid I'd start a fire." Uncle shook his head. "That would be more dangerous than the coyotes."

Coyote howls pierced the air.

"You lead and just drag it on the ground behind you," Jesse insisted. "Ethan and I can stamp out the fire."

Uncle stood still for a moment, staring off into the grass. The path toward the wagon haunted Ethan with the loss of speed. Had he done something wrong? Would his shield work when they needed it? It had never failed him before. He cinched up the straps on his shield, hoping that would give him the confidence he lacked.

Another round of howls caused Uncle to break his silence. "We'll do it! I just hope we can find a rise before they close in on us."

Uncle turned to the big rock and dragged the tip of the sword down it, cutting the stone in a perfectly straight line, leaving scorch marks on either side and freeing a chunk of rock near the bottom of the boulder. Jesse tried to pick it up, but he immediately dropped it.

"OW! That's hot!" He blew on his fingers.

It would have been comical under any other circumstance, but this was a serious situation. Didn't Jesse see this was real danger, why was he playing with a hot rock?

Uncle continued the motion onto the ground and dragged the sword tip behind him. "Gramps, find that praire dog trail and flatten down the grass on either side as you go. Boys, make sure that fire gets stamped out."

Ethan rushed to obey, but Jesse took a minute to cover the fist-sized rock in a handkerchief to pick it up.

"C'mon, Jesse, quit fooling around," Ethan demanded through gritted teeth.

"I'm not foolin' around," Jesse retorted as he held up the rock. "This here's a good coyote-conkin' rock! I've been lookin' for one of these since last night."

Ethan's jaw loosened to let out a sideways smile. Jesse didn't have a holy weapon like Uncle's sword or Ethan's shield, and the only thing around here for miles was prairie grass. "Good thinkin'! Maybe Uncle will make me a coyote-conkin' rock too!"

A coyote howl punctuated Ethan's sentence.

"Boys! " Uncle barked, "Get a move on!" He was already ten yards into the prairie dog path.

The boys rushed to fall in behind Uncle, stamping out the little whisps of flame in the grass that flared up as the sword passed. Uncle repositioned Ethan's pack, so it was slung from his shoulder by one strap, freeing up his hand to push away any prairie grass Gramps failed to tamp down as they passed. Uncle looked awkward, and Ethan felt guilty about not carrying his own pack. But Uncle was moving so fast that it was all he could do to keep up, while ensuring the fire was out.

The coyotes must have sensed their movement because the howls intensified and closed in. Finally, after twenty minutes of battling through the prairie grass, Ethan looked back to see a little whisp of smoke coming up behind them. *Oh no, what if it grows? I need to fix it.*

He was about to say something when Gramps hollered. "Well I'll be!"

Ethan turned and couldn't see through Uncle and the prairie grass on either side. "What, Gramps?"

"It's them no-good, egg-stealin' prairie dog's mound," Gramps replied. "And it's bigger than you, mountain man!"

Uncle harumphed at that and picked up the pace.

"Really?" Jessie added. "Let me see."

Coyote barking and movement in the grass to their left broke the train of thought. Instinctively, Ethan turned in that direction and brought his arm up just as a coyote burst through the grass, leaping toward him.

It rebounded off the shield, knocking Ethan to the ground, but saving him from the beast's claws and fangs.

Uncle swept the flaming sword up from the dirt awkwardly, trying to take a combat stance to engage the beast. But the uneven load he was carrying on his back made him falter.

Jesse threw the coyote conkin' rock, hard and true, at the beast, knocking it out. The canine slumped on top of Ethan's shield.

"Hey! Help! I can't get out!" Ethan thought the live coyote was heavy, but the dead weight was crushing the air out of his lungs.

Uncle closed the distance and kicked the coyote off of Ethan. "Jesse, give him a hand up."

"Sure thing! Just let me find my rock." Jesse searched the grass near Ethan with his hands.

"No time for that!" Uncle commanded.

"But it's a good coyote-conkin' rock!" Jesse complained.

"I can get up on my own," Ethan huffed. "It is a good rock! Let Jesse find it."

"Pah!" Uncle huffed. "Both of you climb up that praire dog mound now!"

"Found it!" Jesse exclaimed.

"Go!" Uncle barked as he turned to follow his own orders.

Ethan got to his feet and ran after Jesse and Uncle up the mound. Gramps was right. It had to be the world's biggest. Usually, prairie dog holes weren't much bigger than a few feet around and a couple tall. By the time they got to the top, they were 10 feet off the ground.

The dirt was mostly hard-packed, but a couple of times Ethan's foot sunk deep into the side of the mound, and he almost fell. When he got to the top, the others were already ready to defend the position as howls erupted again.

Jesse, rock in hand, stood back-to-back with Gramps, and the oldster was ready with his walking stick. Uncle stood between them and slowly set Ethan's pack on the ground.

He had the flaming sword out and scanned the praire grass like he expected the coyotes to rush them. "Ethan, take up the spot to my back."

"Yes, sir!" Ethan rushed to take up the position. He lifted his arm, and the armor piece took on the form of a tower shield bigger than him.

He smiled, as he felt the electricity course through his body. The Light powering his shield created a safety bubble around them. They were going to be OK. God was with them. He brought it down to the ground to anchor it, and the dirt fell out from underneath him. In an instant, the Light went out as he slid down a hole, the light fading away above him. He conked his wonkus at the bottom of the fall, and the darkness became complete.

Sweat beaded Aiden's brow as he worked with Logan to wedge the big branch they'd carried from the grove underneath the wagon. His heart felt a little lighter from having an extra set of hands. Mother held the branch up in the air, while Logan clamped it to the wagon's hitch with his hands. Then Aiden wrapped leather tie-downs around them tightly to take the flexibility out of it, so it could act as a lever. Then they tied the yoke to the tongue and branch in a cross.

"The wagon is very heavy, Aiden. Are you sure this will work?" Mother asked.

"All we have to do is raise long enough to push the wheels under to the right place. I think the lever is long enough with all the weight you moved to the front. It should work," Aiden replied. "If you and Logan can push down, I can roll the wheels into the right place."

Mother's raised eyebrow told Aiden she wasn't really sure, but she was willing to try. Aiden threw out a bunch of grain again, and the crows flew after it, leaving the wagon free of them.

Aiden got into position with his hands on the axel, and Mother and Logan grabbed either side of the yoke.

"Three, two, one, push." Mother pushed with great effort, and Logan pushed so hard he came off the ground, but the wagon only barely shifted before they gave up.

Mother let out a great sigh. "Aiden, it's not enough."

"I think if we can push it down, maybe it will shift the stuff on the seat enough to stay down. I'll come help you." Aiden raced to the front.

He joined Logan on one side, with Mother on the other, and counted down again, "Three, two, one, push!" This time, the back of the wagon lifted off the ground, but they couldn't quite drive the yoke all the way to the ground before they tired out.

"We were so close." Aiden huffed.

"We need more weight," Mother replied.

"What about the birds?" Logan asked.

"They don't weigh that much. But it might be worth a try," Aiden said.

"Not on our end. What if the crows picked up on the wagon's back?" Logan asked.

"I'll see if they can figure that out." Aiden went back to the wagon's rear and snapped his fingers toward the crows. The spotted one looked up at him and cocked its head. "Can you and your friends lift this?" Aiden grabbed the top edge of the wagon gate for emphasis.

The bird cawed at him but then went back to eating grain. Aiden let out a deep sigh. His distraction had worked too well.

Father groaned, and Aiden's attention was drawn to the sight of his wounded back. It still looked awful, but Mother appeared to be right about leaving it in the air to dry it out. Still, they needed to hurry. What could he do to make the birds help?

He put the grain on the ground to take their weight off the wagon, maybe the opposite? He got some grain and carefully let it pour through his hand along the top edge of the wagon gate. The spotted crow flapped up to the gate and began pecking at the food. Half a dozen crows joined in, then Aiden looked intently at the crow and whispered, "Please pick it up." He stared into the crow's eye. "Please!"

It motioned its beak toward the front, almost like it was saying, "Go on, let's get moving." So Aiden ran to where Mother and Logan were waiting at the hitch. "OK, let's do this!"

The three of them pushed down with all their might, while the crows grabbed the wagon gate and flapped their wings with abandon. The wagon lifted all the way up, this time knocking the last of the grain off the top of the gate.

"We did it!" Aiden cried.

"But how do we push the wheels under?" Mother asked. "If you let go, the whole thing will tip, and those birds won't lift forever."

The crows let go and flew back to pick grain off the ground to emphasize their point. But it seemed like the position was stable enough they might be able to maintain it.

"Mother, try sitting on it." Aiden gritted his teeth as Mother's weight shifted. "You too, Logan."

Logan followed suit, ensuring his entire weight was on the yoke. Aiden tried to let go, but he could feel it slipping up. "Arrgh . . . Any other ideas?"

"You said special horseshoes before," Logan said.

From where he sat on the yoke, he pulled a ripe, red fruit out of his pack. "Hey, horsey, want an apple?"

Aiden looked at his friend with an upraised eyebrow. But Logan was focused on the closest Clydesdale.

"Here, horsey, horsey, horsey," Logan continued.

It seemed to accept the offer by coming forward. Logan held it up behind his head, forcing the horse to place its feet right next to his to eat the apple. Logan let it eat, then placed his hand on the horse's ankle. The horse turned its foot up and backward like it was preparing to be shod. "Hammer." Logan reached out a hand to Aiden.

"OK." Aiden put his knees on the yoke, so he could free his hands to give Logan the hammer.

Logan tapped the hammer a few times on the shoe. Then grabbed the horse's hoof and placed it on the yoke. The horse pushed down. "Go quick, Aiden!"

Aiden hopped up quickly and ran back to the wagon wheels. He groaned with effort and managed to push them into place just as the horse picked up its foot.

The tongue lifted a little but not much, because the rear came down on the axel.

"Logan, you did it!" Aiden cried. "That was a great idea. How did you know the horse would do that?"

"It's not big deal." Logan's cheeks were a little pink. Aiden thought he might be a bit bashful at the praise. "Pa taught me everything about horses. They get in the habit of stamping down right after a shoeing."

"I'm sure your father would be very proud." Mother patted him on the shoulder. "Aiden, is everything lined up correctly?"

"Let me see?" Aiden crawled under the wagon. "It's not quite right, but I think I can whack it into place with the hammer. Logan can you bring it?"

"Sure." Logan ran around the wagon's side and lightly tossed the hammer to Aiden. In his hand, the hammer glowed, and Aiden hit the axel. It moved half an inch to line up the broken carriage bolt hole with its spot in the frame on the left side of the wagon. He did the same on the right, and everything was in place.

"Hey, there's a box of penny nails out there. Can you hand those to me and the wood we brought back?"

"Sure," Logan said.

"Once you bring those over, I'll need you to climb under here and help me." Aiden pulled the carriage bolts out of his pouch and put them in the broken sockets on either side of the axel, while Logan put the supplies under the wagon.

"Can you hold this wood right here?" Aiden picked up one of the pieces of wood and held it centered over the left bolt socket. Logan held it in place, and Aiden quickly nailed four nails into the log from different angles. They did the same thing to the other carriage bolt, then crawled out from under the wagon.

Mother must have read Aiden's mind because she had already undone the reinforcement of the wagon hitch and had the horses back in their places. "Are we all ready, son?"

"We just need to reload the wagon," Aiden responded.

"Logan, do you mind helping us a bit more?" Mother asked.

"No problem, ma'am." Logan saluted her, which pulled a slight chuckle from Mother.

"I'm going to prepare your Father to put him back in the wagon. But please hurry," Mother replied.

Working together, the boys reloaded the wagon lickety split. Then, they used the shaft of Logan's spear and the end of the large branch to make a litter out of Father's bedroll. With a bit of help from the crows, they all managed to lift Father into the bed of the wagon.

As Mother and Aiden were climbing into the wagon's seat, Aiden spied smoke to the northwest, beyond the watering hole. "Hey, Logan, can I see your spyglass?"

"Sure." He handed it to Aiden.

Aiden looked in the direction of the smoke. It was hard to make out with the trees, but it seemed the barn was on fire. He tried to sit still, and it got very clear for just a second. Then he saw a person as big as the barn door pass through his field of view. "Giant!"

"Giant! What do you mean Giant?" Logan clambered up on the wagon. "Let me see."

Aiden handed him the spyglass, and Logan cried, "That's my farm! It's on fire! Giants! No!"

He dropped the spyglass and moved to jump off the wagon when Mother grabbed him. "No, Logan! Wait!"

"I can't wait! They're under attack! They need me!" Logan cried.

"Logan, didn't your father say he'd go to safety rather than fight?" Aiden asked.

"Yes! But . . ." Logan responded.

"Logan, let me look." Mother held out her free hand, "Aiden, can you hand me the spyglass."

She refused to let Logan go, which made it awkward for her to look through the glass. She sat for what seemed an eternity. "There is one giant there, for sure. I can't tell if I'm seeing the same one more than once from this distance. The fire looks unstoppable at this point. Tell me what you told Aiden about your father's plans."

Logan's face was pale, but he'd stopped struggling to get away from Mother. "Pa said if anything happened, we would find shelter in the garrison at Blooming Glen." His head slumped as he continued, "He didn't want to fight, but he thought the Mighty Mercenaries would take us in for what he called old times' sake."

"Well, I'm not sure about his reasoning, but that is our destination as soon as we find the Wellspring of Life." Mother set down the spyglass and turned Logan by the shoulders to look at her. "If you were my child, I would want your father to keep you out of harm's way. I would not want him to let Aiden go running off to fight giants by himself when there is another way. So you're coming with us."

"But-b-but"—Logan stammered—"they'll be looking for me. I can't just go with you."

"There's no telling whether the giant will come here, too, or even follow your parents to Blooming Glen." Logan's eyes got big at that, but Mother continued, "However, we are Light Bearers. You will be safer with us than on your own, especially when we gather the rest of our family."

Logan let out a deep sigh and looked down. "I guess you could be right."

"Do you think your family will look in the watering hole for you?" Mother asked sternly.

"Well, y-yah, m-maybe." Logan stammered.

"We'll leave them a message telling them to find you in Blooming Glen. Ok?" Mother responded

Logan stood there shaking and staring off in the distance.

Aiden put a hand on his shoulder. "We'll take you back to your family. We promise."

"OK." Logan nodded slowly. "I'll stay with you."

"Aiden, turn the horses around and drive close to the watering hole." Mother let go of Logan and began digging around under the seat. She pulled out the slate and wrote while Aiden turned the horses.

> Logan is safe
> with our family.
> We are taking
> him to the garrison
> at Blooming Glen

When they reached the rocks around the watering hole, Aiden stopped the wagon. Mother hopped off and found a place with a protective overhang to place the slate. When she got back on the wagon, she said, "Let's go, Aiden. We've lost half a day, and there's no telling how far we'll have to backtrack to find the trail to the Wellspring of Life."

Logan's gentle sobbing broke Aiden's heart, because he knew exactly what it was like to lose your family.

Lauren glanced over her left shoulder while Chance pounded the thick prairie grass beneath his hooves as they ran next to Tye. The inky black plume of Censer smoke was still to their north and moving eastward. The knot in her stomach tightened at the thought that they might not intercept the Censer bearer in time to prevent Father from entering a double-Darkness zone. Lauren wished Aiden were here to help them stay on the fastest course to the enemy. Unfortunately, the Censer seemed far enough away that a slight miscalculation in the direction might have them overshoot and miss it entirely.

Tye must have been worried about the same thing because she stopped at the next rise. The giantess took deep breaths, and it was clear the race across the prairie was winding her.

"The direction has shifted slightly." Tye spoke between gasps of breath. "Originally, it looked like the smoke was moving straight east. But then it turned more to the north after they crossed the stream bed. Now it's going straight for that farm."

"Oh no!" Lauren gasped. "We have to get there first and warn them."

"Agreed, but I don't know if we can." Tye shook her head. "It's going to be a fight when we catch them."

Lauren nodded. It had to be a formidable foe crossing the deep prairie grass at that pace with a Censer. She'd seen Skull Crusher carry one on his back in the night, but now it was broad daylight. Whoever it was with the Censer had to be taking it in a cart or something. So it made sense that crossing the creek might cause them to change directions a bit.

Regardless, showing up to that fight entirely out of breath and exhausted wouldn't do them much good. They'd lose before it even started. "So, what do you recommend?"

"As much as I hate to say this, we can hope the people at the settlement will slow them down a bit." Tye took a deep breath. "Then we'll come in unexpectedly from the enemy's rear. We might catch them in a battle on two fronts then."

"That sounds good." Lauren pursed her lips not sure that was really going to work. But what else could they do?

"We'll conserve our energy as best we can," Tye said. "We'll drive Chance at a trot for twenty minutes, then walk the same period. Then, when we get close, we can pour on the speed at the end overtake our enemy."

"OK." Lauren nodded and then caught something out of the corner of her eye. "Do you see a cloud of dust off to the west?"

"Yes, but it could be anything." Tye shielded her eyes with her hand. "At this distance, it's too hard to tell if it's friend or foe."

"Whoever it is they are following the Censer's path." Lauren offered.

"Then it might be a foe worse than Refi'Cul and his Steele Brothers." Tye stared into Lauren's eyes. "Whoever is carrying the Censer may have been careless with a campfire, or the molten core of the Censer may make it hot enough to set the prairie grass aflame as it passes."

"Oh no!" Lauren's mouth dropped. She'd heard about the devastation a prairie fire could cause. It was too easy for people to become surrounded by flames and lose breathable air.

"If it is, we need to be in front of it when it comes to that waterway." Tye pointed to a cut in the grass in the distance. "The wind is slight today, so the fire shouldn't jump the stream."

"You're right! Let's go!" Lauren snapped the reins, and Tye took off in a jog to match Chance's speed. The coyote pack had grown to a dozen and picked up the pace, darting back and forth ten yards behind them. But the longer they traveled, the further they fell behind.

The miles flew by, but Lauren soon realized the Censer was moving faster. She wanted to push their speed, but she knew that wouldn't help. They would be done for if they showed up spent from a mad race across the prairie.

Maybe the people at the settlement might prove a match for whatever minions of Darkness carried the Censer.

Two hours of carefully managing their speed brought them close enough to start to see the settlement in detail.

"Look! The Censer has stopped moving!" Tye pointed.

Sure enough, the Censer's smoke billowed at the top of the hill marked by the settlement. That flared Lauren's hope that the people at the farm might thwart the Darkness-minions' plan.

That hope vanished as she realized the fields below the settlement were on fire!

"Ethan! Ethan! Can you hear me?" Uncle's muffled voice called from somewhere above.

The back of Ethan's head hurt, and his shield covered his face. The dirt in his mouth tasted horrible. He had to spit it out to reply.

Jesse called down, "Ethan! Please be OK!"

"I'm stuck!" Ethan croaked. "The dirt is pushing down my shield."

A muted set of coyote howls wafted down to Ethan, and it made him wonder if Uncle even heard him.

Ethan could barely make out Uncle's voice, "That hole's too small for Gramps or me. Jesse, if we lower you down on a rope, do you think you can dig him out?"

"Yes, sir," Jesse replied.

More howls, and Ethan lost the conversation. Were they fighting the coyotes now? Ethan's heart raced. He couldn't tell how much dirt was on top of him. What if the coyotes got them before they could come to help him. Was he going to die buried in a no-good, egg-stealin' prairie dog hole? He started to hyperventilate. *God please help! I need you!*

"Ethan, I'm coming!" Jesse called from above.

I'm going to be alright, I need to calm down.

Ethan worked to slow his breathing in the tight space under the shield.

After what felt like hours, the dirt to his left shifted a little. "Ethan, I'm here."

Ethan slowly took a deep breath before responding. "I'm so glad!"

"Give me a minute, and I'll dig you out," Jesse offered.

Ethan pushed up on his shield while Jesse dug, in the hope of getting out faster. It loosened, then popped up, smacking Jesse in the face.

"Ow!" the other boy cried.

"Oh, I'm so sorry!" Ethan apologized.

"If that's what you do to people who are helping you, I'd sure hate to be your enemy." Jesse chided, while rubbing his forehead.

Ethan laughed and rubbed the back of his own head.

"He's out!" Jesse called up.

Any response from above was blocked out by the sound of howls, snarls, and thumps from Uncle and Gramps fighting the coyotes.

"Uncle! What's going on up there? Are you OK?" Ethan cried.

"We're holdin' our own; you two sit tight," Uncle called as his fiery sword flew over the hole.

Ethan picked up his shield, and it took on a faint light that illuminated the space they were in. "They're going to need this." Ethan scanned the dirt-walled chamber they stood in. He was surprised at how deep and open the space was, he expected a prairie dog mound was a bunch of tiny tunnels. But this was some kind of natural cave. A spiral ramp of dirt ran around the chamber from the bottom of the tunnel up to the top. However, his fall destroyed a good three-foot chunk of the spiral from top to bottom.

He pointed to the damage. "I don't think we can climb back up that way."

"Gramps has the rope tied to him," Jesse gently tugged on the rope attached to his waist. "But your Uncle was holding on to him with one arm while I came down. So we can't get up while they're fighting."

A sudden tug on the rope jerked Jesse up and almost off the floor. "Gramps!"

"I'm alright!" Gramps hollered down. "You just watch out for them no-good, egg-stealin' prairie dogs!"

That put Ethan on edge. His first scan of the room showed him three praire dog tunnels coming into the chamber. He might be able to belly crawl through two of them. Jesse was his size, so he could probably make it too. But his blood went cold at the thought of prairie dogs flooding in from all three at once.

"If you can hold the rope, we can come to help you!" Ethan yelled up the hole. He watched as Uncle's sword swung low across the opening a little too close to the rope, catching it on fire.

"Oh no! Gramps!" Jesse called out.

"What you tryin' to do, big man, set me on fire?" Gramps yelled.

"Gramps, stop, drop, and roll!" Ethan called. That's what Father always told him to do if he got caught on fire. Stop, drop, and roll. He wondered if he had dumped father out of the wheelbarrow and just had him roll if his burns wouldn't be so bad now. Ethan hoped Gramps wouldn't suffer the same fate.

"What?" Uncle yelled back over the din of battle.

The boys couldn't see what happened next, but the rope fell into the hole with the far end on fire.

"No! Gramps! Are you OK?" Jesse yelled

"Fine, fine. You all just stay safe down there," Gramps replied. "We'll figure this out once we've beaten back these coyotes."

The boys looked at each other with worry crinkling their eyebrows. Ethan was relieved that Gramps wasn't on fire but hated feeling helpless. *God, please help Uncle and Gramps fight the coyotes.*

"Hey, Ethan, do you see a light down there?" Jesse pointed to the tunnel with the biggest opening.

Looking over the shield, Ethan's eyesight was blurred by its radiance. "I'm not sure."

"Lay your shield down for a second," Jesse said.

"OK." Ethan complied, and now he could see a faint glow at the end of the tunnel, where it connected to another tunnel. A pale green light reflected off of a shiny rock near the top of the junction.

"I see it now!" Ethan replied. The hue of green was very inviting and somehow familiar.

"Maybe that's another way out, a tunnel that might go up at a slope we can crawl up or something?" Jesse offered.

"Uncle! We think we found a way out!" Ethan called up.

"I can't help right now!" Uncle called back. "Just sit tight and stay safe!"

Jesse stepped closer and whispered, "They need our help. We can't just stay here and do nothing."

Ethan took a deep breath. He didn't want to disobey Uncle. The last time they did, it broke the big man's heart. But Jesse was right; they needed Ethan's shield. But he wasn't sure the tunnel with the light was the right answer either.

"I heard these prairie dog tunnels can be really complicated and curvy, almost like an anthill," Ethan explained. "What if we get lost?"

"Maybe we just go to the corner and see; then we can turn around and come back if it's not going somewhere good," Jesse offered

"How about we use the rope?" Ethan tugged on the line around Jesse's waist. We'll leave the end here and follow it back?"

"We can try that," Jesse said. He picked up a big clod of dirt and wrapped the rope's end around it. Then wound up the rest of the cord and hung it over his shoulder. "I'll let it out as we go."

"Hey! We think we found a way out!" Ethan yelled up. "We're going to check it out."

The only acknowledgment from above was a rain of dirt as Jesse's pack fell unceremoniously down the hole. Jesse grabbed the strap in one hand, and the boys looked at each other and shrugged.

"Look out!" Uncle called down. "Get out of there!"

"That was a bit . . . late," Ethan hollered up only to see a flurry of flailing legs and fur descend toward him. Ethan jumped away just as a coyote hit the ground with a sickening crunch.

Jesse scrambled away from the beast, dragging his pack with him toward their chosen path. "We gotta get out of here!"

Ethan picked up his shield. "Let me go first to light the way."

"We don't have time for that!" Jesse argued. "It's bigger than the hole. Leave it!"

The coyote stirred, slowly regaining consciousness.

"Just wait." Ethan cinched it to his wrist and the shield shrunk to the size of a small kitchen bowl, but still provided enough light to illuminate their path. "See."

The coyote growled and snapped at them but didn't stand.

"Go, Ethan! Go!" Jesse cried.

Ethan was already in the hole, crawling as fast as he could. Jesse followed, dragging his pack with the strap wrapped around his ankle. He was almost on top of Ethan despite the dead weight of his bag.

By the time they got halfway down the tunnel, Ethan had relaxed slightly. He could hear the coyote growls and snaps fading behind them. But it didn't seem interested in following them. He wondered if that crunch was a broken bone.

Jesse must not have made that same assumption because he kept pushing Ethan to move faster. Finally, near the end of this leg of the tunnel, they had to belly crawl under a rock sticking down, and Ethan felt it dig into his back as he scurried under it. He blew out a sigh of relief when he made it to the intersection with the other tunnel. It was a bigger space, and he could sit on his knees and catch his breath while Jesse got through the tight spot.

When Jesse joined him, Ethan said, "I don't think we'll have to worry about that coyote."

Jesse sighed as he nodded. "Yah, it must have hurt something pretty bad to not come after us. We got excited about nothing."

All of a sudden, there was a high-pitched whine from the coyote. They peered back through the tunnel. Prairie dogs! Lots of prairie dogs! Attacking the coyote.

Ethan had never heard of the little creatures attacking like carnivores. The coyote's yelps send shivers down Ethan's spine and his heart began to thud in his ears as he realized Jesse and he were next.

Aiden's mind had gone blank in the monotonous clip-clop of the horses and bouncing of the wagon. He'd lost all sense of the world, but followed the path of trampled prairie grass back to the trail. Mother's bowed head told him the ride might have rocked her to sleep. If he wasn't making sure they stayed on the path, he might just have done the same.

A muted cry from behind shattered his daze. Aiden pulled the reins to bring the wagon to a stop and turned to see Father writhing on the bedroll.

"What can I do?" Logan offered as he looked about the back of the wagon.

Mother jumped off the driver's seat and into the back. She grabbed a water skin and poured it on a rag that had fallen from Father's brow which she checked with the back of her hand. "He's burning up! I don't understand it. He was starting to recover."

"Look! We're in a double-Darkness zone." Aiden pointed to the sky. In the wide-open prairie, the Darkness was much easier to detect in the sky than in the tree-filled land of the Bjorn Born. But somehow the change just crept up on him while he was mesmerized by the trail.

"How is that possible?" Mother asked. "We passed through here last night, and this didn't happen."

"I don't know." Aiden shrugged. "A Censer must have moved."

"Moved?" Mother was desperately dabbing Father's forehead with the wet rag. "I thought it was a network; wouldn't that alter something?"

"Maybe? But I know Skull Crusher wore one on his back once," Aiden replied. "Maybe whoever was guarding the one Lauren and Tye went after ran off with it or something . . . to escape them."

"Skull Crusher . . . network? What are you all talking about?" Logan asked.

"It's complicated; I'll explain later," Aiden responded as he turned to urge the horses on.

"What are you doing, Aiden?" Mother put a hand on his shoulder.

"I guess we have to turn around to drive Father out of the double-Darkness zone." He whipped the reins, and the horses started moving. "A single Darkness zone is bad enough."

"Wait," Mother pulled on his shoulder until he turned to look her in the eyes. "Can you tell how far we are from the path?"

Aiden pulled on the reins to stop the horses again, "Logan can I see your spyglass?"

"Sure," Logan handed him the device.

Aiden peered through it, looking for any sign of the beaten trail to the wellspring. Once he found it, he scanned around to make sure it was the actual beaten path, and not just some dirt crossing their wild ride from the night before. Movement caught his eye.

He steadied his gaze and saw Uncle, flaming sword in hand, on top of a small hill. A coyote lunged at Uncle as Ethan fell through the top of the hill.

"Mother! It's Uncle and Ethan, and they're in trouble!" Aiden cried.

"Where?" Mother stood up and took the scope from Aiden.

"Follow the path to where the trail crosses, then look off to the left," Aiden explained.

"You're right! I see your Uncle, Jesse, and Gramps. Where's Ethan?" Mother asked.

"I think he fell in a hole."

"That explains Gramps putting a rope on Jesse." Mother put down the spyglass.

"Aiden, drive us there as fast as the horse can go," Mother ordered, as she squatted down next to Father.

"But what about Father?" Aiden asked, not really wanting to know the answer.

"He's in the Lord's hands now. There's little we can do about it but pray . . ." Mother's voice trailed off, and Aiden could tell she'd started to cry. "We have to save your brother . . . and the others. Go! Before I change my mind."

Through tear-filled eyes, Aiden whipped the reins, and the horses jolted down the path. Over the creaks and clip-clop of the horses, Aiden barely heard Logan say, "Ma'am there ain't much I can do, but would it be OK if I prayed with you?"

Ethan's blood pumped in his ears at the thought of having to fight a whole horde of prairie dogs in this tight space. They needed a way out and fast. To the left, the tunnel got smaller and darker almost immediately. A small hole at the top of a cave-in pulsed with green light.

There was no way to dig through the cave-in quickly. But tunnels snaked off on either side of it. Ethan could feel the tension in his face raise his eyebrows. "Which way?"

"I think to the right is probably a big circle back to where we fell, so left?" Jesse pointed.

"OK, you go that way," Ethan pointed. "I'll follow behind you and be able to block the tunnel with my shield."

"You got it." Jesse immediately started in that direction.

The tunnel was small enough that they still needed to crawl, but Ethan could easily sit on his knees and turn around. He would pause every few feet to check for prairie dogs behind them, while being careful not to pin or crawl on the rope around Jesse's waist as they moved. It was a long rope, but he wondered just how far they could go.

The tunnel took two more turns, and they had to decide which way might lead them toward the light without any clear indication. If anything, the tunnel was darker than before. His shield leaked just enough light around it to avoid tripping on the uneven floor.

After a third turn, Ethan realized the tunnel was angled down and not up. So whatever the green light was, it wasn't the outdoors. He started to worry that they were sending themselves to a dead end with ravenous prairie dogs soon to be in hot pursuit. The rope was quickly running out, but that might not even matter, because he definitely didn't want to turn around and face the prairie dogs. He hoped Uncle and Gramps were OK, because they'd lost all notion of what was going on above them.

Ethan ran into Jesse when he stopped short at a big opening.

"Hey!" Jesse called. "I think that's the snow globe."

"Really?" Ethan couldn't see through Jesse but finding the snow globe would be a real blessing. "Do you see anything else that's good?"

"It's all our stuff, and lots of other things too." Jesse exited the tunnel into a big opening. He moved to put on his pack, while still attached to the line, and almost tripped Ethan with the cord.

He stepped through, and carefully turned his back to the tunnel they had just exited. Ethan held up his shield, and it took its full size and illuminated the room. The chamber was similar to the one they had fallen into, but didn't have the spiral ramp around it. Instead, off to the left and right, there were more tunnels. He feared they might all be teeming with prairie dogs at any minute. He wondered if they would guard their hoard the way dragons did.

"There are tons of little treasures in here," Jesse commented. "Not much of it useful to us, but things I'm sure people are missing. Those no-good, theivin' prairie dogs."

"Well, go grab the snow globe. I'll watch the tunnel," Ethan said.

"Look! This dagger is giving off the Light," Jesse called from behind Ethan.

"Good, we might need it to fight those prairie dogs." Ethan turned to look at Jesse's prize.

Jesse held it up. "It's perfect. I'm keeping it."

It was a steel dagger with a dark emerald at its hilt. A wave of dread flowed over Ethan. His mouth dropped, and he barely managed to whisper, "That's Mama's dagger."

"Really?" Jesse's expression turned from victorious elation to concern. "I'm sure she's alright. Those theivin' prairie dogs are sneaky. Must have snuck away with it before the coyote attack."

"Yah, I guess you're right," Ethan said to convince himself more than to acknowledge Jesse's point. "Let's just take the snow globe . . ." Ethan's words failed him as he noticed the snow globe no longer had its faint glow, and the white flakes had settled. It was making little pops as occasional sparks came out of where the metal label used to be.

"What is it?" Jesse asked expectantly. "Do you see the prairie dogs coming?"

"No, I think they might have broken the snow globe." Ethan put the shield on his back. "Guard the tunnel so I can check it out."

"Are you sure?" Jesse's scrunched-up eyebrows told Ethan that the dagger hadn't given him much confidence to defend them.

"It'll just take a second." Ethan picked up the snow globe. Jesse relented and tried to take a combat stance in front of the tunnel they'd just exited.

The metal plate with the words *Wellspring of Life* had been ripped off while the prairie dogs were traveling with it. He was amazed the glass hadn't broken. The label had covered some kind of technology Ethan had never seen. There were tiny bright red and green strings with metal ends melted to gold metal lines on a green background.

Inside, two black strings were connected together with a gold metal tip on the end. The tip rested next to the gold lines and occasionally popped a spark. The tips were just the right size to plug into a socket next to the green line.

Ethan turned to Jesse. "Hey I think I know how they broke it." The snow globe popped to acknowledge Ethan's finding. "Should I fix it?"

"I guess so." Jesse's wide eyes told Ethan he wasn't any more sure than Ethan was. "Hurry up so we can get going."

Ethan carefully plugged the ends of the black strings into the socket, and pops and sparks came from the gold metal, but the globe came to life, snow falling again, and the arrow appeared, pointing directly at the large stone in the wall opposite the tunnel they'd just left.

Ethan looked where the arrow was pointing, and there was a blue-white handprint glowing on the wall. He hadn't noticed that handprint before. Putting it there had to be quite a feat, given it was a big stone underground. He wished Aiden were here. He'd know how they did it.

"Hey, Jesse, check this out!" Ethan pointed with his free hand.

"Is it a way out?" Jesse cried, "they're coming!"

"I don't know." Ethan sized up the handprint; it seemed just his size. "Maybe, let me check."

Ethan scrambled over the prairie dog's treasures, almost tripping on the debris. He wanted to investigate the things on the floor, but the dagger erupted into flame, and Jesse almost dropped it.

"That'll keep the prairie dogs back while I check this out." In his mad scramble over the prairie dog's treasures, Ethan slipped but managed to place his hand on the glowing handprint in the rock as his momentum carried him forward. Suddenly the stone disappeared, and Ethan fell through the empty space where the stone had been.

"Tye! The field is on fire! What shall we do?" Lauren cried, pulling Chance to a stop at the farm's gate. Flames engulfed the path ahead, and there was no way to travel that path without succumbing to the fire. Luckily, the wind was blowing away from them and toward the structures on the hill in front of them, or they would be overwhelmed by smoke. However, there was a slower moving backfire inching toward them.

Tye stopped cold and gulped big breaths of air. "There's nothing we can do for the settlement." She shook her head between breaths. "The Censer is still stationary. Whoever has it will have to get out soon, or they will be lost in the fire also."

"The fire will spread beyond the farm." Lauren pointed at the backfire. "If we're not careful, we're going to be caught in the middle of it."

Tye turned to the northwest. "If the enemy takes the Censer away to the north or west, the threat of a double-Darkness zone will go away as they try to outrun the fire." Tye took a couple of deep breaths. "But if they go to the east like they have been, that's when we have trouble." Tye paused again to catch her breath.

"So we go to the east and try to catch them." Lauren finished Tye's thought in hopes that might give Tye a chance to catch some more breath to continue the chase.

Tye nodded and took a couple deep breaths through her mouth and out her nose before continuing, "Yes, they will try to leave by a gate to the east if that is their direction. If we can find a gate or another break in the fence, that's where they will go." Tye turned and followed the sod wall, not waiting for Lauren's response.

Lauren pulled on the reins, and Chance took off after the giantess. He was already developing a thin lather, and really needed a long rest. Her heart hurt for her trusty steed, but they had to intercept the enemy at all costs.

As they found the corner of the fence, their assumption proved true. The Censer was coming toward them—fast.

They raced up the east side of the fence, hoping to catch the enemy unaware. A rumble grew louder as they ran. A loud whoosh and a crash came from the farm, and the girls realized the buildings must now be ablaze. Lauren tried not to think about the poor family that owned the property. They must have lost everything. She couldn't imagine how devastating that must feel. If her own family weren't Light Bearers the same fate may have befallen their farm.

The rumbling intensified, and suddenly, ten feet in front of them, a moose shot over the fence, pulling a two-wheeled buggy with a Censer on the back. It felt like it flew forever, before landing obscured in the tall grass to their right. The thud was deafening, but then it just kept on going. Fire flared to their left, and ice flowed through Lauren's veins as she realized the fire might overtake them.

"Tye! We've got to move!" Lauren cried as she wheeled Chance to follow the cart.

The buggy was only fifty yards ahead of them, but they'd already been running half the day. They weren't going to catch it unless it slowed significantly, but they needed to do their best, so they followed at a trot, trying their best not to wind themselves.

When they slowed to give Chance a walk break, Tye said, "Did you see who that was?"

Lauren shook her head. "No, I couldn't tell for sure, all I know is he was wearing black."

"It was Skull Crusher. No true Warden would wear that color. He took the Censer and now he has a chariot." A tear ran down Tye's face. "He'll be unstoppable."

Ethan fell through the nothing that had been the large boulder in the wall. He was utterly baffled as he crashed hard on purple-hued crystals. He caught himself with his free hand, and it stung badly, but he almost lost the snow globe as he rolled to the opposite shoulder to take the weight off his hand. Unfortunately, that wasn't much better because he hit hard there too. The crystal floor was completely unforgiving.

He looked up in the direction he'd fallen, and there was a gap in the crystal the size of the big rock but elevated three feet off the ground.

Jesse peeked his head in. "Are you OK?"

"Yah," Ethan noticed another glowing handprint in the crystal just to the left of the opening. "Quick, jump in! I think I can close it and keep the prairie dogs out!" Ethan set the snow globe on the ground and started to stand, then realized the handprint had gone out and the portal was closing. So he picked the globe back up, the blue glow returned to the handprint depression in the wall and the portal reopened.

Jesse took a step back to hop through. "Hey! Oww!" The dagger fell from Jesse's hand just outside the opening as he was jerked from view.

Ethan scrambled to his feet to help his friend, which was difficult while still holding the snowglobe. When he got to his feet he peered back into the prairie dog's treasure chamber. The rope was taut around Jesse's waist and kept him from leaving the tunnel, where a host of glowing eyes were bounding toward him.

"Jesse! No!" Ethan put a hand on the edge of the portal between rooms to try to push up and over, but it bit him. He looked down, and a sparkling blue light ran around the edge of the portal.

Ethan inspected the edge and realized that he might have sliced his hands open if he'd pushed much harder. "I can't get out!".

"The dagger! Throw me the dagger!" Jesse yelled as he pushed his feet into the ground with all his might to try to scramble away from the prairie dog horde.

Ethan was able to reach over the lip of the portal and grab the knife without cutting himself on the blue boundary. It was a big dagger for a little boy. Jesse had been wielding it two-handed. Ethan wasn't sure he was strong enough to throw it all the way across the room to Jesse. The dagger seemed to read his mind and shrunk itself to the size of a kitchen knife.

"Here goes!" Ethan flipped it over in his hand to throw it by the blade the way Uncle did. It flew in a perfectly twirling arc, just like Ethan hoped it would. But the knife kept flying past Jesse to land just beyond his feet, transforming to full size when it came to rest. Jesse gave up fighting the tug on the rope and slid toward the dagger. He barely managed to grab it.

Three prairie dogs burst from the tunnel just as Jesse managed to slice the rope.

"Watch out Jesse!" Ethan called, the twenty feet between them felt like miles, with Ethan trapped on the other side of the portal.

The rodents leapt for Jesse, and he brought the dagger up defensively. It burst into flame, and the rodents on either side veered away from the fire, but the center one wasn't fast enough, and its fur caught ablaze. It cried a piteous howl and rolled away from Jesse as the boy stood on shaky feet. His balance was off, due to the pack on his back, and it took him a moment to get on steady feet as he backed away from the tunnel where prairie dogs poured. He waved the flaming blade in their direction.

"Jump through, and I'll close the door!" Ethan called, then turned and held his hand at the ready over the glowing palm print in the wall. Jesse sprinted away from the prairie dogs as fast as the pack would let him, and the prairie dogs chased him in hot pursuit. Finally, he got to the portal and leapt over the sharp edge just as they caught up with him.

He landed flat-footed on the crystal floor. "Ow! That ground is hard!" the flame on his dagger went out.

Ethan put his hand on the depression in the crystal, and the portal changed to a giant transparent crystal.

He turned to help Jesse up. "Tell me about it; I landed on my hands and knees." He rubbed his knees for emphasis.

Ethan looked over his shoulder and could see through the crystal that the room they'd come from was filling up with prairie dogs. He didn't understand it at all. The walls went up so high they were lost in the dark above, and the blue light of his shield played oddly off the purple crystals, except for the clear one that made up the portal. He was still baffled by it all and turned to his right to see what Jesse thought.

Jesse was just shaking his head back and forth ever so slightly as he inspected the clear crystal. "Well that's interesting, I wonder—"

A loud cracking noise, like a rock splitting, came from behind them, followed by a scraping sound. Ethan whirled to see the violet crystal wall behind them had split open, and in the distance, stood a three-tiered white fountain flowing with clear water.

His breath caught in his throat.

Is that the Wellspring of Life?

Between Ethan and the fountain stood a five-and-a-half-foot tall woman, dressed in a pale blue, sleeveless dress, and her body was white crystal. She had some of the same complex angular features Iron Sister did, like her cheekbones, but each part of her fingers was its own crystal. In addition, she had wavy hair that flowed as if it were white milkweed floss.

She just stared at the boys for a minute with her unblinking amethyst eyes. The hair on the back of Ethan's neck stood up, and he was about to try to introduce himself, then she raised a gold object to her right temple area. It began emitting odd sounds that could be words in different languages. Finally, he heard "Greetings" from a playful voice that didn't fit the woman before them.

"Well howdy to you too," Jesse blurted out.

"Ah I see." The woman shook her head, and each hair flowed with a brief orange light, cascading down her back. "Zourians! Your people should have no ability to come here. What is that in your hand?" The color in the strands of her hair strobed as the crystals of her eyebrows slightly covered her eye jewels.

"Well, we found this snow globe." Ethan held up the snow globe with its broken base facing towards her. "My daddy's hurt bad, and the snow globe said Wellspring of Life, but the prairie dogs broke it."

Her face seemed to soften at the mention of Father's injuries. "Bring that to me." She held out her free hand but kept the gold object to the side of her head with the other.

Ethan looked at Jesse, and they both shrugged. "OK, my name's Ethan, and this is Jesse." He started to close the gap between them. "What's yours?"

The corner of her mouth cracked just a bit, and a melodious hum came from her body, rather than the device. Then the machine said, "That is how my people know me, but your people lack the ability to say it. You may call me Krystal."

He held out his hand to shake in greeting. "Nice to meet you, Krystal."

She cocked her head, and a wave of pale blue coursed through her hair. It seemed as if she didn't know what he was doing.

Ethan felt he should help her out. "It's polite to shake hands when you meet someone new."

"I see." Krystal held out her hand, and he tried to shake it, but the hard edges of her finger crystals made a firm handshake impossible. Once he managed to get a loose grip, she didn't have the practice to actually shake. Ethan wanted to explain it because everyone knew how to shake hands, but before he could continue, she interrupted.

"Now that we have your greeting out of the way"—her hair coursed with hues of orange—"give me the snow globe."

Ethan couldn't tell if the sharpness in the tone was from the device, or if she meant them harm.

"Don't do it, Ethan." Jesse stepped up and pointed the dagger at her, but it had no flame. "She'll take it, and we'll never leave this place."

Krystal's eyes narrowed, and her hair went red. "I am not going to steal the snow globe. I have no use for it."

Ethan looked at Jesse with a raised eyebrow. Why did she want to see it if she didn't need it for anything?

"I merely want to inspect the damage." She pointed the index finger of her free hand at the globe's base.

"Oh!" Ethan handed it to her. She attached the speaking device to the gold chain around her hips and carefully took the snow globe from Ethan. Then she turned and walked toward the fountain in the other room.

Ethan wasn't sure if they were invited to go with her, but he was afraid she might shut the door and lock them away in this room, so he followed her. Besides, that fountain just had to be the Wellspring of Life.

Jesse matched pace with Ethan, dagger still drawn, so Ethan put a hand on his friend's, hoping he'd put the weapon away. Instead, Jesse shook his head ever so slightly but did move to a less-aggressive stance as he walked.

Ethan didn't like Jesse's attitude right now; what was the blade going to do against someone made of crystals? If the dagger were on fire, he knew it would cut through metal and rock. Her hand had been hard as stone when he'd shaken it, the blade wouldn't do anything to her without the fire. So there was no reason to be rude by threatening someone who might help them. However, he felt having an argument right now would be even ruder, so he bit his lip to keep it back.

When she got to the fountain's base, she set the snow globe on its flat edge, then, with both hands, retrieved some objects from a shelf inset into the crystals on the wall to the left.

"What are you doing?" Ethan asked.

She let out a humming melody, then orange light cascaded through her hair as she seemed to frown. She tapped the device on her hip with her free hand.

"Oh, you can't talk to us without that," Ethan said. "Sorry."

A green light cascaded through Krystal's hair, accompanied by a brief tone. Was that her way of saying "no problem"? He'd met the tiny Bjorn Born, giants, and the Iron Priestesses on this trip. They all spoke his language . . . well, kind of. But this was really hard.

Krystal squatted down, and her gown flowed out around her feet as she held the crystals she'd gotten from the shelf up, one at a time, to look at the snow globe. Her hair flowed blue, and she emanated a slight bass tone.

Ethan wondered if she was humming while she worked. Jesse's tapping foot interrupted Ethan's musings.

Ethan let out an exasperated huff. Didn't he know that she was their only chance to save Daddy?

Krystal's hair went from blue to purple, and she returned the items to the shelf. She picked up something else from the shelf and palmed it.

Ethan wanted to know what she'd found. "Well? What's the deal with the snow globe?"

Krystal's hair went to orange again, and she raised a finger. Ethan assumed she was telling him to wait just a minute. He started tapping his foot now. Her hands were free; she could tell them what was going on. Jesse must have been feeling the same way because he had his free hand on his hip and brows furrowed.

Instead, she picked up the snow globe in both hands and carried it to Ethan. She offered it to him, and he took it. Then she took the device from her belt and put it to her temple. "The snow globe is so damaged I'm surprised it brought you here." Her hair strobed yellow. "I can feel an odd vibration from the power core at best, it can return you to Zoura."

"What does that mean?" Jesse beat Ethan to the question.

Her hair coursed orange. "You are young. I do not know how to explain this." She looked up at the ceiling for a moment, then her hair turned blue. "This snow globe opens a secret door to my world." She waved her free hand around the room, and Ethan noticed she was still palming something. "There are many like it that open doors elsewhere."

"OK, I get that, ma'am," Jesse said. "But this place seems way bigger than the prairie dog mound. Something's not right."

Krystal's hair flowed orange again. "Maybe we'll meet again when you're older, and I can explain it more. But for now, there is little time."

"Yah! We've got to take the water from the wellspring to daddy," Ethan interrupted.

Krystal's hair turned white, and her head shook slightly from side to side. "Little Ethan, I don't think this fountain is what you are looking for."

"B-but!" Ethan stammered. "It has to be." It was big, and the whole place felt special. Surely this was what he was looking for.

"With the damage to the snow globe, I cannot tell if it was meant to bring you here or somewhere else." Krystal took a knee and met Ethan's gaze with her amethyst eyes. "You keep saying you think this is the Wellspring of Life because it was on the snow globe. Do you know where that name comes from?"

"Well yah, the Good Book," Ethan replied

"The Good Book, yes that's right," Krystal replied. "What does the Good Book say about it?"

Ethan looked up at the ceiling and took a deep breath, then let it out. "I think it was something like protect your heart because it's the wellspring of life." He put his hand on the lantern symbol on his breast plate. "This armor it guards my heart. This place is a fortress, and that's the heart, right?" He pointed at the fountain.

Krystal seemed to crack a slight smile, and her hair took on a deep blue color. "That is very observant, but there is another verse you might know. 'Understanding is a wellspring of life unto him that hath it: but the instruction of fools is folly.'"

"Hey, I've heard that," Jesse exclaimed. "Gramps always says you can't teach a fool nothin'."

Krystal let out a sharp melody that Ethan thought might be a laugh. "I don't know who set you on the path here, but I think understanding what I'm about to tell you will be far more valuable than the plain water in my fountain." She cupped her free hand, scooped up some water and let it run through her fingers as she continued, "The man you know as the Bishop is not of Zoura, and he has come through a secret door in hopes of controlling all its people by cloaking the land in ancient Darkness."

Ethan's mouth dropped. He knew the Bishop was a bad guy, but hadn't thought about the whole world being cloaked in Darkness.

"You are of the Light, and you can beat back the Darkness," Krystal continued.

Ethan nodded. "Yes, ma'am, my shield makes the bad dogs go poof."

"But the Bishop is consolidating his power, and even now he is using the Iron Mountain to bring forth a Calamitous Drake through a secret door to spread the Darkness to the farthest reaches of the land."

Ethan cocked his head. "A Calam a what?"

Krystal's hair pulsed black. "A dragon."

Both Ethan and Jesse gasped.

Krystal continued, "It's foul breath will be capable of isolating even those of you who shine the brightest, where you might be defeated one by one."

Fear gripped Ethan's stomach. Their bedtime prayers at home always said to keep the dragons away. He didn't believe it could hurt them if God was on their side. "What are you saying? The Light won't be able to help us defeat the dragon?"

Krystal held up a hand palm out. "No, I'm sure faith will always find a way through. But I believe fighting the Calamitous Drake will come at a great cost."

Ethan's face fell, and a tear rolled down his cheek. The memory of his friend Nicolas falling to the hell hounds was a considerable burden. Jesse put an arm around him.

Krystal's hair turned pink. "While I cannot provide the healing waters you hoped for from the Wellspring of Life, I may be able to provide the understanding that is worth much more."

Krystal held out her palm to reveal three cut gems. Ethan rubbed the tear off his face and looked at them. They were clear but reflected the light in amazing ways.

Krystal continued, "The Bishop is not of your world, and if he were sent back to his own, the threat to Zoura would be eliminated at the source."

The stones mesmerized Ethan for a moment as he tried to understand everything she was saying. But it just didn't add up. "What do these jewelies have to do with anything."

"If you strike the Bishop with a holy weapon made with these jewels, he'll be instantly sent through a secret door to a prison he can never escape."

Ethan grabbed one of the gems between his forefinger and thumb and stared into the facets, trying to see the prison inside. There were no bars or a cage in there, it just seemed to just be a jewel, a really nice one with lots of pretty light. If he turned it just right he could see a tiny reflection of himself, but that all. It didn't glow the way the stone in the dagger did. So how could it have any special powers? Jesse took one as well and looked it over similarly.

"It doesn't seem that special," Ethan replied. "The snow globe looked alive."

"Yah, It just doesn't feel that special. Not like this one." Jesse turned the dagger over in his hand to show the gem on the bottom.

"A skilled artificer will have to install it properly to give it the life you seek." Krystal held out the third one between finger and thumb. "Take this and be careful. They are the only thing that can truly rid you of the Bishop and the Darkness he brings to your land."

Ethan pocketed the stone she offered, and the other he was holding. It was probably better that they were not all in the same pocket, so he nodded to Jesse and pointed at his friend's pants pocket. Jesse complied.

"But, Krystal, my Daddy's the only artificer I know, and he's hurt so badly." Ethan pointed at the fountain. "Are you sure that water won't help him?"

Her hair lit up pink. "It's just water."

Ethan was so desperate to help his father that he couldn't let it go. "But maybe your water is better."

Her hair turned orange, and Ethan was starting to understand that meant she was annoyed. "I'm sure my water is not 'better.' It is pure and clean. It will slake your thirst or put out a fire, but it's just water. However, if you insist." She walked back to the shelf and picked up a finely crafted crystal jar, which she dipped into the fountain. She put a lid on it before offering it to Jesse.

"This feels fragile," Jesse said as he set his pack down and carefully placed it top up in the upper half of the bag.

"It is the only container I have, and as I said, it's just water. To the right person, I suspect the container itself is worth a king's ransom, as its craftmanship is impossible on Zoura."

Jesse's eyes got big at that, and he took a second to repack around it to protect it even more.

Krystal continued, "I wish you good fortune taking it to Ethan's Father, but I don't believe it has any special properties to help him. This fountain is a monument to the knowledge of my people, not a healing spring."

Jesse put the pack back on with a grunt. Ethan wished he had a way to help his friend carry the load. When they found Uncle, he'd be sure to retrieve his pack and help Jesse carry stuff again.

"Uncle!" He whirled to look at his friend. "We need to get going, Jesse! Uncle and Gramps need our help!" Ethan turned toward where they came in.

"Yes, you should go now." Krystal urged. "The power supply is on the verge of failing, and if you don't leave soon, you'll have no way to open the secret door."

"Thank you, Krystal." Ethan looked over his shoulder. "Will we see you again?"

"I do not know, young Ethan." Her hair turned pink, "But I do hope you prevail against the Bishop, and we might meet again in celebration."

"Amen," Ethan said to that.

Then he turned his attention to the wall where they had come through. The handprint glowed but much less brilliantly than before. Krystal was right. The power must be failing.

Ethan put his hand on the activator, and the crystal faded away to show the prairie dog hole. The room with the treasures was free from the rodents, but they could hear scurrying in the side tunnels.

Ethan got on his hands and knees, and Jesse stepped on his back and over the portal's threshold. Then Jesse turned around and helped pull Ethan up and into the prairie dog den, avoiding the sharp edge of the portal. When Ethan was safely on the other side, the snowglobe made a loud pop, followed by a puff of smoke and extreme heat.

"Ouch!" Ethan dropped it on the ground, and the portal behind them disappeared.

The random scurrying stopped, and then hundreds of little feet began pouding towards them. Jesse's dagger lit up. Ethan could feel the tingle from his shield go up his back.

Ethan moved the shield from his back to his arm, then looked at Jesse. "If them no-good, egg-stealin' prairie dogs want a fight, let's give it to them!"

Ethan and Jesse stood back-to-back in the prairie dog's treasure chamber and slowly circled, trying to detect the direction the rodents might attack from.

"We need to find our way back to Uncle and Gramps. Do you see the rope?" Ethan asked.

"Yah, over there in a jumble." Jesse waved the dagger toward a pile of prairie dog treasures.

"How can you be sure?" Ethan asked.

Jesse stopped circling, "Look at the ends. That's our rope."

In the silvery-blue light of Ethan's shield, the burnt ends of the rope stood out in stark contrast to the yellow rope fibers. "Well, should we at least grab it?"

"No time," Jesse barked as the first prairie dog poked its head out of the tunnel to their left.

The tunnel straight in front of them was the one they'd come through, and it was starting to fill with eyes, but the one to the right looked free from attackers. "I guess we try that one." The boys scrambled over debris as they made their way to the tunnel to the right.

A half dozen prairie dogs, including the one burned by the dagger earlier, gathered to the left, then raced forward in force to cut them off.

"Go faster!"

Jesse poured on the speed, and Ethan turned to run full tilt behind him. Jesse's pack slowed the boy down, so Ethan backed off, feeling it would be better to block up the tunnel with his shield than try to have Jesse navigate backward and defend them with the dagger.

When Ethan got fully in the tunnel, he could squat walk without hitting his head, so he turned his back to Jesse and held up his shield on his arm. It reformed to a circle almost as big as the tunnel. It would be easy to wedge into the bottom of the tunnel to block it completely. But then he'd have to leave it behind. He wasn't doing that. Maybe its light would be enough to keep those no-good, thievin' prairie dogs at bay.

"E!" Jesse hollered. "Which way? I can't tell."

They'd come to a *Y* intersection, and it was unclear where to go. Both sides seemed had a slope up. Then Ethan caught a slight sensation of a breeze from the tunnel to the right, followed by the scent of rotten something. He crinkled up his nose and didn't like the smell, but that had to be the way.

"Hey! That way." Ethan pointed with his head in the direction they should go.

A sudden shove to his shield knocked him into Jesse, and they both toppled in that direction. Ethan recovered in time to block the rodent's assault by slamming the shield down on two of them—who'd poked their noses through underneath it. They squealed and backed away. Jesse regained his feet, and they both hurried up the tunnel.

The slight breeze grew as they got farther away from the *Y*, and it got warmer as well. Jesse coughed and gagged a little. Ethan realized the warmth was from smoke slowly filling the top of the tunnel. But it wasn't the smell of burning grass. The smell was worse than burning a rotten dead skunk. Ughhh.

"E! I think there's a fire out there."

Ethan gagged and realized it might be the dead coyotes on fire. Did that whisp of smoke he saw earlier catch the prairie on fire? Were Uncle and Gramps safe? "I think you're right; we've got to hurry."

Jesse's eyes were wide. "Shouldn't we go back? Doesn't smoke rise? Deeper in the tunnel would be safer, right?"

"I don't know, let me see." Ethan moved around Jesse to look at the tunnel.

There was a deep hole at the end of the tunnel, just like the one he'd fallen down. But there was a narrow ramp to one side up and out, a prairie dog–sized hole, that seemed to be dumping little whisps of black smoke into the tunnel as the breeze blew outside.

"No, we should get out. It's too easy to be overwhelmed by the prairie dogs in here."

"OK, then what's the play?" Jesse nodded.

"If we carefully crawl up that way, you could climb on my back and then out that hole." Ethan pointed off to the left.

"But what about you?" Jesse asked, then had a coughing fit. "I'm not sure I can pull you up after me."

"Uncle and Gramps shouldn't be far," Ethan said, with more conviction than he had. A gagging coughing fit hit him for a moment, then he continued, "We've got to escape before this place completely fills with smoke. Do you have a better plan?"

"OK, let's do this." They got down on their hands and knees and crawled around the sloped edge to the hole. When they got there, Jesse drew his dagger and hacked away at the hole to make it big enough for him to fit through.

"Ready?" Ethan asked.

"Ready!" Jesse stepped up onto Ethan's back.

"Ow!"—his own coughing interrupted him———"hurry up!

Jesse threw his pack out first, and then climbed up. Dirt rained down on Ethan as the edge of the hole collapsed. Jesse managed to use his momentum to keep going and didn't fall back in.

"E!" coughs were followed by a thump, cutting off Jesse's words.

"Oh no! Jesse." Ethan stood up, hoping to sneak a look at what was going on up there. The hair on the back of his neck rose as a hand grabbed the back of his shirt from above.

"Uncle! I'm so glad you found us!" Ethan cheered, followed by a fit of coughing. Ethan was pulled all the way out of the ground and then kept going higher. "Uncle?"

The hand carrying him turned him around, dangling him six feet off the ground.

To Ethan's utter horror, he now faced Skull Crusher.

"My, my, those prairie dogs do collect such treasures in their holes, don't they?"

Skull Crusher sneered a big evil grin at Ethan, then put a whistle to his lips and blew. That close to his face, Skull Crusher's putrid breath made Ethan gag. He wished his shield were on his arm so he could conk the giant in his wonkus with it. With Jesse flat on the ground under Skull Crusher's foot, Ethan felt utterly helpless.

In the distance, coyotes howled, and the giant pointed with his free hand toward the mound where Uncle and Gramps stood back-to-back. The coyotes around the rise stopped cold in their frenzied attacks, allowing Uncle a clean kill on one of them. After that, however, the coyotes took up the call and then circled the mound out of Uncle's arm's reach. They slowly collected—two dozen pacing beasts.

"The dutiful Uncle." Skull Crusher turned Ethan around to face Uncle. "Catching me from behind on the wharf was crafty, but you'll have no such tricks this time, frontiersman." The giant spat, then pulled a dagger from his belt and sliced it across the top of Ethan's chest.

"No!" Uncle cried and leapt down the hill toward Skull Crusher only to be pushed back by the threat of massed coyotes.

The blade severed the straps holding Ethan's shield and barely sliced through his shirt and skin.

"Ow!" Ethan's eyes welled with tears at the pain.

The shield dropped to the ground, and the giant took the foot holding Jesse in place on the ground and kicked the shield into the prairie dog hole. Then he motioned with the dagger for the boy to stand up.

"So, who's this? A long-lost cousin and your grandfather?" Skull Crusher whispered in Ethan's ear. That sent a chill down Ethan's back. He was sure the giant meant to kill them all.

"That's Jesse and his grandpa," Ethan explained as he fought back tears of terror. "We just met them. Don't hurt them, please."

"Where are the rest?" Skull Crusher turned Ethan to face him once again. "Your sister and the traitorous Tye?"

"Right here!" Tye yelled from behind.

Ethan's heart leapt at the sound of her voice. "You're in big trouble now!"

Skull Crusher whirled and Ethan saw Lauren pulling her pony to a stop and raising her spear to strike.

"Sissy! You came!"

Skull Crusher grabbed Jesse in his other hand and raised the boys in front of him.

"You coward! Using little boys as a shield? You are no Warden." Tye screamed through deep, gulping breaths. Ethan realized from the lather on the pony that they must have been running full-out for a long time in order to catch him.

"You get 'em, girls!" Uncle called from the top of the prairie dog mound, still surrounded by two dozen coyotes.

"Yah! Get that no good house-crushing giant!" Gramps called.

The way Skull Crusher was sidestepping to his left, with the boys held out front, made him a challenging target. Ethan prayed for Lauren to take a shot with her spear, but she held off.

Skull Crusher suddenly dumped Ethan on the seat of a buggy and slammed Jesse on his lap. Jesse's backpack almost smothered Ethan. "Sit boys, while I teach these girls a lesson in true power."

Without his human shield, Lauren threw her spear on target, only to have the smoke of the Censer on the back of the cart swirl and block the shot. The spear bounced off and returned to Lauren's hand. This sent a chill down Ethan's spine as he realized Skull Crusher's buggy was protected by the Darkness.

His fear was driven away by a sudden quack overhead. "You're in big trouble now!" Ethan goaded Skull Crusher. If Daddy Duck destroyed the Censer, then Lauren and Tye would surely defeat the evil giant.

However, the cover Skull Crusher made for the Censer kept Daddy Duck from connecting his beam of light directly with it. Ethan had to find a way to take that cover off. He wished Aiden were here, he was always better with mechanical stuff.

Skull Crusher laughed maniacally and jumped into the cart next to Ethan, squishing him from the left side. Ethan couldn't tell what was worse at this point, being sat on, being squished from the side, or feeling the sting of the cut on his chest.

"I'm going to enjoy running that little pony of yours into the ground," Skull Crusher yelled, and then whistled the moose pulling his cart into action. He scooted to the left in his seat and raised his giant battle hammer in one hand. The moose turned and raced toward Lauren and Chance.

Lauren could feel Chance quake with fear at the sudden turn of events. The poor pony was exhausted, and it would be impossible for him to outrun a moose even on a good day. Maybe she didn't have to outrun him, perhaps just outmaneuver. Being attached to the cart, the moose couldn't turn as fast as Chance could.

"It's OK, boy. He can't hurt us." She patted Chance on his lathered neck. More for her own confidence than his, she said, "We can do this. Get ready to run."

For a brief moment, Lauren thought about jousting the giant's chariot like she'd done the coyotes the night before. But she was afraid the Darkness shield would cause her weapon to bounce off, and she'd be slammed by the hammer. Better to avoid the right side of the chariot altogether.

"La'Ren, while your people have brought us to this place. It is an honor to fight with you to rid the world of this liar." Tye moved to her side, sword in hand. It wasn't on fire. That was a bad sign.

Oh, God, please help Tye stop doubting the Light.

Tye and Lauren split right and left, respectively, as the moose-drawn chariot drew down on them. Skull Crusher anticipated this move, because he whistled the moose to a sudden jerking halt to one side. The cart skidded unnaturally across the prairie grass, and he leaned out with the hammer as far as possible.

Despite her attempt to dodge, the weapon connected with Tye, and she fell with a hard thump to the ground.

"Ha! There will be no help for you now girl!" Skull Crusher howled as the rapid turn allowed the chariot to nearly line up with Lauren and Chance as they raced away. However, Jesse nearly flew out of the wagon, and it was Ethan giving him a bear hug that gave both boys enough mass to stay in the seat.

Skull Crusher pulled his hammer arm in, and he let out a high whistle from his teeth. The moose reacted with speed, and they were off like an arrow.

Jesse squished Ethan further into the seat, but Lauren could hear her brother's voice yelling. "Run, Sissy. Run!"

"Shut up, boy!" Skull Crusher bellowed. "I'm the one doing the running—running her down!" He cackled maniacally.

Lauren pulled Chance hard to the left, making a sharp turn. She dared a glance over her shoulder as she wheeled the pony. Skull Crusher jerked, trying to make the same move. This time Jesse was thrown out and away from the wagon and not into Skull Crusher. Ethan wasn't ready for it, and his friend began to sail out of the cart. Ethan reached for Jesse and only managed to snatch a small bag from the top of the other boy's backpack, while Jesse flew out of the cart. The boy landed with a hard thump on his hands and knees.

Skull Crusher slammed his left arm into Ethan's injured chest. "Don't get any ideas about joining him, boy!" The giant whistled again, and the moose took off once more.

"The Censer will keep you in your place, while I put your sister in hers." Skull Crusher whistled again, and the moose seemed to put on even more speed.

Lauren began to weave back and forth in front of Skull Crusher. She thought if she could convince him to commit to a turn in one direction, then she could pull hard in the other and circle behind him. Then, out of the corner of her eye, she noticed a shape closing fast from the right. Lauren realized that the way the smoke was swirling around the cart prevented Skull Crusher from seeing what was coming.

Lauren and her pony slowed, and turned toward it.

"No, Sissy! He'll get you!" Ethan called.

The corner of Lauren's mouth turned up ever so slightly. The giant was in for a big surprise. Lauren looked over her shoulder hoping to see the look on his face.

"Shut up, boy!" He cuffed Ethan in the mouth with his free hand and turned the cart to follow Lauren, only to end up face-to-face with Aiden driving the horse-drawn wagon straight at the cart!

"What!" The moose dodged back to the left in time to barely miss the wagon rolling over it.

Lauren wheeled Chance to chase after Skull Crusher.

Aiden kept driving straight forward, through the coyotes on one side of the prairie dog mound. A rainbow arced out of the wagon toward Tye's unconscious body. Sparkle Frog!

"Now you're in trouble!" Ethan hollered.

A whole murder of crows and the geese swooped in, driving the coyotes away.

Aiden pulled the wagon to a stop. "Uncle, help Gramps climb in!"

Lauren's heart leapt at the turn of events. They were going to put an end to Skull Crusher once and for all. She kicked her heels into Chance's flanks. Maybe she could pull Ethan from the cart while Skull Crusher was distracted by the others.

While Uncle and Gramps made their way down the mound, Aiden and a new boy his age jumped out of the wagon, seeming to act as a rearguard to keep the coyotes away from the horses.

Skull Crusher stalked straight for them.

Lauren's heart leapt into her throat. She had to pull Ethan to safety before they collided.

She urged Chance on and closed to the side of the cart. "Ethan, quick jump on."

"I can't. I'm stuck!" Ethan pointed to his neck. It looked like Skull Crusher had used one of the tarp's tie hooks to pin Ethan's shirt collar to the wagon. "Watch out!"

She turned to see a hole in the ground just a few feet in front of them. She wasn't prepared to have Chance jump it, so she pulled him hard to the left and reined him in. Then glanced to see how Skull Crusher reacted to the hazard.

The giant didn't seem to care about a bump in the road. He was bearing down hard toward Aiden and the prairie dog mound. He and the new boy were faced the wrong way, and didn't see the danger racing towards them. Uncle was on the other side of the wagon, and Mother was in the back, helping Gramps.

Chance was huffing hard, and she could feel the pony quiver underneath her. Their quick turn put the giant out in front again, and she didn't think her friend could put on another burst of speed to catch up.

"Aiden, danger!" Lauren cried with all her might.

Aiden and the new boy turned as one to face Skull Crusher's charge.

"Logan! Log splitter!" Aiden called, pointing his little hammer at the ground. The new boy held a hatchet in both hands to the ground, with the line of the blade facing the oncoming giant.

Lauren was completely baffled by the boy's actions. They should be getting out of the way. Before she could say anything, Aiden raised his hammer over his head, holding it in both hands, and slammed it down on the back of the hatchet. A thunderclap sounded from it, and a bright blue line of force erupted from the blade, scattering the coyotes and birds in all directions. The blow must have been too much for the crows, because they scattered in all directions and kept flying. However, Uncle's geese and Daddy Duck fluttered to a safe landing in the wagon.

The blast ripped a jagged two-foot-wide tear through the ground from the hatchet to the hole Lauren had dodged earlier. The prairie dogs must have had a massive underground tunnel system, because dirt around the rip in the ground fell in wide, jagged cracks.

The moose managed to keep its footing and leap to solid ground, but the cart wasn't so lucky. The right wheel fell into the hole, slamming the base of the chariot into the ground. It slid to the right and into the hole, as the moose scrambled in the loose dirt to not be pulled down too.

Skull Crusher screamed and launched himself out of the cart and onto the back of the moose, leaving Ethan stuck in the cart. The giant sliced the ties to the buggy, and the moose managed to right itself on the other side of the crack in the earth.

Aiden and the new boy gave each other high fives and jumped back into the wagon. Uncle had finally seated himself on the bench, reins in hand, when a war horn sounded.

Lauren looked off to the left where she thought it was smoke from the prairie fire, but it wasn't. It was the dust of another giant, riding on the back of a bison, with two dozen more of the beasts thundering to Skull Crusher's aid.

Everyone's attention turned to the approaching giant and his bison herd. Chance whinnied and reared. The poor pony was so frightened and exhausted Lauren could feel his anxiety in her legs.. He was no match for this battle and might already have been ridden near death.

She hopped off of him and quickly pulled the strap that held his saddlebags in place so it could fall off. She didn't have time to do more. Tears in her eyes, she hugged his neck and urged him on his way. At first, he stood stock-still, unsure of what to do. Then the giant let loose with another horn call, and the coyotes took it up, rallying around the bison and the horn bearer.

Chance ran off, following the path the wagon had just torn through the grass.

Uncle hopped out of the wagon and pulled his golden breastplate from the back. Mother reached over the wagon's side to help him fasten it. Skull Crusher, mounted on the moose, jumped over the crack in the ground created by Aiden and Logan, but the giant halted within ten yards of the Censer. The moose tore at the ground, seeming desperate to charge into battle.

Lauren realized he was counting on its shielding to protect him until the other giant and the animal army were in range to provide overwhelming force. If they weren't so spread out, they might have been able to climb into the wagon and outrun the enemy, but as it was, all they could do was stand and fight.

God, please help us with this new enemy.

Lauren had seen Jesse take a tumble out of Skull Crusher's chariot. She was about to help him but noticed he was making a beeline for Ethan. That fall must have hurt, but he didn't seem fazed by it. He must be one tough kid. If he was going to help Ethan, it might be best if she got Tye back on her feet.

When she got there, Sparkle Frog sat on the back of Tye's head, proudly preening himself. That should have been enough to wake Tye up if it were a normal hit. Just to be on the safe side, she fished Meow Meow out of her dress pocket and placed him next to Tye's nose. He licked her nose, and she began to wake. Daddy Duck landed next to them and quacked. She was glad for Aiden's feathered friend's presence, but she was so overwhelmed she couldn't see how he could help.

Ethan was still stuck in the cart and it might fall in the hole any minute. Lauren had to get him out before it fell. The thundering of bison hooves was beginning to shake her teeth. Then there was Skull Crusher. She had to make a decision. Help Ethan, take down Skull Crusher on her own right now, wait and see if the new giant would be more reasonable. *God please, help me know what to do.*

Maybe if she could prove Skull Crusher was the one who knocked Tye out, then they'd listen. She doubted it. But regardless, she needed to try.

"Sissy! Help!" Ethan called from across the way.

She looked down at the collection of animal friends. They'd done amazing things before, maybe they could do something now so she could focus on Skull Crusher, "Can you go help Ethan?"

Daddy Duck quacked and took to the air, with Sparkle Frog just a second behind him. Meow Meow looked up at Lauren for just a second, as cute as a button, and then vanished. Lauren did a double take. The kitten just popped out of existence right before her eyes. Lauren thought he might be able to do that, but she'd never seen it happen before.

"Ethan! Is Meow Meow with you?" Lauren yelled.

"Uh . . . yah! How'd he get here?" Ethan called back.

Before Lauren could answer, Tye slowly crawled to her knees. "Is that you La'Ren?"

"Yes, I'm here. We have big trouble," Lauren replied.

The giant and herd of bison came to a halt ten yards from the wagon and formed two rows of a dozen. At this distance, Lauren recognized Tye's father, the Master Warden. He walked his mount forward two paces. "What is this, Skull Crusher? Have you taken the power of the humans as your own?"

"Only in your service, my Master Warden." Skull Crusher sure sounded a lot more obedient than Lauren believed he was.

He'd said he was going to run them all down with it. She doubted it was Master Warden's purpose to kill his daughter.

"My service was to drive them into Lord Refi'Cul's trap. Then we would be rid of the Steele Lord and his kind, once and for all," Master Warden bellowed. He pointed his spear where the family stood defensively around the wagon. "This does not appear to be driving them to the Steele Lord?"

"But, Master Warden—"

Master Warden turned his weapon on Skull Crusher. "What of my daughter? She was supposedly captured by these humans."

"Here, Father. I'm here" Tye stood tall with Lauren's arm around her waist, helping her stand.

"You see even now, the humans are trying to hold her hostage." Skull Crusher accused and whistled his mount to move sideways. "Shall I dispatch her, my lord?"

"The child?" Master Warden mocked. "My daughter was banished on your word alone, Skull Crusher. Yet I do believe there is more to this story than you told."

The giant leader turned his spear tip to the air and his face softened as he looked at Tye. "Daughter, disarm the girl and return to the tribe."

Tye placed her hand on the back of Lauren's neck, "Do as he says, give me your spear."

The firmness of Tye's grip on her neck told Lauren she was serious. Was this the final betrayal? Was Tye really turning her over to the forces of Darkness? Tears pooled in Lauren's eyes.

"No! Tye! Don't do it!" Mother cried from the back of the wagon. "Please, Tye, please don't hurt my girl."

"It's OK, Mother, it's OK." Lauren squeaked out through quivering lips while handing Tye her spear handle.

As Tye's fingers wrapped around the weapon, its light went out, and Lauren was sure Tye was lost to the Darkness.

Aiden gritted his teeth in frustration. He'd only seen Father for a moment before hopping back out of the wagon to defend it with Uncle and Logan. But the double-Darkness zone was exacting a heavy toll. There were places where the burns had turned from pink to angry red to black almost before his eyes. They needed to drive Father out of here right now, before it killed him!

Doubly worse, the prairie fire on the horizon was closing in. All it would take was a little bit of wind, and the fire would overtake them in minutes. Tye's father had to know that, so why were they fooling around?

Aiden wasn't about to let that happen. From the way the ground broke, he knew they all could find some cover from the firestorm in the caves below. However, the cut in the ground was at least twenty feet deep, so even if they survived the fall, how would they climb back out?

All eyes were on Tye holding Lauren captive. His cheeks burned at her betrayal. As much as they needed to take Father to safety, they also needed to rescue Lauren. They should have never let her go off with Tye after the giantess betrayed them in Spring Fields.

Slowly, he let out a deep breath to clear the fog of his anger and find a way out of this. *God, please help us.*

First things first, he needed to get Father out of there. So Aiden backed away from where he was clustered defensively with Logan and Uncle, and headed toward the wagon seat. He motioned for Gramps to bend down, then whispered in his ear, "Can you drive Father and Mother out of here if the chance comes?"

"Whatcha thinkin', boyo? You going to break the ground again and swallow them giants?" he whispered back. "And what about Jesse?"

"He looks like he's taking care of himself." Aiden nodded in Jesse's direction, where he'd just picked up Ethan's shield from a hole in the ground. "But if you circle back to the left, you should be able to pick him and Ethan up as you drive past."

"Alrighty, when you give the signal, I'll go." Gramps nodded.

"You'll know," Aiden gave him a quick two-finger salute. Earlier, he felt more than saw the fault line through the prairie dog caves. He couldn't feel the same thing out toward the giant and the bison, but he had an idea. "Logan, when I say to, hit my hammer with the back of your hatchet, OK?"

Logan nodded. Aiden closed his eyes and tried to feel the earth in front of them. "Uncle, when things go crazy, go help Gramps save E."

"Gotcha," Uncle slowly side-stepped toward the back of the wagon.

Meanwhile, Tye had closed the gap to where Master Warden stood holding his giant spear in both hands at his waist. Skull Crusher came closer hefting his massive battle hammer onto his shoulder.

"Father, I give you La'Ren of the tower," Tye said as she approached with Lauren's spear in her right hand and Lauren's neck in her left. She stopped next to Skull Crusher.

Aiden felt so lost right now. Tye was supposed to be of the Light. How could she betray them again when she didn't have the daggers telling her what to do? It was one thing when those Darkness daggers had control of her. But now?

Aiden wanted to rush out and save his sister, but the odds against them were too high in the midst of the Censer smoke.

They needed an opening to disrupt the enemy, but what?

Master Warden's tanned right bicep flexed as he held his spear in one hand and pointed it accusingly at Lauren. The spear's shaft was as thick as Lauren's thigh, and the chiseled flint spear point was almost as big as Uncle's sword. A wave of dread passed through Lauren as he spoke.

"So this is the girl that talked you into betraying our people and waylaying Skull Crusher."

"No Father," Tye shook her head and slightly loosened her grip on Lauren's neck. Now her hand merely rested at the base of it. Lauren didn't know how to react to this. Was Tye just tired and losing her edge, or was this all some elaborate ruse?

She closed her eyes and took in a deep breath. Unfortunately, they were at the edge of the smoke from the Censer. So her deep cleansing breath turned into a hacking cough, to rid herself of the foul pollution. *God, please help me shine my light in this dark place.*

"Not the girl? Skull Crusher insists that this is *the family* Lord Refi'Cul so desperately wants to destroy." Master Warden bent to look into Tye's eyes.

"Refi'Cul is a liar and Skull Crusher is his mouth piece!" Tye hissed.

Lauren gasped at the ferocity of Tye's accusation. Maybe she was on her side after all. Skull Crusher broke Lauren's thought with a deep laugh.

"You're going to allow this *girl* to slander me?"

Skull Crusher's emphasis on *girl* cut Lauren to the bone. He was a liar, and she was about to go off on that point, when Master Warden cut in.

"That *girl* is my daughter, and following the trail of destruction left in your wake has made me wonder where your loyalties truly lie." He pointed back to the growing prairie fire. "A true Warden does not carelessly set the land ablaze."

"But—" Skull Crusher started.

"I am speaking." Master Warden cut Skull Cusher off.

Hope blossomed in Lauren's heart. Would Master Warden listen to their side of the story?

He continued, "I am now wondering if I was too quick to listen to your tale, and not give this *girl*, my daughter, the chance to tell her own story. "

"You would take a woman's word over mine?" Skull Crusher blurted out.

That made Lauren's blood boil. What did that have to do with anything? This guy lied so much his pants should be on fire.

The Master Warden turned to the wagon. "You there, frontiersman." Master Warden walked toward the wagon while Tye, Lauren, and Skull Crusher stayed put. "Skull Crusher tells a story of how you ambushed him to take my son from him. Why don't you tell me the tale."

"Beggin your pardon, Master Warden, you've lost your way. I'll not allow the humans to speak lies to influence the Wardens." Skull Crusher reached into his pouch and pulled out a rough-looking furryball. He squeezed it, and a crunching sound came out of it, then he pulled his arm back to throw.

Tye whipped the end of the spear up and connected with his arm as he threw. The blow kicked the furball into a lazy arc right past the Master Warden's head. It came apart in flight and trailed yellow dust as it went. Lauren could almost see the Master Warden inhale it as little welts started to erupt all over his face.

"You are a stupid girl." Skull Crusher yelled. "You've killed your father to save a wretched human!"

A wave of horror went down Lauren's back as Master Warden began to gasp and claw at his face.

"Now!" Aiden cried as he slammed his hammer into the ground.

Logan followed up with a swing of the back of his axe onto Aiden's hammer. A wave of power fanned out from the strike, leveling the praire grass, knocking most of the bison to their knees, and scattering the coyotes in front of the wagon. Logan hit it again, toppling the rest of the bison as Gramps kicked the horses into high gear.

Tye still had her hand loosely on Lauren's neck. She looked up at the giantess, hoping to see a sign that she was on Lauren's side. But Tye just stood there, dumbfounded with her mouth hanging open.

As the wagon started to gain speed, the boys ran beside it. Mother reached and hauled Aiden up, and they both pulled Logan in just as the wagon began moving too fast for him to keep up.

"Let's get, E, Gramps!" Aiden called, as the wagon completed its turn back to where they'd started. Lauren's heart leapt, they were going to make it. They just needed to put Skull Crusher down, once and for all!

"Father!" Tye cried as her hand slid off Lauren's neck and expertly grabbed Lauren's still dull spear shaft in both hands. "No! I didn't do this! You did, you evil fiend!" Then, she thust the blunt end of the spear into Skull Crusher's gut with the full fury of her rage.

He wasn't prepared for the assault, and staggered under the first blow. He didn't fall and managed to back away, barely blocking the incoming blows.

Uncle was rushing toward Tye and Skull Crusher, and the wagon had circled around the far side of the chasm. Help was on the way, and there would be no way out for Skull Crusher now.

Lauren saw her opening to end this quickly and dove behind Skull Crusher. When the giant backed up from Tye's onslaught, he tripped on Lauren and landed hard on his back. Lauren rolled out from under his feet. "Tye, give me my spear. I can end this now."

"No, he has disgraced the Wardens and harmed my father. Vengeance is mine!" Tye dropped Lauren's spear and reached for the hunting knife in her belt as she leapt to attack him on the ground. He managed to roll away to the left, moving him closer to the Censer and the chasm. Tye merely slammed her blade into the ground.

Skull Crusher finished his roll, coming to rise on one knee while Lauren retrieved her spear.

Blue light poured out from around her hands, flowing into a blue glowing point on the end. "Tye, go help your father, he's dying. I'm no healer; see if there's something you can do!"

Tye got her feet back under her and paused as Lauren's spear flew through the air. Skull Crusher had gained his feet also, and now had his hammer in hand. Instead of dodging Lauren's spear or attempting to block it with the hammer, he took a huge step backward. This put him back in range of the Censer. Its web of black tendrils encircled him just before the spear reached its mark, protecting him from the blow. The spear *popped* back into her hand.

"Come to me!" Skull Crusher called out, putting the coyote whistle to his lips. "Let's rid ourselves of these humans once—"

Uncle tackled Skull Crusher in the legs from behind. The giant fell face-first and lost his hammer as he threw out his arms to catch his fall. Uncle was quick to his feet and stole the giant's weapon from him. "Now, Lauren! I think he's out of the Censer's smoke."

Lauren's spear had returned to her hand, and she threw it again. Only faint whisps of black smoke surrounded the giant this time. But it was enough to deflect the spear up and over the giant's forehead. Before the spear could fall to the ground, it reappeared in her hand.

Skull Crusher's face was red as he got to his feet and dodged back in range of the Censer. "Frontiersman, that's the second time you've attacked me—like a coward—from behind. There won't be a third."

Lauren could see Uncle straining to wield the giant's hammer. "Uncle, it's not worth it. Just throw it away and use your sword."

"That's not gonna knock him out of position." Uncle huffed as he circled with the hammer. "That fiery blade's just going to bounce off the shield."

Tye must have changed her mind about tending to her father because she turned and sprinted toward him. "Destroy him with his own weapon!"

"Girl, there's time to return to the Wardens! The Censer will heal your father," Skull Crusher called out as he pulled a hunting knife from his belt. "Come, let us finish these humans together."

"It is your Censer that did this to him!" Tye knelt next to her father, where he'd fallen on his back. Lauren could hear him choking on the liquid coming out of his mouth. Tye rolled him on his stomach, resting on her thighs. "God, please help put an end to Skull Crusher and the dark power killing my father."

Lauren's attention was drawn to Skull Crusher as he stepped in her direction to avoid Uncle's wild swings. She threw again, but the smoke protected him. However, it took his focus long enough for Uncle to strike. The hammer came down hard on the giant's thigh just above his knee. The leg crumbled beneath him, and Skull Crusher let out a howl. But Uncle's follow-through was slow and ungainly. The giant was able to grab the hammer and jerk Uncle to him. Uncle released the hammer, but his momentum carried him into Skull Crusher's grasp. The giant squeezed Uncle in an unbreakable grip with one arm and placed the tip of his hunting knife on his temple.

"Drop your weapon, little girl." Skull Crusher called as he slowly pivoted on his bad knee to face her. "Or this time, I will have your Uncle's Skull."

Ethan was well and truly stuck in the cart. He just couldn't move his body in the right place to fix anything the way he was seated with his collar pinned to the seatback. He was glad he saved the crystal jar from breaking on the ground when Jesse went flying out of the cart. But he had no idea how it would help him right now. So, he carefully set the bag that held it on the seat next to him, hoping it wouldn't roll away while he figured out how to escape.

It looked like Jesse might be coming to help. But he was on the other side of the chasm, and half the cart was hanging in mid-air over the hole in the ground. If Jesse tried to jump on from his side of the rift to help him, he was sure it would tip over, and they would end up upside down in the prairie dog hole—again—this time with the cart on top of him. Besides, some really mad prairie dogs were running around down there looking up at him.

The giant on the white moose had come to a stop, and he seemed to be talking a lot, so nobody was paying attention to Ethan. Suddenly, Meow Meow appeared on his shoulder, then proceeded to scratch at his collar.

Lauren called out to him from behind. "Ethan! Is Meow Meow with you?"

He tried to look over his shoulder to see her, but was still stuck. "Uh . . . yah! How'd he get here?" Ethan called back. He waited a second for her reply. When nothing came, he turned his attention Meow Meow. "Can your little claws cut me free?" Meow Meow hopped up on the edge of the seat and started to claw at Ethan's collar.

Sparkle Frog arrived and croaked at him like he was wondering if Ethan had a bump or a bruise. "Not right now, buddy, but if this thing tips, I'm going to be all bumps and bruises." Sparkle Frog took the hint and hopped onto the wheel on the upper side to add his weight there.

Jesse finally got to where Ethan's shield had fallen. The hole was now open, and Jesse could retrieve the shield without falling in.

"I've got your shield," Jesse hissed.

Daddy Duck landed next to Sparkle Frog. A little white dot was shining on whatever the duck looked at, like the spot on his crown was a mirror. The duck seemed to be looking for the right angle to shine his light on the Censer, but with the way it was protected with the oilcloth, he couldn't find a spot.

While Meow Meow worked on his collar, Master Warden and Skull Crusher started to argue. Master Warden started to move toward Uncle, and Skull Crusher threw something at him. Then Aiden yelled, and Gramps started the wagon moving.

Meow Meow drew his attention away from the action by licking his ear. Ethan got the idea that he should try to pull free. So he bent forward with all his might, and the collar ripped free from his shirt. This allowed Ethan to turn around and look at the Censer.

What Skull Crusher had done was hook Ethan's shirt with one of the mounting straps for the Censer. Ethan tried to pull it free, but it was just too heavy. However, that created a really odd pucker in the side of the tarp that was hanging over the crevasse.

The wagon pulled to a stop next to Ethan and Aiden called, "C'mon, E! We need to go."

"No! We need to break the Censer," Ethan called back. We just have to shine light in the hole over here!"

Ethan indicated the spot on the side of the wagon.

"Ethan, we need to go, come right now," Mother demanded.

"Mother, I can jump on and cut it open really quickly," Aiden offered.

"No if you touch this, it's likely to fall in," Ethan cried.

"Hey, what about me?" Jesse called from across the chasm, where he held up Ethan's shield. Everyone turned to look that way, including Daddy Duck, which reflected a spot of light off the shield and back into Aiden's eyes.

"That's it!" Aiden called. "Jesse turn the shield to point that light into the hole Ethan's talking about."

Jesse complied, but nothing happened. "Now what?"

"Well that should have worked, " Aiden replied with a shrug. "The angle must need to be just right. I don't know, E, the light goes straight. There's no way to just pour it in there."

"Boys! Your father is fading fast! We have to be off!" Mother pleaded.

"Hey, Jesse," Ethan yelled as he pulled the crystal jar from the sack on the bench. "Do you remember what Krystal said about the water?"

"Well, just that it was pure, and you could drink it." Jesse raised an eyebrow.

"Or put a fire out," Ethan responded. He pulled the cork out of the crystal jar and began gently pouring water into the crack in the Censer cover. A slight hiss began to emanate from the Censer. Jesse turned the shield slightly, and the beam hit the vase perfectly. Ethan poured a little more vigorously, and the Censer stopped issuing black smoke.

"E! You did it!" Aiden called from the back of the wagon.

Mother stood beside his brother, holding her arms out to pull him up. "Come now!"

The Censer made some wild gurgling noises, and Ethan could feel something powerful was about to happen. He handed the vase to Aiden while Meow Meow caught a ride on Ethan's shoulder. Mother pulled them up into the wagon, and Sparkle Frog leapt up too.

Suddenly the cover burst off the Censer, and clear white mist shot out of it, filling the sky. Every trace of Darkness over them vanished in seconds.

A gentle rain began, and all of the corruption in the area slowly washed away.

"Get him, Lauren," Ethan cried from the back of the wagon.

Lauren was so excited by the change in events she almost threw her spear at Uncle instead. But Skull Crusher knew his danger and lifted the frontiersman as a shield for his face. The giant whistled, and his moose started to lope towards him slowly. Lauren noticed that as the rain fell on it, the moose seemed to age.

"No!" Skull Crusher screamed, "You wretched moose! I should have fed you to the coyotes!"

He twisted slightly, keeping Uncle as a shield. It looked like he might be trying to move toward Master Warden's moose to make a get away. She had to down him before he made it there. But she couldn't find an opening to make a throw. *God, please don't let him get away!*

"Lauren! Don't worry about me!" Uncle cried. "Just stop him!"

"Quiet, you!" Skull Crusher used his free hand and bonked Uncle on the top of his head. He slumped, and the giant had to adjust to the dead weight.

Lauren wasn't fast enough and missed her shot. As she looked for an opening, a blur caught her attention behind Skull Crusher. Something raced toward him, but the giant's bulk and the mist from the Censer blocked a clear sighting.

There was a sudden whinny, and Skull Crusher stumbled forward, dropping Uncle. The giant kept his feet, but was now fully exposed. Lauren could also see the attacker. Chance! The little pony had reared up and kicked the giant!

Lauren let loose with her spear, dropping Skull Crusher face-first into the dirt and on top of Uncle. She rushed up to her trusty steed and hugged him. The pony whinnied in appreciation. He was so brave! Then she turned to congratulate her brother, and finally got a good look at the Censer spraying a fine white mist in the air. Her words of congratulation were lost to Tye's scream for help, "I think he's stopped breathing!"

Lauren raced to see how she could help, and crouched next to Tye. "We have to find a way to cleanse the poison in his lungs!"

Mother's voice rang out from across the chasm. "Bring him here, maybe the pure vapors will help him?"

Master Warden's moose approached his fallen master. As Tye attempted to pick her father up, the moose bent its front knees to lower its body some. Lauren attempted to help Tye, but Master Warden was just plain huge.

Tye struggled through the task of putting him on the beast's back and quickly guided the animal around the crevasse to where the Censer sat spraying it's rain of life. Jesse, Ethan's shield in hand, joined Lauren as she followed the moose around the crevasse.

Mother had dismounted the wagon and had Gramps pull it away a bit to make room for the moose. She stood next to the Censer. "Just hold his head near one of the cracks that the white mist is escaping."

"Yes, I see." Tye strained to keep her father held in the right position. After a moment of everyone holding their breaths, Master Warden began to cough severely. Black goo being seeping from his mouth and nose. Tye gasped and started to pull him away.

But Mother put a hand Tye's back. "No! It's working. He has to cough up the poison."

So they continued to hold him there, all of them gathered around.

"Hey!" Uncle waved off to the west, "That fire's comin' fast it's going to be on us in no time."

Suddenly, clouds formed in what had been a sky filled with smoke from the Darkness. A lightning flash lit the sky, and rain began to pour down.

Uncle looked up eyes wide. "Well I'll be."

The Master Warden's coughing turned from black goo to red blood for just a handful of coughing fits, and everyone was worried he was not going to get better. Then it turned clear, and Mother said he was no longer in danger and they could lay him down. After he was on the ground his breathing settled to a rattling wheeze with an occasional cough.

"Hey, missy!" Gramps called from the back of the wagon pointing at Father. "The rain's a-washin' the dark stuff out of his boils and blisters away!"

"E! You found the Wellspring of Life!" Aiden patted him on the back.

Ethan raised an eyebrow. "Well not exactly. I just put the water from Jewely lady's pool into the Censer. She said it was just water. But I didn't believe her."

"Jewely lady? What are you talking about?" Lauren asked.

"Well, the snow globe got broken, and it just opened a secret door. We met a lady, and she had a really pretty fountain—oh wait! And she had these!"

Ethan dug in his pocket and pulled out the two jewels. "Jesse, show yours."

Jesse found his and held it up.

"She said that the Bishop isn't from Zoura. He used a secret door, and he's trying to open another to bring a Clammy Dragon or something. It sounds really bad." Ethan continued, "So we need Daddy to get better, and he can make weapons to put the Bishop back in his secret place, and we can beat the Dragon."

Jesse held up Mother's dagger with his jewel next to it. "Yah she said if we put these stones in a weapon like this one we can lock that Bishop up forever—whoever that is."

"Well all this time I done thought the wellspring you all was lookin' for was in the hidden grove up yonder to the north east." Gramps pointed off in the direction of the beaten path they'd abandoned to take their stand on the prairie dog mound.

"That destination hasn't changed," Mother said. "It's still a safe place where wounded warriors can heal." Mother held her hand out toward Jesse, who was still holding her dagger up for everyone to see. "May I?"

He did a double take and then stammered, "Uh, yes, ma'am."

"You hold on to that jewel for safe keeping for now, OK?" Mother raised her eyebrows to him.

"Yes, ma'am." Jesse tucked the stone back into his pocket.

Tye looked up from where she wept over her father. "I have been so foolish. Can you forgive me, and please take my father with you as well?"

"The Savior's grace forgives all." Mother put a hand on her shoulder. "Of course, we will take you with us. Everyone, please help put Master Warden in the wagon. Both he and Father may be clear of the Darkness but I'm afraid the mist alone is not enough to heal their wounds."

"What about Skull Crusher?" Aiden pointed to the giant's unconscious form with his hammer. Uncle had regained consciousness and now sat on the giant's back with Skull Crusher's hammer across his knees. The decrepit moose stood at the giant's feet, almost like it was guarding him.

Tye pulled her dagger from her belt. "I will show him justice." She turned from the wagon and started to stalk forward. Aiden set his jaw. Tye was right. They needed to be rid of him once and for all.

"No! Wait!" Lauren called from the back of the wagon. "He was under the influence of the smoke the same as you when you held the daggers." A memory of Nicolas waking up in their home, unaware of the evil he'd done, came to Aiden's mind. Was Skull Crusher the same way? Was the giant just a puppet, like so many others?

"Well, I'm not sure's I get all of that, young missy," Gramps interjected. "But that there giant destroyed our home. So Tye can give him what he's got comin' to him."

Aiden was about to come to Lauren's defense when Jesse broke in. "Yah! He brought the Darkness to our home!" He lifted a big rock. "This here coyote-conkin' rock would give him the what for!"

"Stop!" Mother yelled at the top of her voice, blazing sword in both hands over her head. Aiden's mouth dropped. The mist amplified the light of the sword, and Mother could have been mistaken for an angel ready to do battle.

"'Vengeance is mine sayeth the Lord!'" Mother slowly pointed her sword blade at each of them. "Every one of us has reason to want Skull Crusher to pay for his crimes. But, we'll not be judge, jury, and executioner to an unconscious and defenseless prisoner."

She hopped down off the wagon, sword flames blazing in the motion.

Tye turned from her advance on Skull Crusher. "He is of my people; I'll not have you tell me what justice looks like for the Wardens."

Mother stopped advancing and squared her shoulders into a stance that said she was ready to fight. Then she held up her right hand and slowly moved to sheath her sword as its fire went out.

"Tye, please listen to me." Mother spoke slowly and softly, which scared Aiden more than when she had the sword out. If she was using her quiet voice, you just knew there was big trouble coming. "The only other Warden that knows the truth of Skull Crusher's betrayal is your father." She pointed her sword to where he lay in the wagon with his feet hanging out of the gate.

"Which is why it is my right to show this traitor Justice." Tye pointed the dagger at Mother.

"But that won't clear your name with the other Wardens." Mother slowly sheathed her sword. "It would be easy for Refi'Cul or a giant under the control of the Darkness to undermine your claims."

Mother stood motionless for a moment. Aiden held his breath as Tye seemed to be mulling over Mother's point. This was a lot more complicated than he thought.

Tye lowered her blade. "So, what would you have me do?"

"We'll restrain him and bring him with us." Mother stepped up to Tye. "Then in the presence of the Light, God willing, Skull Crusher will answer to your father in front of your people, clearing your name once and for all."

Tye let out a deep sigh, and Aiden found himself doing the same. "Very well. You are wise Mother of La'Ren."

As the tension in the group subsided, Uncle asked, "So how exactly do you think we're going to be haulin' him with us?"

***

With Tye's help, they harnessed two of the bison to the cart with the Censer, then tied Skull Crusher to it's seat. To make room for Master Warden in the main wagon, everyone stood around the wagon except for Gramps. They positioned the Censer cart in the front of the line—with the wagon behind. The idea was that the mist from the Censer would flow over their wounded fathers as they traveled.

Tye stood with the bison at the front of the line, and Skull Crusher's moose stood chewing the tops off prairie grass next to where Skull Crusher sat in the cart.

Something about that moose just looked pitiful to Aiden, maybe the swayed back or its patchy fur. But it didn't need to be going on this long walk with them. So he ran up to it and released the pack straps. As they fell off its back, he encouraged the beast, "You're free; you don't need that nasty giant any more."

The Moose stood still, bowed its head, and seemed to frown like it was sad. That made Aiden want to free him even more.

"Tye, can you tell him he can go?" Aiden asked.

Tye turned from her post at the front of the procession, put two fingers in her mouth and let out a high-pitched whistle. The moose gently shook its antlers, and stood its ground. Aiden noticed that a reddish milky cataract covered one of its eyes. Part of him pitied the animal even more for being half-blind, but something about that eye sent a shiver down his spine.

"A'den of the Tower, a moose, does as it chooses," Tye explained. "We can only suggest. But, for now, best to just let it tire and wander off on its own."

"Yeah, Aiden, stop foolin' around; we need to get a move on," Uncle called from where he stood next to the horses.

"OK, but we might want these supplies." Aiden tried to pick up the saddlebags, but they were too heavy. "I can't do it on my own."

"Alright," Uncle huffed, then waded through the half trampled prairie grass.

While Aiden waited, he inspected the packs and found a map case. "Hey! Look what I found." He unlatched the top, pulled out the linen map, and handed it to Uncle.

Uncle unfurled the map. "Well I'll be. This here's a map of the whole area between Spring Fields and Blooming Glen!"

Aiden's heart leapt. Would it show them where the Wellspring of Life was? If it did, and Skull Crusher had the map, would the rest of the forces of Darkness know about it too?

"Let me see."Uncle stamped the prairie grass in front of him flat and laid the map out on top of it, then took a knee. Everyone else gathered around.

"Well, there ain't nothin' labeled 'Wellspring of Life,'" Uncle explained. "But this here path looks like the one we are on. See where the dam was, and that crossroads way stop, and the waterways match the creeks we've been tracking. Then ended up at 'The Grove of Righteousness.'"

"Well that's an awful high and mighty name for a bunch of trees, don't you think," Gramp interjected.

Mother gasped. "No, not high and mighty at all, the Wellspring of Life is there! Just down the trail from us!"

"Really? How do you know?" Aiden asked.

She tapped her armor. "The Breastplate of Righteousness guards the heart! That grove must be guarding the heart of the prairie!"

"Well all be!" Gramps slapped his knee. "I guess I done had it wrong that's just the right name."

Everyone's faces brightened. They were going to find the wellspring for sure. But something in the back of Aiden's mind left him unsettled.

He stared at the map, then pointed to the middle of the lower lake. "Do anybody else see a little X there, in pencil? Its really faint, might be a speck in the linen."

"That's definitely an X," Uncle replied with an upraised eyebrow.

"That's where we found Gramps, Jesse . . . and the Censer!" Aiden's mind raced. If there were more little X's on the map, that would tell them where the whole network was.

"I see another little *X* on that hill on the other side of the lake." Logan tapped the map excitedly.

Aiden searched the map some more. "Here's one! It's right where Sissy and Tye should have found the next one."

"We didn't find one, but that must be it in the buggy," Lauren offered.

"If that's the case," Aiden put his hand flat on the map to gauge the distance between Censers, "then we should find the next one here." He pointed at the Grove of Righteousness. In the middle of the tree symbols there was a very tiny *X*.

A collective gasp went up from the group as a shudder traveled down Aiden's spine.

Tye was the first to recover. "That explains the Darkness in the blood of the prairie. He has corrupted its heart. Yet another crime Skull Crusher must pay for." Her hand went reflexively to the knife at her belt.

"So what do we do, now?" Lauren's eyebrows were furrowed, and Aiden realized just how exhausted she must be by the lines under her eyes. She'd ridden halfway across the prairie and back in the last day, and he was feeling the strain from his wild ride the night before.

"Your father has stopped declining, but he's not healed." Mother waved her hand to the back of the wagon. "Tye's father is also in bad shape. We have to take them both to the wellspring."

Uncle stood up and looked at Lauren. "Yer Ma's right. I know where all in strung-out shape, but we gotta get them help now."

"Yes, we must clear the heart from the Darkness to win back the prairie," Tye added.

Lauren took a deep breath and nodded "Of course we must." But Aiden could tell she was speaking more confidently than she felt. They had the Light and each other, but were they going to be a match for what waited for them at the Wellspring of Life?

As evening fell, the beaten path abruptly ended at a wall of dense, corrupted foliage. In the failing purple light, raspberry vines with thorns the size of swords hung with berries the size of melons across the path. The edge of the grove was a choked mass of discolored and enlarged plantlife. When the party was twenty yards from the wall, a half dozen cougars slunk out from the few gaps at the bottom of the wall of foliage, and four brown bears broke through bushes to the right. Owl hoots rang out from the treetops.

Tye whistled the bison to a stop and pulled out her sword. It erupted in flames, and she looked back at Lauren. "Do we fight?"

The bears stood on their hind legs and roared as the cougars began to stalk to their left. The screech of hawks joined the owl's calls as dozens of birds launched into the air.

"I'm startin' to not like these odds," Uncle interjected as he pulled his own flaming sword from its scabbard and turned toward the bears.

Lauren didn't like the odds, either, but then she remembered their fights with the coyotes. "Ethan! Quick, stand on the wagon with Gramps! I don't think they'll break the bubble of your shield. "

"Yes, I think she's right." Mother grabbed Ethan under his arms and lifted him up to the wagon's seat. "Raise your shield, and shine your light."

"Yes, Mama." Ethan took his shield off and strapped it on his arm. The protective bubble barely covered the back of the wagon to the horse's hindquarters, and the same distance around.

"Jesse! You get up here with that coyote-conkin' rock of yours!" Gramps scooted to the middle of the seat to make room.

Uncle ran up to the bison on the right. "Tye, I got this one covered; you watch the other."

"Of course," Tye replied as she backed toward her bison.

"Lauren, watch the horse on your side, and I'll do the same on mine. Aiden, Logan, fill in between the horses and the bison," Mother ordered.

"Yes, ma'am," all three children replied. Lauren took a deep breath. It was a good plan. The Censer's mist went out about twice as far as Ethan's shield, so maybe it would provide some protection too.

"What about the moose, Mother?" Aiden asked as he took up a position next to it.

"It may be old and lame, but it's still a moose," Tye said. "It will care for itself."

"Enough lolligaggin'. Let's move out!" Uncle called, and Tye responded with a two finger whistle.

They moved forward, and the army of corrupted animals charged. But as the first dive-bombing hawk hit the edge of the mist, it screamed and awkwardly pulled out of the dive. It spiraled for a second, then banked in a slow circle around the edge of the mist.

Uncle's Geese and Daddy Duck flew up to meet it and an unusual flock of hawks and owls formed up with them.

"WOW!" Aiden called, "I sure wish we had the Light Censer when we met Gramps. Those crows wouldn't have given us such a hard time."

"Hey now!" Gramps called. "Them crows were pretty useful, if you recall."

Lauren had to laugh, despite the tense situation. The fight with those crows was such a mess. It felt like it was years ago, but it'd only been two days. Her attention was drawn back to the cougars as they hit the mist. They howled for a second, then seemed to have a moment of confusion. Like the hawks, they changed course and took up a position stalking along the edge of the mist on the bears' side of their formation.

Lauren let out a deep sigh. The last time they'd fought a cougar, the beast almost ate Uncle. She was glad to see them turnining to face the animals that were still affected by the Darkness. The odds were definitely in their favor now. Would they want to be friends once the Censer was destroyed? The thought of a pet cougar seemed very enticing.

As the edge of the mist began to fall on the grove, the largest bear roared, and all four faded back into the woods, having never crossed the mist.

"Do you think the bears are still a danger, Uncle?" Aiden asked.

"I think we'll be just fine as long as them cougars are watchin' our flank." He pointed his fiery sword to where the big cats were patrolling their perimeter.

The cart and the wagon rolled on, and the mist began to fall in earnest on the grove. The vines at the center of their advance began to shink, along with the berries and thorns.

Lauren's eyes went wide at the rapid transformation before them. The Light Censer power was amazing.

By the time the bison reached the edge of the woods, all of the overgrown foliage blocking the path had returned to normal-sized healthy growth, and the way ahead was clear.

"Wow!" Aiden cried. " I wonder if we took the Light Censer to the Bjorn Born village if the thorns would shrink like that?"

"Well, we should try it!" Ethan blurted from the wagon seat.

"One thing at a time," Mother interjected. "Let's hurry your Father to the wellspring."

Lauren had to agree with that. The last time she'd checked on Father, the mist seemed to be healing the black lesions and deep red blisters brought on by the double-Darkness zone little by little. But it wasn't perfect. The skin on his arms looked stretched and scarred, almost too tight for his body. All while his muscles looked weakened, as though he'd been starving for months.

She wished desperately that they'd been able to intercept Skull Crusher before he'd put Father in the double-Darkness zone. Her heart ached that they had been too late to protect him.

Once they fully entered, the grove was oddly cooler than the prairie they'd just left—more than just an evening chill. In the mist, a shiver ran down her back. After about fifty yards, the path took a steep slant down and seemed to have a curve to it. The longer they walked, the less defined the woods around them became. It would have been pitch black, if it weren't for Ethan's shield and their holy weapons.

The path continued its gentle curve to the right and down in a broad circle. She walked along the outside edge of the curve. Between the limited light and the horses blocking her view, she couldn't see what was at the bottom.

"Aiden, where are we going?" she asked because he was on the other side of the horses.

"Looks like there's a pool down there," he responded.

So there was a literal wellspring here. But would it have the healing properties Father needed?

"And a Censer—"

A "QUACK" from Daddy Duck cut Aiden's description short. Their feathered friend flew off to the right, then straight up through a break in the trees above them.

"Wait, Daddy Duck!" Aiden called. "Where are you going?" The whole group pulled to a stop to watch what the bird would do.

Lauren didn't have long to wonder as a brilliant beam of light blasted from above, illuminating the whole forest brighter than the noon day sun. A plume of black smoke roiled up from below, fighting against the light.

"No, Daddy Duck! Stop!" Aiden hollered with his hands cupped around his mouth! "We can use the water on it and make another good one!"

Unfortunately, Uncle's geese had joined the wayward duck and dissipated the smoke by flapping their wings. The beam blasted down, and then disappeared with a loud thump. The ground shook, and Lauren knew he'd destroyed the Censer.

"Daddy Duck!" Aiden complained.

Lauren's mouth turned down in disappointment. What would it be like to have two Light Censers they could take with them? That would surely keep them safe from dark forces.

"It's okay, Aiden," Ethan called from the wagon's seat. "I don't have any more of the special water." He picked up the crystal jar from the back of the wagon and turned it upside down for emphasis.

"But didn't you say that the lady told you it was just plain water?" Aiden retorted while the group started winding down the trail again.

"I don't think she was right." Ethan squinted his eyes, "Those Censers have lava in them. Regular water wouldn't just cool it off. There was something special about it."

"I don't know, Ethan," Jesse interjected. "She was pretty insistent that it was just water."

"Well it doesn't matter, your duck broke it." Ethan stuck his tongue out at Aiden.

"Boys!" Mother barked. "Enough of that, we need to get your father to the wellspring."

The entire group's pace picked up until the path flattened out at the bottom next to the pool, which seemed to be fed by a bubbling spring surrounded by four stone mounts, one in each cardinal direction. They were the right size for the Censer and covered in soot that must have been from its explosion. In the center, the spring bubbled and seemed to be slowly washing the Darkness out of the pool around it.

"So Mama what do you think?" Ethan cocked his head, "Is this the 'real' Wellspring of Life?"

"Of course it is!" Aiden blurted as he leapt from the back of the wagon into the sand next to the pool.

Mother squinted her eyes like she was about to correct Aiden's interruption, then shook her head, "God willing it this wellspring has the healing your Father needs. Let's get him into the water."

Lauren's heart leapt at the thought that they might finally heal Father from his grievous wounds. He looked so frail right now. She stood to climb out of the wagon, and Mother put a hand on Lauren's shoulder.

"Wait!" Mother held up a hand. "We need to put our Censer in the middle first. It needs to force the rest of the corruption out of the pool, or we'll be doing more harm than good."

"Yes of course." Tye whistled the bison to a stop and yanked the Censer out of it's mounts. She was sprayed with mist that quickly soaked her leather jerkin and pants. She seemed oblivious to the water as she waded into the pool, watching the mist from their Censer drive back the black goo.

Once she placed it in the stone mounts, it seemed to begin sucking up water from the spring under it, because the mist blasted higher into a plume that reached the tree tops. It didn't fall down as Lauren expected, instead it seemed to get carried by the wind all around them. It was hard to tell, but she thought it might be healing all the trees that had surrounded the Darkness Censer.

Gramps pulled the wagon to a halt as close as he dared to the pool, and Uncle quickly ran to the wagon and opened the tailgate. "Tye, can you give me a hand?"

"Of course," she responded, wet hair plastered to her face.

She waded back through the pool that was now completely clear, and together they gently pulled Father out of the wagon and carried him to the pool.

Mother joined them and knelt in the pool as they laid him down. The water was barely deep enough to cover his whole body, so mother sat cross-legged in the pool and put his head in her lap. Tears streamed down her face.

Lauren and her brothers stood over Father, wracked with tears. *God, please let this be what Father needs to heal.*

Meanwhile, Tye and Uncle worked to put Master Warden into the pool. Once he was situated, Tye sat with him to keep his face above the water.

The giantess looked up at Mother with tears streaming down her face. "So what happens now?"

Through her own tears Mother replied, "We pray, and hope this is the miracle we believe it to be."

***

Morning came after a sleepless night on the poolside stone. More than anything else, Lauren wanted her father to be better. As she rubbed sleep from her eyes, she was shocked to see Father shrouded in a wool blanket and sitting up on a wooden supply box next to the fire.

"Daddy!" Lauren leapt from her covers and raced to embrace him. She stopped short when he looked up at her. His eyes were sunken in, and she could see the definition of his cheekbones, like those of a starving man. He reached a hand toward her, and his arm was wickedly scarred and shrunken.

Lauren's heart broke. "No! This can't be! Daddy, you're supposed to be OK. We found the Wellspring of Life. It was supposed to make you all better."

Mother stepped away from the fire and put her arm around Lauren's shoulder. Tears streamed down their faces as they walked toward Father, where he reached up with feeble arms to hug her.

With a raspy voice, he said, "I was in the Darkness too long. The poison was powerful. No one could have done more."

Lauren's heart ached. Father had been so strong, so powerful. Now it seemed Gramps was more vibrant than he was. "Oh, Daddy! I'm so sorry. We tried so hard! We just couldn't catch Skull Crusher. I'm so sorry!" Lauren was wracked with guilt and regrets.

Father just held her for an eternity, then gently reached up and touched her cheeks in each shaking hand. "No, my sweet, sweet Lauren. You did not fail me. We must all guard our hearts because they are the Wellspring of Life."

As tears filled his eyes, his head sagged. "I let pride guide me. I did what was right in my own eyes and strayed off the path. It was easy to be washed away when the flood of Darkness came."

Father shook his head. "This is not your doing. It is mine alone." He pulled her back into a hug, and Mother joined them.

Lauren didn't understand what he was saying. Before she could ask more, Tye approached. "What of my father?"

"We are not yet sure." Mother pointed to where Master Warden lay, eyes closed in the pool. "The vapors are making his breathing steady, and he may recover, but the poison was deep in his body."

Tye's mouth drooped as Mother continued, "He may need to breathe the vapors every day from now on to live a good life."

"I see," Tye said very softly.

The few pieces of Lauren's heart that were still whole shattered at her friend's pain. She let go of Father, turned, and embraced Tye. A few moments passed in tear-filled silence.

"Mother," Ethan asked sheepishly as he wiped the tears from his face. "Are we going to finish our mission . . . without Daddy?"

"What are you thinkin' boy?" Uncle blurted with a sharp bite in his tone. Ethan's face fell, and the big man softened, "I'm sorry, didn't mean to snap. We saved yer Ma and yer Pa."

"But—" Ethan started.

Uncle reddened as he interrupted, "There ain't no other mission. It's time to head home."

Lauren didn't like Uncle being sharp with Ethan, but he was right. Father was in no shape to fight. Their mission was done.

Mother held up an open palm to Uncle. "Please, let's hear him out.

"Last night, you said we were close to Blooming Glen." Ethan pointed up the path. "So it wouldn't be long to go light the tower there. Isn't that what we're supposed to do, shine our light over the whole wide world?" He spread his arms out wide. "I promised the little girl I'd shine my light for her."

Deep down, Lauren knew Ethan was right. They couldn't let the Darkness continue to cover Zoura. So many other families were suffering.

Father cleared his throat as if to speak, when a light splash caught everyone's attention.

Master Warden coughed and spoke weakly in a raspy voice. "Lord Refi'Cul means to trap you in Blooming Glen. He plans to make it a stronghold of giants and Steele Brothers for the Darkness." Tye ran to him, splashing through the pool, knelt, and hugged him fiercely.

What resolve Lauren had gained from Ethan's plea was only paper-thin, because it blew away at the thought of another battle.

Everyone watched as Father forced himself to his feet. He wobbled, and Mother came to his side. "Though my wounds are grievous, I do not regret the fight. The Darkness only wins when Light Bearers do nothing. We cannot allow that stronghold to stand." His knees gave out, and Mother grunted as she took his weight and helped him to sit softly on the log.

Aiden pulled out his little tack hammer and held it up in the air. It radiated bright blue light all around. "I'll do it; I'll demolisth that stronghold!"

Something in Lauren broke, and she had to stifle a laugh. How was that little tack hammer going to destroy a stronghold full of giants and steele brothers.

"Me too!" Logan held up his hatchet, and its glow amplified the light. "My ma and pa were going to Blooming Glen. We have to save them."

"I'll protect you with my shield!" Ethan knelt in front of the boys and slammed his shield down.

"I ain't got nuthin' but this coyote-conkin' rock, but I'm up for some payback!" Jesse said as he held his rock in both hands above his head. It seemed that even radiated in the light.

A disturbance in the water pulled Lauren's attention from the boys. Tye stood and pulled the Sword of the Spirit from her belt. "La'Ren of the Tower, if you'll join me, I, too, will demolish this stronghold."

All eyes were on Lauren. She picked up the shaft of her spear in one hand and stamped it on the ground. Blue light erupted from around her hand, covering the shaft and building up the speartip. "Yes, we need to shine our light over the whole wide world."

Tye's sword burst into flame, and Lauren's heart surged with relief that her friend was truly back in the Light.

Lauren wiped her face with her free hand, then she took a deep breath and slowly let it out. She looked at Uncle, "Are you up for some stronghold demolishing?"

Uncle stroked his beard. "Yah, I think I could demolish a stronghold or two, what about you, old-timer?"

"Well you did trade me that pony fer a ride to Blooming Glen, and I got relation that aught not be livin' in a stronghold of Darkness. So it sounds mightly tempting."

The only one who had remained silent was Mother. She was on her knees next to Father, head down and sobbing.

Lauren stepped toward her, and the others lowered their arms and circled closer around. "Mother, will you allow us to do this, to demolish the stronghold?"

She looked up at Father. "I just got you back. I know this is right. I can't let the children go on alone. But I can't leave you here all alone, either. You're too weak to fend for yourself."

Father put a shaky hand on her shoulder, but said nothing.

Lauren knew Father was barely able to even sit on the log, and Master Warden wasn't in any better shape. If they left them alone, how would they survive?

Gramps cleared his throat with gusto, stood up, twisted his body side to side, then bent down and touched his toes. "As I see it, missy, I'm feelin' twenty years younger here in this mist. So how's about I take care of these two wounded warriors, while you all go do some stronghold demolishing?"

This made sense to Lauren, and he did seem to have a spring in his step. She let out a sigh as she contemplated the situation. Between the protection of the Light Censer and how hidden the path was, they would be unlikely to run into any trouble.

"Besides," Gramps pointed to the far side of the pool and the path to it. "I've got a whole army of the beasts of the field and birds of the air by my side."

Lauren had been so focused on Father when she woke up, she didn't notice the bears had come in the night to lap at the pool and were now sleeping next to it. The cougars patrolled the path, and predatory birds filled the trees all around them.

Ethan approached Mother. "Mama, does that mean we're going to go light the tower?"

She snuffed back her tears and wiped her face on her arm. "Well, I don't know anyone who sings 'Light of Mine' better."

Ethan's face beamed at Mother's praise, and Lauren's heart felt a sense of ease, despite the looming danger. Mother was right; his little light was very, very bright.

Uncle slapped his thigh to catch everyone's attention, "Well that's settled, then, but we've got one last thing to deal with."

"What's that?" Lauren asked.

"Skull Crusher!" Uncle pointed to the buggy they'd tied him to the day before. A collective gasp went up from the group, and the feeling of hope and direction washed away from Lauren's mind. "Somehow the villain escaped in the night."

"Let's get him!" Aiden called, and the boys shook their weapons.

She picked up her spear at the ready, in agreement.

"Keep yer britches on," Uncle demanded. "From the rope and the tracks, that old moose of his, chewed the ropes free, and managed to get him on its back." Uncle stepped to an open part of the path. "There's moose tracks leavin' but no giant tracks to go with them. That moose seems like it's about to be lame—one of these tracks is dragging out of position."

"Well then, let's go and finish him!" Tye yelled. "I knew we shouldn't have tried to capture him. He'll always be in the shadows, working to destroy us."

A wave of unease ran through Lauren's stomach. She'd just seen Tye come back to the Light. But now, the giantess seemed to be slipping back into Darkness. Lauren hated

Skull Crusher too, but it wouldn't have been right to kill him when he was defenseless. Besides, her spear packed a wallop.

"Tye, I'm not sure he's a threat right now," Lauren offered. "When my spear hits people, it knocks the Darkness out of them. When he wakes up fully, he's likely to be lost and confused."

"Listen to La'Ren of the Tower," Master Warden rasped. "Skull Crusher is a fiend, but there will be time for justice. For now, you must demolish the stronghold."

She knelt next to him. "But, Father—"

"I have spoken," The Master Warden said with finality.

Refi'Cul pulled his horse-drawn, black-lacquered chariot to a halt, as he met a moose-riding Heath Warden coming the opposite direction from Blooming Glen at the top of a hill overlooking the city. The smoke from the Censer enveloped them, and Refi'Cul inhaled in a deep breath of its calming vapors as the giant addressed him.

"They wave the white flag, my Lord!"

"What?" Refi'Cul was incredulous. "The 'Mighty' Mercenaries giving up without even drawing their swords?" The Steele Lord felt a broad smile crack his metallic lips.

Journey Leader leaned in to advise. "It may just be to parlay, my Lord, or a trap. Those mercenaries are not to be trusted."

Refi'Cul stared off into the horizon as he contemplated this development. "Tell me more of the city."

"It's open, my Lord." Scout pointed toward the city, where it was just barely visible in the distance. "I saw a few refugee families struggling to cross the prairie grass on foot to the east and some others entering by the road. But otherwise, there was some standard horse-and-wagon traffic. Nothing going south, but open gates and traffic going in."

Refi'Cul put his hand to his chin and cocked his head in thought. Working in dispatch for the Bishop, he'd met many Mighty Mercenaries. With the exception of Knight Protector sent to the children, not one of them seemed particularly clever. Had his reputation preceded him? Were they really going to just accept his rule? "You're sure they have the white flag up?"

"Yes, the Mercenaries always have their colors flying where they garrison." Scout pointed to the tower barely visible in the center of the city. Something was at the top, but it was hard to make out as more than a tuft of white cloud.

Since Master Warden's squads returned without him, Refi'Cul now had three dozen giants, plus two dozen Steele Brothers to mount an assault. More than enough to overwhelm a normal city garrison. But if they were waving the white flag, he might be able to take it without a fight.

"Very well," Refi'Cul turned to Journey Lead. "Stay here with half of your men, and I will leave half of mine in your charge as a rearguard and reserve."

"Yes, my Lord Refi'Cul," the giant slammed his right fist on his chest.

"Second Brother!" Refi'Cul bellowed.

"Yes! M'Lord," The Steele Brother responded.

"Take a dozen men in reserve with the giants. Journey Lead is in charge," he said in a booming voice. Journey Lead's grin widened at the apparent promotion. Refi'Cul waved Second Brother closer and whispered, "If it doesn't appear he is following my will"—Refi'Cul checked to make sure Journey Lead had moved out of earshot— "dispose of him."

Second Brother's eyes got big. "M'Lord, what of the other giants? I'm not sure we could take them all."

"Those sandals they wear make their ankles vulnerable." Refi'Cul pointed. "A quick slice there, and the mighty will fall. Your Steele will protect you to make the strike."

A wicked grin crossed Second Brother's metallic face. "Yes, M'Lord."

"Now go. It looks as if I must parlay with the master of the garrison."

*****

An armored mercenary flanked by a standard bearer and a soldier with a bugle around his neck rode out of the city as Refi'Cul approached.

When they got within twenty feet of each other, both sides pulled to a halt. At this distance, the armored mercenary bore a distinct resemblance to Knight Protector, only twenty years younger and with a full head of black hair. He raised an open palm. "Peace be with you, my Lord Refi'Cul."

The Steele Lord's face split ear to ear in a grin of pride. He had not yet met this man, and already he knew to call him *Lord* Refi'Cul. This would go well.

"And also with you," rolled off Refi'Cul's tongue as sweet as syrup. "Shall we parlay?"

"If it pleases my Lord." The man climbed off his horse, despite his entourage's shocked and confused looks.

That told Refi'Cul all he needed to know. This man was a true mercenary. While he could be the offspring of Knight Protector, he was no devotee of the false light. Refi'Cul dismounted the chariot and waved off his honor guard as they approached.

Refi'Cul closed the gap with the mercenary leader. "You have the pleasure of knowing my position, who are you to parlay on behalf of Blooming Glen?"

"I am the Garrison Master of the cadre defending Blooming Glen." He turned and indicated the city.

"I was under the impression that Blooming Glen was a haven of the false light and that the Mighty Mercenaries here were under its power." Refi'Cul prodded.

"I hate to correct you, honorable Lord Refi'Cul, but you are mistaken." The man took a deep breath, and Refi'Cul realized it was to control the quiver in his voice. "While some within my ranks believe in the 'false light' as you call it. This cadre has but one master: The Code."

Garrison Master's entourage looked at each other with hints of concern in their eyes. Then the bugler shrugged.

Refi'Cul pressed the man. "Tell me of The Code."

Garrison Master cleared his throat. "It's straightforward, my Lord; we serve whoever has the most coin, as long as they don't try to have us harm women and children or destroy the common folks' livelihood."

His entourage nodded in agreement with this. This was very interesting. After his run-in with Knight Protector, he expected these men were all dedicated to the false light. But they were indeed just mercenaries.

"I see, and if I told you I had access to the wealth of the Iron Mountain, would you believe I had the most coin?" Refi'Cul quipped.

A grin crossed Garrison Master's face. "Why yes, m'Lord, that's the very reason we came to parlay."

Those in the entourage widened their eyes. It was clear the troops might not be completely bought in. Refi'Cul snapped his fingers, which made an odd metallic noise. "First Brother, show the man some coin."

First Brother picked up a chest from the back of Refi'Cul's chariot and brought it forward.

The Dark Lord opened it. "Would this be enough for a down payment for your ongoing support?"

This time Garrison Master looked back at his men. Their countenances had changed. Clearly, deep down, they were just as greedy as their leader. "Why yes, my Lord, it would."

"Are you certain all your men will be onboard with this." Refi'Cul furrowed his brow. "The last thing I would want is a follower of the false light derailing our plans from inside these walls."

The smile on the Garrison Master's face broadened. "I thought you might ask that." He pointed two fingers toward the bugler, who gave his horn two short blasts.

A moment later, a box wagon came out of the city gate, filled with a dozen men, bound and gagged. Garrison Master gestured to the group. "As a show of good faith, I've taken the step of 'detaining' the potential troublemakers for the moment."

Refi'Cul smiled ear to ear as he turned back to the Steele Brothers and the giants. "The renown of Refi'Cul Lord of the Iron Mountain has spread across the land. Even the Mighty Mercenaries know where they'll be paid best!"

A cry rose up from his men that, despite their earlier misgivings, was taken up by the giants as well.

"Call in the rear guard. We revel in the city tonight."

Another cheer rose from his soldiers. He waited for it to die down.

"But first, we have one piece of business to take care of . . ." He trailed off for dramatic effect. "Garrison Master, is it against your code to put the detainees to work?"

Garrison Master looked taken aback. "Well, no, my Lord, but they'd have to be under supervision."

"Very well then, I'm sure I can find some supervisors among my soldiers," Refi'Cul responded.

A great laugh erupted from the giants and Steele Brothers.

"May I ask what the work will be, my Lord?" Garrison Master said.

"Of course, there's a tower that needs to be taken down!"

***

Refi'Cul stood on his chariot, beaming with glee at the sight before him. The dozen Mighty Mercenaries who were pledged to the Light stood chained together straining with heavy ropes attached to the beams at the top of the tower that mirrored the one on the evil children's farm. Steele Brothers cracked whips at those who didn't put their whole back into it. Two giants stood at the base of the tower opposite them with massive two-bitted axes.

The entire town was gathered around the spectacle, many of whom were wailing and weeping. The Mighty Mercenaries loyal to Garrison Master had created a cordon around the work site supported by the giants, and the Steele Brothers formed a tighter circle around Refi'Cul.

Journey Leader stood at the Steele Lord's side and asked, "Why this, my Lord? Surely there are better ways to destroy this monument? A fire would be easy enough?"

Refi'Cul frowned. "Oh no, that would be too easy. Fires happen all the time. That sets no example to the people."

Refi'Cul waved his hand to the giants at the base of the tower, and they swung their mighty axes. "Having these so-called Light Bearers rip down this beacon of hope in front of the people will ensure they see the folly of their ways."

The sound of axes chopping into the tower punctuated his sentence.

"I see." Journey Leader rubbed his chin.

"When it has fallen, I will give them new hope in the true light."

Second Brother cracked a whip towards the men pulling on the ropes. They heaved as one, and a horrendous cracking sound erupted from the tower's base. This startled the men, and they let go of the rope. The tower wobbled in the air and seemed to settle back into place. Then one of the giants gave it a shove. Cracking sounds grew in severity as the tower leaned toward the Light Bearers.

Realizing their doom was at hand, they tried to scatter, but their chains kept them locked together—and Refi'Cul just smiled.

He hadn't planned on a public execution, but this would be an even better example to these people. Then, he'd be rid of this symbol and any agitators that might try to upset his plans.

However, a bald man among the men yelled, "As One!" And the chained Mighty Mercinaries got themselves together in time to avoid the falling tower.

It slammed into the ground with enough force to scare the horses attached to Refi'Cul's chariot. They reared, and he pulled hard on the reins. He would not have some beasts ruin his moment of triumph. They settled down, as wails and deep sobs erupted from the crowd.

Refi'Cul's brow creased, however, when he realized the tower was still basically intact. He'd expected it to splinter and crack on impact. However, the only real damage was to the base of the main supports. It looked like it could be put back into place as if nothing had happened. Maybe the giant was right, perhaps he should have burned it down.

No, this is my finest hour. Only the giants could put it back in place, and the giants are with me. He let out a deep metallic sigh, "People of Blooming Glen, do not despair. I bring you the true light. You will all be blessed by its crimson glow."

He waved to the captain of his honor guard, and they rushed to the back of the chariot and put two poles through the wooden base they'd added to the Censer at the farm. Then, they worked together to free it from the chariot. Four of them carried the Censer, while the other two resumed their guarding positions on either side of Refi'Cul.

"Place it on the center of the fallen tower for all to see," Refi'Cul demanded.

The honor guard followed his orders and double-timed it to the tower. Once there, the giants with the axes joined them, and they helped the Steele Brothers lift the whole thing onto the side of the building. The Steele Brothers clambered up on the fallen tower and centered the Censer with the carrying poles stretching from one side of the tower to the other.

Then they stood back-to-back around it and put their right hands to their chests. "For the true light!"

Refi'Cul, the rest of the Steele Brothers, and Journey Leader followed their lead. Looks of confusion crossed the face of the rest of the giants. *That will never do! The giants are going to need some lessons in the true light, or the townsfolk might get the idea we aren't a unified force and try to win the giants to their side.*

Now that the Censer had sat in place for a moment, the smoke around it circled up into the waxed canvas cover over it, then boiling out, its ominous red glow slowly filled the sky.

"Blooming Glen, I bring you the true light. All must embrace it's saving glow." He slammed his right fist into his chest. "For the true light."

This time the giants and the Mighty Mercenaries joined in the salute, repeating, "for the true light."

Many of the townsfolk joined in as well, some vigorously like the soldiers, but some were slow to respond, and many did not say the words at all.

Then he realized the Light Bearers had all fallen to their knees weeping, and their hands were clasped in prayer. *Maybe a public execution would have been better.*

. . . to be continued in <u>Demolishing the Stronghold</u>

If you enjoyed Wellspring of Life, please share your review

Good Reads

Amazon.com

Acknowledgments

A book like *Wellspring of Life* takes a tribe to make it happen. I found my tribe at the <u>Realm Makers Consortium,</u> and I'd like to thank the following people for their contributions to *Wellspring of Life* and their encouragement on my writing journey.
Sarah Grimm
Kalyn Cummins
LoriAnn Weldon
J.J. Johnson
Ted Atchley

The Iron Sharpeners
For their witty critiques and helping me shape Mother into a character worthy of the tale.
Catherine Bonham
Anna Tan
Elisabeth Warner
Kara J Lovett
Rachel A. Greco
Lauren Thornhill

The Realm Makers
For helping me shape the powerful forces in the story in unique and interesting ways.
Scott Minor
Becky Minor
Carla Cook Hoch
Jenelle Leanne Schmidt
Kandi J Wyatt

Phyllis Wheeler
C.E. White
James R. Hannibal

The Light Bearers
These readers valuable feedback to keep the series
engaging and fun for the whole family.
Samuel Hagberg
Thalia Beatrice Schertzer
Reece Bonnin
Samantha Welch
The Heil family: Isaac, Elizabeth, Nathan, Noah, Anna &
Andrew

About the Author

Allen Brokken is a teacher at heart, a husband and father most of all. He's a joyful writer by the abundant grace of God. He began writing the Towers of Light series for his own children to help him illustrate the deep truths of the Bible in an engaging and age-appropriate way. He's dedicated 15 years of his life to volunteer roles in children's ministry and youth development.

Now that his own children are off to college, he's sharing his life experiences at home school conferences and through his blog and newsletter at
https://allenbrokkenauthor.com/subscribe

You can get sneak peeks of the ongoing adventures of Lauren, Aiden, and Ethan (plus their pets!) and the #dadjokeoftheday on all the major social media platforms.
@allenbrokkenauthor

Towers of Light Series

The series insightfully examines Christian values from the perspective of three small children, facing insurmountable problems . . . and succeeding, by faith and grace alone.

Book 1 _Light of Mine_: Discernment
The Darkness has taken their parents. Can Lauren, Aiden, and Ethan discern who to trust before it takes them too?

Book 2 _Still Small Voice_: Conscience
Lauren, Aiden, and Ethan want to follow their conscience to save their parents, but their Uncle has other plans. Will he see the light before it's too late?

Book 3 _Fear No Evil_: Courage
Lost and alone in a valley of Darkness, will Lauren, Aiden, and Ethan find God's courage to find redemption and each other?

Book 4 _Armor of God_: Faith
Lauren, Aiden, and Ethan race across the Heathlands on a quest to arm themselves with the Armor of God. Will their faith give them the power to save their father?

Book 5 _Wellspring of Life_: Redemption
Lauren, Aiden, and Ethan must find the legendary Wellspring of Life. Will they be able to share it's living waters before it's too late?

Book 6 _Demolishing the Stronghold_: Victory
Lauren, Aiden, and Ethan return to the Iron Mountain. Will they defeat the Darkness in their land once and for all?

Want to find more Secret Doors to Amazing Places?

A twelve-year-old girl discovers a link between the father she's never known and a mysterious shop where the snow globes open portals to other worlds. An adventurous science fantasy for readers who like to explore.

"Snow Globe Travelers: Samuel's Legacy will appeal to science fantasy lovers of all ages
   and it's most highly recommended."
   —READERS' FAVORITE, A FIVE-STAR REVIEW

EleonoraPress.com

www.ingramcontent.com/pod-product-compliance
Lightning Source LLC
Chambersburg PA
CBHW051131190726
48290CB00006B/1798